Curious Cousin

Book 6 of the Masterson Files

By

Andrew Allen Smith

Curious Cousin: Book 6 of the Masterson Files

Dedication

To each and every person who has a dream and the courage to make it real. This book is for you as book six of the Masterson files becomes a reality. It is with presence of mind that I see this book as a gateway to move and look forward to the amazing projects I will find in the future, all because of a dream.

Prologue

The cold wind was the least of Jonathon Michael Masterson's problems. His entry into Ukraine had been easy. The passports and official papers the United States government provided were legitimate, and Michaels's fluent Ukrainian helped him get past the most skeptical border guards. His entry into the country and subsequent acquisition of a weapon and a location had been easy. This time the target was a Ukrainian mobster, which turned out to be more difficult for Michael.

Michael had spent weeks trying to get close to Anton Petrikov. His contract was to determine the impact of the elimination of Anton, followed by his termination, if it was deemed feasible. To do this, Michael did something he usually didn't enjoy. He socialized. Michael attended party after party and, in doing so, moved closer and closer to the Petrikov household. He began determining the social and economic impact on Ukraine and the city structure. Michael had a team supporting him, and that, too, was unusual. Michael's usual contracts were clean and clear and almost always involved eliminating a target and then moving on. In this case, the target would not be neutralized until the impact was determined.

During the weeks Michael was in Ukraine, he met Yuri and Gaston Petrikov, Anton's sons. Michael was fascinated with Yuri's approach to the world and how mature he was for his age. Gaston was still playing video games and trying to get close to his older brother. Gaston was always an underfoot annoyance. Yuri was constantly having his bodyguards take Gaston home. Yuri was not a fan of his father's dealings, but Michael couldn't take a chance that Yuri wouldn't understand his actions, he said nothing and instead listened intently.

Michael continued walking and felt the wind cut through his jacket like a knife. It wouldn't be long now, and he would be at the safe house. Once at the safe house, he could take his time and be extracted later. The safe house was off the grid; the safe house was as it should be, safe.

Michael thought of Abby and hoped he would get to see her again. He realized he should have never taken this job. His greed for the large payday might be his undoing. Tarkington had told him that no one else had been able to get close and that it had to look like an accident or at least natural causes. At first, Michael refused, but the $500,000 payday made the job much more appealing. He had plenty of money, but he would be far more comfortable if there were a little more.

When Michael heard the sirens wail, two blocks remained to reach his destination. There was sound everywhere, and Michael mused for just a moment that the sirens were so different in Ukraine than in the United States of America. Everything was different. Every house was a potential threat, and as he passed each, he scanned windows with his peripheral vision watching for movement or any chance that he would become a rapid and convenient target.

One block left, and he saw the lights in a reflection ten blocks behind him. Michael didn't want to take the chance of turning around and drawing attention to himself. He continued walking with a mighty brisk walk that so many people in the area seemed to have adopted. It wasn't so much walking as it was lumbering through the streets. The sirens continued coming closer. Michael considered running but knew this was an emotional response and ignored it. Running would ensure his capture and potentially his death. He counted down as the sirens got closer and closer, gripping the 9mm in his pocket, wondering how many would be in the car or truck.

Michael slowed his breathing and prepared himself as the sirens were directly upon him. He took a deep breath and continued his walk forward, only to have the police van pass him at high speed without slowing or paying him a bit of attention. Michael took another breath and chastised himself for having any emotion at the moment. He put too much pressure on himself, and because he did, he could have compromised everything he had worked for so far. In his mind, he laughed, but on the outside, he didn't even smile as he reached the door to the modest stone building, used his key, and went inside.

The freight elevator was in front of him. He lifted the double gate and stepped into the car-sized elevator. Pulling the gates back down, he used the lever to move the elevator upwards until he reached the top floor. The machinery was old. It churned the gears and pullies, but it was made strong and was more reliable than most modern systems. With a hearty *clunk*, it hit the highest floor.

Michael stepped out of the elevator into the large warehouse area where he had lived for weeks. It was well-heated and spacious but still relatively modest. What once was a large warehouse was now an open area for him to wait for the manhunt to pass. On this top floor, he had exercise equipment, a bed, a couch, a tube television, a few bookcases with a variety of books, a punching bag, a few dartboards, and four chairs with a table. There was a small kitchenette; it was just enough for him to feed himself. In a far corner was a restroom with a shower. Michael could hear the shower dripping through the night even with the door closed and might have time to fix it now.

To one side was a car. It wasn't just any car; it was a 1969 Mustang fastback he found in a barn while in the country with Yuri. Yuri laughed at him for being interested in the car, but Michael thought it would be fun to work on. He had it towed to an old man in the next city over. The old man got it running while Michael was doing his research. It wasn't perfect, but it gave Michael something to work on while he waited. Now it appeared he would have time to work more on the engine and clean up the car. At its worst, it could still be driven easily in the city. Many older cars sat in front of older homes.

Michael decided to shower first and walked to the far corner. Next to the restroom were a few dressers and a hamper. Michael took off his clothes, put them in the hamper, and then walked into the restroom and showered. As the hot water ran over him, he became more and more frustrated with his performance today. Killing Anton was just a job, and he did it without remorse. Somehow his friendship with Yuri had caused him issues, and he realized he could never afford to get that close to someone again while doing a job. He told himself that since the beginning, but obviously, he had not listened this time. Michael considered the issue and knew that sometimes you had to let go.

Michael finished his shower and got out. He dried himself off, combed his hair, and folded the tower neatly. He then placed the towel over the towel rack and walked out of the room naked. As he reached the dresser, an odd feeling crossed over him, and he realized something was wrong. He heard the familiar sound of a Glock 17 being chambered. Michael stopped.

"It was you wasn't it," the voice asked in Ukrainian.

"I am unsure of what you are talking about," Michael replied in Ukrainian.

"I was sure it was you," the voice said, "turn to me so I can see you."

Michael turned around with his hands up slightly. He was at an extreme disadvantage, mostly because he was naked. He had the advantage of home turf but had no idea how many others had their guns trained on him.

"Chekhov?" Michael said, "Is that you?" Michael couldn't see anyone, and Chekov was hidden in the shadows.

"Of course, it is me. No one else would come; no one else would believe it was you. I saw, and knew you were not the sheep you pretended to be. I knew you were the wolf, and protected Yuri from your treachery."

"What are you talking about Chekov?" Michael said.

"Do not insult my intelligence, I knew it was you all along, and I thought you were trying to kill Yuri. Instead, now Anton is dead. I will take you back so you can face Yuri's wrath."

"Anton is dead? Since when? Is Yuri okay? Let's go see Yuri together," Michael said. "Do you mind if I get dressed?"

"I am tempted to drag you to Yuri naked, but that might make him soften his heart for you. Get dressed, but remember my gun is pointed at your head, and if you do anything I do not like, I will have no problem killing you like you did Anton." Chekov replied.

"I don't know what you're talking about," Michael said as he reached into the top drawer and pulled out underwear and a T-shirt. He put them on and then put on socks, another shirt, a sweater, and a pair of tactical pants. All the while, he was watching as he moved to try to get the exact location of Chekov. "Yuri is my friend; why would I kill Anton?"

"I am not sure why you killed my uncle, but he trusted you, and Yuri thinks of you as a friend. Why did you do this?" Chekov asked.

"I didn't kill anyone," Michael lied. "I doubt I could be around a dead person for more than a few minutes."

"Liar," Chekov spat; "You are a killer, and soon you will be Yuri's play toy."

Michael reached into the drawer, pulled out a baseball cap, and put it on. As he turned, he finally saw a glint in the corner and realized it was Chekov. There was little to see. He must have been wearing dark clothes. The matte black Glock reflected very little light, but the barrel was steel. Michael could see the circular barrel and the glint of Chekhov's eyes in the dim light.

"Well, let's go see Yuri and get this worked out," Michael said.

"Yes, let's go see Yuri," Chekov said as he walked into the light.

"Why didn't Yuri just come with you?" Michael asked.

"He didn't believe that you lived in this district, and he wanted to be with his father even though he was dead." Chekov looked down for a moment. "You have hurt my cousin and my friend, and I will see you suffer for this. His brother, Gaston, is unaffected; he is a brat."

The timing was right, and as Chekov looked down, Michael quickly reached into his hat and pulled the knife from the brim. He threw it and hoped his aim was good. The knife struck clean through Chekov's hand and lodged inside the handle of the Glock.

"Liar!" Chekov screamed as he fired the weapon wildly.

Michael dove for the couch and grabbed a handful of darts. As he stood, he threw the darts one at a time at Chekov. Each dart was on target. One embedded in Chekov's hand, one in his knee, one in his other knee, one in his shoulder, and one directly in the sternum. None of the darts could cause a fatal injury, but Michael knew they would buy him a few moments. Michael ran towards Chekov and tackled him. There were no martial arts or amazing combat moves, instead, Michael swung and pushed each of the darts deeper. The Glock jammed from Chekov's inability to move his hand well with a knife through it. Michael saw this and pulled the knife from Chekov's hand, then plunged it into his eye socket. Chekov spasmed as his body decided it was no longer alive.

The intrusion made Michael second-guess himself. He had no idea who or how many others knew where he was. He had no idea how much time he had before his doors would come crashing down with dozens of armed thugs. If that happened, Michael would die.

Michael looked at his hands and clothes. They were covered in blood now. He cleaned up quickly and changed clothes again. This time careful not to carry any weapons.

With deliberate movements, Michael collected the papers necessary to get out of the country. He took enough money to get over the border and a little more. Michael also packed a small bag, and he put a second set of papers in the bottom of the bag. Only a careful search would find the second set of papers. Michael surveyed his safe house, wrapped Chekov's body in a large garbage bag, and sealed it. From there, he put the body in a freezer in the far corner of the warehouse. The freezer had a lock on it, and Michael hoped he would be out of the country before anyone found Chekov's body. If the power stayed on and if the freezer was not touched, it was unlikely the body would ever be found.

Michael looked at the car he intended to rebuild over the next week. It wasn't meant to be. It was five minutes to the bus station and a twenty-one-hour bus ride to Bucharest. It would be uncomfortable, but there would be no raised eyebrows for a young student traveling by bus. Michael closed the door and locked it, then took the freight elevator down and locked the building. He owned it all, and as long as the government was stable, the local banks would pay for utilities indefinitely.

Michael looked around at the warehouse area and all of the empty buildings. This building had cost him almost nothing, and the paper trail to him would be impossible to find. The payoff for the job was more than worth it, but Michael would miss the building and the freedom it gave him. He threw the bag over his shoulder and walked to the bus station. No one else came for him, there were no sirens, and in the end, only Chekov had suspected him.

Michael walked to the bus station and purchased a ticket to Bucharest. He waited with a variety of students and older men and women, getting ready to go to far-off places. After only a few hours, he boarded a bus for the start of his long trip home. As Michael looked at the city through the windows of the dingy bus, he considered the contrasts between life in Ukraine versus life in Kentucky. If a person had been to Appalachia, they would almost think the two were one and the same. Michael pulled his hat down and kept his ears open, listening for anything out of place. There was nothing, only the rattle of the poorly maintained bus making its way to safety.

Chapter 1

The hills of Ivel, Kentucky, were clean and unfettered with the hustle and chaos of the world. Jonathon Michael Masterson stood in a simple but tasteful living room looking out over a pristine valley. The sky was clear and blue, a type of blue that seemed more powerful in the hills of Appalachia. A hawk flew past while a turkey vulture circled a death that only it could detect somewhere far below. Trees spanned as far as anyone could see, and Michael looked out over them all, paying attention to movement and details and enjoying the moment. Michael was tall, at 6'2", he dwarfed many men, and he worked out at least daily, giving him a strong frame and handsome rugged looks that made him attractive. His dark black hair was disheveled, and he wore black shorts and a matching black t-shirt.

Michael watched the hawk as it folded into a thin bullet and dove towards the ground. Something below was about to change its role in the world. It was about to become prey. Michael considered his life only for a moment and how so many before had become prey, his prey. That time was gone now, changed by a single job. A man who hired him to kill but lied to Michael and became Michael's target instead. Recent events had opened that world again, but Michael was not interested. Michael wanted to retire.

The house he stood in was recently rebuilt, and Michael was happy with the work. He loved his other houses, but this one had special memories. It was here he felt his Kentucky roots, and the beauty of the area was unparalleled. The house was built into the side of a cliff, the limestone allowed a solid anchor while the hills afforded Michael a defensible area in case of visitors. He owned 700 acres, and the house stood near the center. Michael acquired the land at a very low price. Even though the price was low, it helped the area when Michael brought in workers. Craftsmen and trade workers had built the first house. Although that house was destroyed, he rebuilt. Most recently, he used workers from the area, carefully picking them for their talents and his ability to trust them, if only a little.

In the end, the house was just a house, but as he heard the near-silent footsteps behind him, he knew that it was those that made a home. Michael turned in a swift motion that would have been a blur to many and grabbed Abby Tarkington. She wore one of his shirts, and her long blonde hair flowed over the black t-shirt. Where Michael was tall, Abby was only 5'4". Abby radiated beauty; if she had been taller, she would have been a model. Michael appreciated everything about her and was always mesmerized by her eyes. To some, Abby may have looked diminutive. They would not know she had grown up an Army daughter giving her a confidence many people didn't have. Like Michael, her mind was quick and always aware.

"Good morning," Abby said as Michael reached for her and lifted her from the ground like a feather. They kissed, and it lingered. Passion grew between them. Michael held her close, but Abby held him as though she would never let go. Even hanging in the air, she was tenacious about holding on, and as her legs wrapped around Michael, he kissed her even more. A moment later, they pulled back and looked at each other.

"Good morning," Michael replied.

"Woof," Abby laughed as she released her legs, and Michael lowered her to the ground. Abby rubbed her back. "We need to get a bed at least and start to get furniture for the house."

"We can do that," Michael said. "You picked out the original furniture. We can get the same and have it delivered, or we could take a drive and go look for some."

"I know how much you hate being out," Abby referred to the fact that Michael didn't want to get in a conflict or run into someone who might know him. Michael never looked for trouble, but lately, it seemed to find him.

"Well, I am trying to retire," Michael laughed as he spoke like an older man and bent over. "I had hoped you would retire with me."

"I am retiring with you," Abby chided. "That does not mean we need to be self-imposed prisoners, does it?"

Michael laughed. He thought for a moment. He had amassed a reasonable fortune working for the government and a series of private companies. His father's gift to him had been a knack for seeing trends and dealing with money, and he turned that into a significant amount. The problem was his profession was eliminating targets. He terminated a very high number of targets, many of whom no one else would consider and as such had amassed a significant number of enemies. It seemed the past came up from time to time, and Michael was forced to get involved again. This created an interesting dynamic. Michael and Abby were both social and did well with people, but they could not entertain or be involved as others would. It would simply allow them to be traced more easily and put Abby or him in danger. It was not that he could not handle it; it was better not to handle it.

"We could make a run to Lexington, but we only have the one car with us. It would stand out as it always does," Michael said, "We need to get something that blends in."

Abby batted her eyes in a gesture of innocence that didn't seem to fit, "What do you suggest, my prince?"

Michael laughed, "How 'bout a trip to Lexington? We can pick up a car and look at furniture while we are there."

"I like it!" Abby said, "I bet we could get the furniture in Pikeville, though, or at least a bed?" Abby batted her eyes again.

"Pikeville is pretty close," Michael said, "We only have the DB9; not a lot of DB9s in the area."

"Maybe, but maybe we can be direct and come back. I doubt we will attract much attention. Remember, this was coal country. There are more than a few high-end cars and well-off people here."

"An exotic car with a fashion model blonde in it and a big guy who always wears sunglasses," Michael recited; "Sounds like a scene in a movie or a book."

Abby's eyes sparkled, Michael always showed her respect and passion, but he slid in the occasional statements that made her just feel good. "I can wear a ponytail and loose clothes, and you can lose your sunglasses and wear a ball cap."

"I don't think I have a ball cap," Michael laughed.

"I am sure we can get you a *UK Wildcats* ballcap at the gas station down the hill. We can be a little scruffy, and the car, well, we won it on the internet if anyone asks. They will all walk away and play on their smartphones if they like it."

"You talked me into it," Michael laughed. "I have been to Pikeville, though, it isn't a lost city; it is a real city in the hills. People walk around just like we are now, not the redneck fantasies in movies or television."

"I know, I know," Abby giggled, "but we want to look a little less refined."

"You mean you won't wear those spiked heels you love so much?" Michael asked with a grin.

"Hey," Abby laughed, "It makes me feel taller, and those heels kick ass. I bet if I wear jeans and those heels, I will fit right in."

Michael scooped her up again, "It's a deal." Michael kissed her again and she was lost in his kiss for a moment.

The two headed to the bedroom. The walls echoed. The house was complete, but there was no furniture, and every sound seemed to make a cascading echo on the large top floor. The two walked into the bedroom, where the air mattress and their luggage sat. The suitcases were open but well organized. The bed was made even though it was an air mattress.

"Not much in the way of clothes here," Abby frowned. "Not like we have a ton of choices."

"Maybe we can go to Lexington this week and get you some clothes," Michael added in a hopeful tone. "I am good as long as we can wash what I have for a while." Michael was usually simple in his tastes. Tactical pants and T-shirts were a constant, and he had several identical pairs. The trick was eliminating the extra thinking necessary when deciding how to dress. Clothes were not important to Michael. There were only a few things in life he really cherished. At the top of that list was Abby.

Abby stripped off her clothes and ran to the large bathroom. She turned on the shower, and the dual heads sprayed water anxiously. As the water warmed, Abby stepped into the streams and closed her eyes. The water ran onto her face and made its way to the drain. She relaxed as the sound of the drain gurgling, and water filled the area with white noise. Abby felt strong hands on her and smiled as Michael caressed her body. She felt the soap on her back as Michael washed her with slow movements as though he were savoring every moment. He washed her hair more carefully than a Paul Mitchel expert. He spent time making sure it was rinsed, and Abby felt soothed. Abby felt him all around her, and then, in an instant, he stopped. Abby turned around.

"Stopping so soon?" she said as Michael soaped his body and washed his hair.

"We will get back here and spend the whole day together," He replied.

Abby thought for a moment. She took his hand and pulled him close, pressing his hand on her breast. Abby kissed his chest, turned, and walked out of the shower. "I see your point," she noted as she grabbed a towel and dried off. Michael smiled and finished washing, then joined her in the bathroom. He picked up a second towel and began drying off.

"We only have two towels, too," Michael laughed.

"We could go to another house and bring things back," Abby thought of the houses in Dubois, Wyoming and the western shores of Michigan.

"A little far, don't you think?" Michael questioned.

"Maybe," Abby laughed, "but it would give us time together."

"We will work it out later," Michael stated as he hung the wet towel and went into the bedroom. As he walked out, Abby rolled her towel and snapped it at his butt. As the towel traveled back, Michael turned and grabbed it.

Abby grinned, "It's my butt."

Michael turned, still holding the towel. He pointed his butt at her, "This butt?" He danced around, then dropped the towel and ran into the room.

As Abby dried her hair, Michael dressed and went back to the living room. He looked out on the land and was once again lost in the beauty of the Appalachians.

Chapter 2

Ronnie Comer was apprehensive as he worked out. Ronnie was used to the physical parts of the workout, but now he had a new challenge. Rachel Brown and Jim Simpson had been sparring all morning. Rachel was constantly trying to beat Jim, and Jim was constantly laughing, playing and enjoying the workout. Today Ronnie had to spar with one of them, which was difficult for him to consider. Many people on base gathered and were waiting for Ronnie to step into the ring with either Rachel or Jim.

The Bluegrass Army Depot in Richmond, Kentucky, was not known by many people. It was a nice facility but was infamous for the storage of particularly bad weapons. The depot spent great time and effort in the art of eliminating those items that were no longer considered viable weapons in war. Things like Sarin gas. It was deadly by contact and by inhaling and had an effect so unspeakable that it could never be used in "civilized warfare."

Ronnie was part of a team originally assembled in this facility when an assassin was targeted by a rogue CIA agent. They had since taken up residence simply because no one would expect a team of highly skilled individuals with a specialized agenda to be stationed at the Bluegrass Army Depot or in a town as small as Richmond, Kentucky.

The base was buzzing with excitement now because Ronnie would soon spar with one of the two best fighters in the area. Rachel Brown was originally brutal and tenacious, and well known in the depot. She had led a group of base MPs. She was particularly arrogant and ensured that everyone followed her lead by pure intimidation. Her fighting style was a combination of mixed martial arts and Tae Kwon Do, making her show a tendency to be overly aggressive. Before Jim arrived, she frequently drafted men in the unit and was more focused on winning than teaching them anything.

Jim Simpson was very good at a variety of martial arts, and it was rumored he was something called a Grandmaster, though he played it down and never admitted to it. When Jim first sparred with Rachel, she was so angry she nearly exploded. Jim had embarrassed, outmaneuvered, and overpowered Rachel so easily that she screamed in pure anger. In the process, Jim kissed Rachel and walked away, leaving the fight and just saying, "You win," which made Rachel even more agitated. After they were assigned to the same unit, they began sparring often, and Jim's carefully nonchalant attitude always seemed to prevail. The more surprising change was Rachel had mellowed to an extent and now tried to help others learn rather than just humiliating them.

Ronnie was apprehensive because both were very practiced and skilled fighters, and he was just average. Sure, he had more than just basic training, and he and Jim had sparred some, but he wasn't in a class near Rachel or Jim. Rachel suggested the bout and said they would flip a coin to determine who he would spar with. Ronnie reluctantly agreed because he didn't want to offend either of them. It was just how he was.

It was nearly six o'clock in the evening, and people were filing into the big gym. Many were standing on the outside edges, and Ronnie saw his unit members show up. Jim and Rachel were busy lifting and laughing in the corner. Terry Drake and Barbara Stone came in, and Ronnie blushed a little. Terry and Barbara were usually not at the facility. They kept the teams' private planes in top shape and were both pilots. Ronnie thought Barbara was an amazing woman. Barbara was nice to Ronnie and very flirtatious, but Ronnie just didn't know if she was serious about him or just playing. He always hoped for more. Barbara was the type of woman he would want to take back to Pikeville.

Alex Brown walked in and sat at a table, nodding first to Ronnie before he sat. He had a series of folders with him. Ronnie was sure it was more paperwork to review or budgets to determine. Their group was involved in many high-profile endeavors. They were not part of any normal unit, so there was always accounting to be done to ensure the unit was well-funded. They also wanted to ensure they were doing good work for General Samuel Tarkington, the head of the division.

Sarena Prince was the last member of the unit to wander into the gym, and she sat across from Alex. Sarena was new to the unit. She was an FBI agent who had been a part of a previous encounter. Their unit was part of her rescue from a rogue group of assassins in Indianapolis. She found a way to talk to General Tarkington and asked to be reassigned to his group. She was exceptional with ballistics and was a weapons expert. Still, she was not originally part of the military and was getting used to all the processes, procedures, and interactions.

Ronnie finished working with the leg machine and walked over to his water bottle and towel. As he tilted back the bottle, he felt two hands on his shoulders. They were strong, and he felt powerless for just a split second.

"It's time," Jim laughed as he held one of Ronnie's shoulders.

"Yep, it sure is," Rachel grinned like an evil cat from his other shoulder. "You shouldn't have worn yourself out; one of us is gonna do that!"

Ronnie looked around the room at all the people that had gathered and wondered if they were there to support him or see another big bout like Jim and Rachel usually put on.

Jim and Rachel led Ronnie to the mats, and the attendees quieted in short order. A murmur was still there, but Rachel's wrath was still a legend. No one dared offend her on purpose.

Rachel began talking, "I bet some of you have heard that Ronnie is going to spar with either Jim or me today. We don't want to disappoint, so we will flip a coin to decide who he will spar with and get it going."

"Wait!" Ronnie shouted, stepping in front of them both, "Ya'll know me, right?"

There were louder affirmations and nods around the room.

"Ya'll know that either Jim or Rachel could beat me blindfolded, right?" Ronnie added. At that statement, Alex looked up, and Barbara and Terry sat down. Men and women began clapping their affirmation to Ronnie's statement. Rachel and Jim looked at each other and then at Ronnie and his newfound bravado.

"I'd bet they both could beat me blind and deaf, right?" Ronnie barked.

The entire room was clapping, and Alex began clapping as well.

"So instead of flipping a coin," Ronnie reached into his pocket, "I challenge them *both*, if they wear these blindfolds and put in these here earplugs."

Rachel and Jim looked at each other, "What are you up to, Ronnie?" Rachel asked.

"I just want it to be fair. Right?" Ronnie said. He spoke to the crowd, "We will all three stay on the mats, and Miss Prince will be the judge. Ya'll think that's fair?"

The clapping got louder, and the base commander came in clapping as well.

Sarena came up to Ronnie, Jim, and Rachel. "Umm, I know fighting, but will someone tell me what's going on?"

"Easy," Ronnie handed her the blindfolds and foam hearing protection. "You make sure they are done up, and none of us cheat, and you call the winner."

"Umm," Sarena considered, "Umm, okay."

"The boy has gotten sly as a fox on us," Rachel said. "What are you up to, Ronnie?"

"I just wanted a chance to win," Ronnie tried to look innocent.

Sarena broke in; "I will put my hands on your shoulders to let you know we will be starting and then pull them off to let you know it is time."

"How will we know when to stop?" Rachel asked.

Sarena looked around and walked to a cooler on the edge of the mats. She walked back, "I will splash you with water to stop. Okay?"

"Yes, that works" Jim smiled.

"Yeah, okay," Rachel said, "Already a sweaty mess, I guess it won't matter."

The three were in the center of the mats, and each put on protective pads for sparring. Ronnie's was dark blue, Rachel's bright red, and Jim's bright green. Jim and Rachel squished the earplugs, made them thin, then worked them in their ears. The plugs expanded, blocking sound. Then they put on the black goggles Ronnie provided. The thick straps made the goggles hold tight, and they would not leak light nor fall off.

"Damnit, Ronnie, Jim did this to me once already," Rachel yelled.

The crowd laughed, knowing she could not hear. She was trying to adjust her voice like someone in the range who forgot their earmuffs were on.

"Good job Ronnie," Jim spoke in a normal voice, "You obviously thought this through, and that is the sign of a true fighter."

Ronnie felt good getting praise from Jim. Jim was a complex man and had been through a lot since the team came together. He was always positive with Ronnie and always supportive. Ronnie knew Jim and Alex had fought together before their team was formed and wondered what Jim was like when he was a soldier.

"Can he hear us?" Sarena asked.

"I don't rightly know," Ronnie was bouncing and perhaps a little nervous.

"You ready?" Sarena asked.

"Yes, ma'am," Ronnie said.

"Here we go," Sarena said. She put her hands on Jim and Rachel's shoulders. With one smooth motion, she jumped backwards and pulled her hands off the two.

Ronnie was quick; taking off the foot protection with a move that could only be called "practiced." He then crept between the two who were struggling to listen and waiting intently.

As Ronnie moved closer to Jim, he swung and nearly connected. Ronnie ducked at the last possible second and felt the red hairs on his head wave in the wind.

"Where are you?" Rachel's voice was a little loud since she could not hear, "You can't leave the mat."

Ronnie cupped his hands together and focused. He took a deep breath, swung, and tapped Rachel.

Rachel went after the punch and swung two times; the second time, she was swinging at Jim. He raised his hand to block. Rachel was not so careful, she kicked forward, and Jim dropped his other hand down to block, only to topple backward off balance.

"I got you," Rachel yelled as she jumped forward, and Jim rolled to the left.

"It's me," Jim obviously recognized the punch, but it didn't matter; she could not hear him.

Rachel stopped and didn't move. Ronnie moved closer to her, and with patience, he got close and punched her again, then rolled away. She swung again and, this time, connected with Jim in the chest.

Jim backed off and rolled away. As he did, Ronnie punched him in the kidney hard and pulled away as Jim returned the punch on thin air.

Jim didn't move. Rachel stayed still, but Ronnie crept between them again. Ronnie tapped Jim in the face. Jim jumped forward into Rachel with a   rapid bounce. Jim checked his punch and began to turn around; as he did, Ronnie hit him as hard as he could in the chest. Jim rolled with the blow, rolled backwards, then twisted back to a standing position.

"We may have been outsmarted," Jim laughed loudly as the crowd murmured and laughed.

Ronnie was behind Rachel and pushed her hard, forward into Jim. She lost her balance and struggled, falling forward with momentum. Jim swung at the movement and hit Rachel in the side of the head, knocking her to the ground.

"Shit," Rachel grimaced. "That hurt."

The group in the gym began laughing, and some began chanting, "Ronnie! Ronnie!"

"Well crap," Rachel ground her teeth. "We are looking like idiots." She knew Jim could not hear her.

Rachel jumped up, and as she was going to move, felt a fist hit her head again. She stumbled, and Ronnie leaned his back against Jim's. As Rachel moved back to get to Jim, Jim began to swing at her but stopped himself and reached around and grabbed Ronnie, throwing him forward to the ground.

"Nice try; her back is much nicer," Jim laughed as he swung at Ronnie again and hit only air.

There was clapping all around them, and Jim struggled to move his feet in many directions. As Rachel moved to him, he grabbed at her and laughed, "Oh, you feel much better. The bumps are in the right places now."

The crowd laughed, but Rachel heard nothing.

"Damnit, Ronnie, fight like a man," Rachel bellowed.

Ronnie hit them both in the ribs on one side and rolled away. The two both moved towards him. In the process, they were no longer back-to-back. Ronnie slipped next to Jim and punched Rachel. She swung at the punch and hit Jim squarely. Ronnie rotated to the other side and punched Jim again. When Jim swung back, he missed Ronnie and barely missed Rachel.

Rachel screamed. She began swinging every way, moving fast and with random jumps and turns. "I will not be played for a fool!" she screamed.

Ronnie watched as she ran back and forth and kept his distance from her, knowing those heavy punches would hurt if they connected. He kept a close eye on Jim, but Jim was just standing still. Rachel screamed again, "C'mere, you little shit." She swung over and over. Ronnie had to move with more and more pure energy. He bounced around like a road runner, trying to get away from a pack of coyotes.

Ronnie didn't see the next blow coming. He got too close to Jim, and Jim swung his leg low and fast and tripped Ronnie to the floor. Rachel was still swinging as Jim grabbed Ronnie's leg, twisted it to an impossible angle, and then moved so his weight was on it.

"Tap out," Jim laughed as he let his weight settle.

Ronnie yelled, "Oh damn, Uncle, Uncle!" He began slapping Jim's shoulder.

Jim stood and ripped off his blindfold.

Rachel was still swinging like a machine as Jim grabbed her and pulled off her goggles. They both pulled their earplugs from their ears. Rachel was red and seething. She looked at Ronnie with pure fury, ripped off both of her gloves, and put her hand out for him to shake. Ronnie took it, and the crowd erupted in cheers.

"You were damn smart," Rachel was very appreciative.

"I still lost," Ronnie said as he rubbed his leg.

Jim looked at the group, many still clapping, "Did you?"

Ronnie stared for a minute and understood. Ronnie smiled as his team came up and patted him on the back. He had been unpredictable, and this changed him in his team's eyes.

Chapter 3

Michael and Abby drove to Pikeville in the DB9. The sleek black car didn't turn as many heads as Michael thought. Numerous high-end cars were in the area, and the DB9 was just another exotic car in the middle of a multitude of exotic cars. It was nearly noon, and the two listened to music as they drove to the local furniture store. The sounds of classic rock reverberated in the well-designed stereo. Michael was impressed with the car made for comfort as much as power and presence.

Conner's fine furniture was in the downtown area, in a nice-looking older building. The painted cinderblock was clean with only a few chips, and the sign "Family owned since 1951" on the corner was inviting and seemed to beckon customers.

"This must be the place," Michael surveyed the building.

"It must be," Abby was almost giddy. "It will be awesome to have a real bed again. I was ready to go to Michigan, just to sleep on our own mattress again."

"Really?" Michael laughed. "We can't have that."

The two stepped out of the car, and Michael put on his newly acquired UK ballcap. His black jacket was a little long, and he straightened it, making him look like just another man in jeans and a black jacket going into a furniture store.

Abby, on the other hand, looked stunning in her ponytail and tennis shoes. It was impossible for her to hide the radiance she projected. Her blue eyes shone in the sunlight, and she walked with an air of confidence that both men and women noticed. As she walked to the door in front of Michael, he could not help but say, "Hubba, hubba."

Abby turned and laughed as she pulled the steel-framed glass door open, and they walked into the building. It took a moment to get used to the light, even though huge LED lights lit the showroom. Michael took off his sunglasses and put them in his front coat pocket.

In the front, couches were spread across the area, and that seemed to radiate further and further back until kitchen tables began, then dressers and bedroom sets with beds galore. Row after row of furniture adorned the area, but no one approached them. Michael and Abby walked to the back of the nearly 50,000 square foot building where the bedroom sets and beds were scattered. Small bedroom setups were placed on squares of carpet and were perfectly clean. A dresser, hutch, bed, and sometimes footstool or chair were placed to entice the customer. Abby ran and jumped on one of the beds near the door.

"This is heaven," she was elated as she lay back on the bed.

"Good mattress?" Michael asked.

"It's not an air mattress," Abby replied.

"Ouch," Michael laughed; "I guess camping is out?"

"We are not camping in our newly built house. If I was camping, I wouldn't care." Abby grinned.

Abby got off the bed and began looking at the different sets one by one as Michael followed, watching her and looking around the strangely quiet showroom.

"Slow day," Michael surveyed the sales area.

"Hmm," Abby replied, then looked around. "Yeah," she said, becoming aware, "A little too slow."

"I was thinking similar," Michael said. "Keep your eyes open."

Abby nodded as they kept walking. "You know, sometimes people have slow days, and it's not always trouble."

A big man in a white shirt with a black tie walked out to them. Michael watched as he came forward. His shirt was mussed, and his tie was crooked. Michael noted the red marks on his face.

"Sorry, kids," the man puffed as he sauntered to them. He could be no more than fifty, but he looked worn and tired.

"We were just looking around," Abby looked around the building as she spoke, seeing the same things Michael had noticed. "Did we come at a bad time?"

The man glanced back at the door, then at Michael and Abby, "Naw, you came at the perfect time. Are you looking for anything in particular?"

"A bed," Abby looked at the door for a split second then back at the man. "We want something comfortable and maybe a little elegant.

Michael raised his eyebrow. The bed in Michigan was a Walnut Sleigh bed. It was rugged and fit the décor of the house. He would not have considered it elegant.

Abby looked over and smiled at him. "So, which mattress would you recommend?"

"Ma'am," the man was in his element now, "My name is Bob, Bob Conner. I tell ya, I know you're looking for a good mattress, but that depends on what you want to spend and how perfect you want to sleep."

"Let's say price was no problem," Abby began.

Michael again raised an eyebrow. Abby smiled at him and winked.

"Well, ma'am, here at Conner's, we aim to please. Now walk right over here. These Tempur-Pedics are rated with super high customer satisfaction. There are others, but these are here and in stock, ready to go home with you. Just lay down on this and see how it feels." Bob pointed to the mattress like a beacon.

Michael slowly panned as the front door clanged. Three men walked in. They were in their late 20s or early 30s, around Michael's age. The three walked towards the office area and saw Bob, Michael, and Abby. They sat down in the front area.

"What do you think?" Abby asked as she jumped on and sank into on the mattress.

Michael sat on the mattress, looking towards Bob, but his eyes never strayed from the three men.

"Feels good," Michael stood backup and looked around, "What do you want to get with it? You know, elegant?"

Abby laughed a little and glanced towards the front of the store as well. She grabbed Michaels's hand and squeezed a little.

Bob smiled and walked with them to a spindle bed that was dark Cherry. The whole set was expensive but not outlandish. He walked in front of them, "How about something like this?" he pointed to the frame, "It is not too elegant that a man would feel bad sleeping in it, but not so masculine that women would want to run from the room."

"A little sexist," Abby seemed serious. Bob was dumbfounded for a moment, not sure what to say. Then Abby laughed, "Just kidding, Bob." She looked at Michael, "What do you think?"

"Want to look around or get it?" he asked, eyes still watching the men but aware of Bob's reaction to the big sale.

Abby looked at the set. "I don't know." She walked around and looked at the different pieces, the cherry hutch, the dresser with an attached mirror, and the nightstands. It was complete, and she made a show of walking around looking.

"I can make you a good deal," Bob pleaded. "We can take 25% off the top."

Michael smiled knowingly at what was about to happen as Abby began walking, looking at other areas but keeping her view close. She turned and looked up at the big man named Bob. "I know your margins here are about 50%, the industry is 45%, but in looking at several items I had already looked at, it is obvious you have padded some a little. I am not an unfair person, but let's say we have money does not mean we have to flaunt or waste it, and if we don't have money, we want to be as frugal as possible. It's easy Bob. You jumped on the 25%, which means this has probably been here for a while. It is eating into time and inventory and affecting your gross profit potential. Let's really deal. If you want to sell this and the mattress, a big sale to say the least, and the other bedroom set over to the side, including another mattress," she pointed to an Oak set a few dozen feet away, "you will give me 30% off the top. We will have someone pick it up and pay cash. No games, no issues. That is my offer, or" Abby drew out the 'or' for several seconds, "we can drive to Lexington."

Bob stood mute, unsure of what to say with a strange look on his face as though he had just been played. Michael smiled a little and kept watching the front.

"I will start up the paperwork," Bob was again excited. As he turned, he looked to the front of the building and, upon seeing the three men, stumbled for only a moment. Bob then walked with conviction to the front office area.

Abby looked up at Michael and squeezed his hand again, "Trouble again?"

"Yeah, seems to follow us. Maybe it's just me," Michael sighed, putting his sunglasses on. The sun-sensitive lenses were now lighter than outside but dark enough to obscure his eyes. Michael and Abby made their way to the front. Michael glanced at the furniture as Abby walked to the counter. Bob was behind the desk and was shaking a little as he filled out some papers.

"Umm, delivery, ma'am?" Bob asked.

"We will send for it," Abby replied.

"Oh, that's right," Bob said and filled out some more. "Let me go put a sold sign on it."

"New furniture is good?" one of the men sitting down asked with a European accent.

Abby turned; "Of course, new furniture is always good."

The three men giggled, and one whispered to another in Ukrainian, "Spending all her money on some worthless wood."

Michael smiled and was silent.

"Do you need help with your furniture?" the man asked. "I could have my men help you."

"No, it's not necessary," Abby reiterated. "We will have it picked up."

Bob returned and handed Abby the receipt. "I need a name, address, and phone number."

"Not necessary," Abby said, "It will be picked up later today."

"I would like a name as well," the man obviously in charge of the small group sitting up from interjected.

"Let me finish with this customer," Bob told the man.

"It is no problem for her to give a name, is it not?" the man made a show of nodding to Abby, "My name is Alexi. I am pleased to meet you." The two men in the chairs laughed.

"I am not impressed," Abby noted without looking away.

Bob came around the counter.

"Of course you are impressed," Alexi pushed his bravado as Bob put himself between Abby and Alexi.

"I told you I was not interested," Bob was obviously upset and angry, "I would like you to leave and leave now."

Alexi grabbed Bob and pushed him to the floor. The two men began to stand, but Michael was behind them and pushed them down. They started to struggle, then both realized a blade was at each of their throats. They settled back into the convenience seats. Bob turned to get up as Alexi drew out a stainless Kimber 1911. As he began to point it at Bob, he felt a barrel against his head.

"Please hand me the pistol," Abby whispered. "I would hate to get your blood on this fine furniture."

"Kill her," Alexi spat in Ukrainian.

There was silence. "They have their own issues to deal with," Michael said in Ukrainian, "and it is her money to spend as she sees fit, do you not agree?"

Alexi turned and saw the two men held by the knives to their throats, "Fools," he shouted in English, "Outmaneuvered by an American."

Alexi swung the 1911 towards Michael as he pushed backward on Abby. She fell back, out of the way of the barrel of the gun. Michael raised his right arm and threw the Hibben throwing knife that had been on the neck of the second man. As the knife left his hand, he swung his arm around and pulled the concealed FN 57 pistol from under his coat. He placed it to the head of the second man, who had started moving. Michael's left hand never moved from the first man's neck. Alexi kept moving with his arc, but his hand was penetrated by the throwing knife. Abby was once again back in control. Alexi dropped the Kimber and grabbed for his hand. Abby pushed him to the ground and slammed her right foot on his back.

"That was stupid," Abby was now more than a little forceful in her tone.

Bob was beginning to stand up.

"Bob, please collect their weapons," Michael was nonchalant about his request.

Bob grabbed a cloth bag from the counter and walked next to Alexi, picked up his 1911 and walked to Michael.

"Slowly, gentlemen," Michael said as he tightened the knife on the first man's neck. Bob walked to the first man, and he began to reach in his jacket, "Two fingers," Michael instrcuted. The man slowed his reach, pulled out a weapon, then put it in the bag Bob held, "Is that a Makarov?" Michael asked. "Find many places that carry the ammo?" The man glared and stared forward, unable to see Michael easily with the knife to his neck. Bob moved to the second man and waited. Michael pushed the FN 57 against this temple. The man reached into his coat and slowly pulled out a Glock 17. "Nice weapon. Bob, please hand the bag to Abby and sit on the chair over there." Michael motioned. "Well, that could have been better."

"What are you going to do?" Bob asked.

"Not sure yet," Michael was contemplating his next move. "What's the story here?"

Alexi was holding his hand, the knife still through it. It had to have hurt, but Alexi didn't whimper. He just stared.

"They just came in last week and said they wanted to buy my store. I said no, but they said I would be convinced. At first, it was just one man, Alexi, but today he came back. I have no idea. They just wanted my store. I don't know nothin' else." Bob paused for a second, "Are you going to kill me?"

"No Bob," Michael's voice was aloof as he spoke with a wry smile, "I am going to buy a bed and a few other things from you."

Michael removed the knife from the first man's neck and walked around, still holding his weapon at the two seated men. He walked to Alexi. Michael glanced at Abby, and she shifted her weapon to the two men, who now looked at her. A woman holding a pistol, but they realized she didn't waver or sway at all. She was in control of the weapon and now, their fate. Michael holstered his pistol and leaned down to Alexi, who still just stared.

"This will hurt," Michael stated, "but I want my knife back."

Michael grabbed Alexi's hand and held it tight. Someone looking closely would have seen the hand turn white with the pressure. Michael grabbed the blade and pulled very fast, and blood surged a little as he did so. He held the blade for a second, walked the short distance to the counter, and picked up a few tissues. He dropped them on Alexi and pulled one more to clean his knife.

Michael walked over to the two men seated. "ID, please."

The men pulled out their wallets and handed them to Michael. "Green cards; Johan and Sven here are not citizens." Michael looked through the wallets and tossed them back. Both men caught their wallets. "I know you are trying to determine how to kill me right now. Personally, I would happily kill all three of you, but it would make a mess for Bob, and he would be torn up about it."

"I don't mind," Bob muttered.

"I have friends in Ukraine," Michael spoke in Ukrainian. "I also have acquaintances in the State Department. It would be best if you left and we didn't meet again, true?"

"Stupid American," Alexi seethed in Ukrainian. "I will not suffer this indignation. You do not know who you are dealing..."

Michael shot Alexi in the head. He fell to the ground and spasmed once, then twice, and stopped.

"Why is it that people always want revenge," Michael said. "I try to give everyone a choice that is fair and right, but people always want to test my resolve."

The two men were not wide-eyed. They looked at Michael, and it was obvious they now had a different opinion of their current situation.

"Sorry, Bob," Michael apologized. "I will get that cleaned up for you."

"Poor Alexi," Michael continued his earlier line of discussion as he walked towards Johan and Sven. "Why are you here?"

"We were ordered to buy this business," Johan was obviously nervous as he spoke. Sven elbowed him. Sven moved over a little.

"Why?" Michael asked.

"We were not told," Johan said. "Yuri wanted it. It is all we were told." Sven hit him in the ribs again.

"You tired of that?" Michael asked.

Sven straightened and realized what it meant as Michael aimed at his forehead.

"No, no," Johan panicked. "It is fine. He is my brother."

"Your brother?" Michael commiserated with him. "When Bob told you no, why did you come back?"

"We were told to get the business," Johan continued. "If it was not for sale, we were to kill the owner and buy it from the next owner."

Bob stiffened. His face became noticeably red.

Michael looked at Bob. "Can you close for a short time while we clean this up?"

Bob looked at Michael and composed himself. He seemed calmer than when the whole ordeal began and nodded with some enthusiasm. "Sure, I'll put up the lunch sign."

"Go ahead and do that," Michael said as Abby walked up, still aiming at the two men.

"Not the day we wanted," Abby shrugged.

"Seems to happen sometimes, but at least it is with you," Michael replied.

"That is a little cheesy, don't you think?" Abby still grinned at the statement.

Bob locked the door and walked back to Michael and Abby. As he passed Alexi, he glared down with an angry look. "I'm sorry, I could have just called the local police, and they would have handled it. I appreciate you getting involved."

"We could have just ignored it," Abby explained. "I am used to scum hitting on me from time to time."

Michael raised an eyebrow. "Just how often is this happening?" he laughed.

Abby grinned.

"What will you do with us?" Johan asked.

"Still deciding," Michael replied. "If I let you go, you might run to Yuri." Michael paused. "This is not Yuri Petrakov, is it?"

The two men looked at each other, "Why is it that you ask?"

Michael pulled his FN 57 again. "I will count to three, there will be no four. Is it Yuri Petrakov?"

The men nodded yes with some timidness.

"Who is Yuri?" Bob asked.

"He was a good man, but when his father died, he went a little power-hungry," Michael replied. He looked at the two men again. "Is Yuri in the area?"

"No," Johan replied. "He has not visited in some time. Alexi's brother, Oleg, is in charge of the Kentucky people."

"The Kentucky people, huh?" Michael was considering his options. "Bob, I am sorry."

"Why?" Bob asked.

"For the mess, of course," Michael replied.

Michael swung his arm and shot both men in the forehead. The FN 57 bullets went straight through, but the force still knocked both men backward in their seats.

Bob put his finger in his ear and wiggled it. "That will make a man deaf. How do you stand it?"

"Earplugs." Michael pulled out a small earplug. "Noise-canceling and amplifying."

"Would have been nice to warn me," Bob replied. "My ears will be ringing for hours."

"Sorry, Bob," Michael said as he holstered his weapon, and Abby holstered hers. "I will have to call to get this cleaned up. It will take a while."

"Won't be necessary, son," Bob was looking at the two men, "I'll have one of the Chaney boys come by and take these three out in carpet rolls. They can drop them in a lime pit, and they will be gone forever. Either that or I am sure the boys have hogs to feed."

Michael raised an eyebrow. "That easy?"

"We run a good clean city, but we don't take kindly to people who get in the middle of our business. Seems I owe you. If you hadn't been here, I might be in the lime pit today." Bob still looked at the bodies as one spasmed.

"Maybe," Michael nodded, "but maybe you would have taken care of them just fine."

"No, son," Bob looked at Michael solemnly, "I am getting to be an old man. You two get out of here. I will take care of this."

"Umm, about the furniture," Abby said. Michael smiled.

"Y'all still want it?" Bob asked.

"We will send a truck by later today," Michael said. "Then you won't hear from us again."

"I can give it to ya," Bob stated. "I mean, seein' as you saved my life."

Abby looked up at Michael and then said, "No, we'll take care of it." She pulled her small crossover purse to the front. She counted out a series of bills. "This is five thousand dollars." Abby said. "It should cover everything with tax and have a hundred and twenty-three dollars left. Keep that for the trouble."

Bob nodded, "You want the receipt?"

"We trust you," Abby looked at Bob with a wry grin, "you wouldn't cheat us."

"Oh, hell no," Bob replied. "Let me let you out." Bob walked to the door and spun the lock. "You want them guns?"

"Thanks, Bob. I am sure you can get rid of them or keep them. I have my own." Michael held the door open as he and Abby left. "You sure you are good with this?"

"Yeah, mister," Bob followed them to the door edge. "Never did get your name."

"Nope, you didn't," Michael said as they left. "The driver will find you."

"I'll take care of the guns then," Bob said as the door closed. He locked it and walked to the phone to make some calls.

Chapter 4

The winds whipped through the mountain hollows and rustled the trees as they passed through the valley. Thick ferns and brush made the areas nearly impassable for most who didn't know the area, but Eleanor Marie knew the bush better than most. In fact, she knew it better than anyone.

Eleanor Marie Comer grew up outside of Pikeville, Kentucky, and was raised as one of five daughters. She was the youngest, and her father gave up trying to have a son after her because it "was just too damn expensive." When he stopped thinking he would eventually have a son, Harv Comer decided to teach Eleanor Marie everything he knew about the land, hunting, fishing, and surviving.

As Eleanor Marie grew older, she went out on her own, and pretty soon, she was familiar with a great deal of the Appalachians. She had become a tried-and-true Wildcat basketball fan and believed the world would never be ready for her unless she proved herself every day.

She was seventeen years old yesterday and worked her way through the brush in an area she had not visited in a while. The growth was thick, and she knew the heavy rains this year had made almost any path not taken overgrown and unwieldy. The thick thorns tugged at her jeans and tried to pierce her leather gloves, but both were thick and would not give in easily. The denim caught but didn't pierce, and Eleanor Marie kept going. It was easy to see she could no longer move without a little help.

Eleanor Marie reached to her side and pulled out a machete. She would love to have one of the good ones she saw on TV, but there just wasn't enough cash lying around anymore. With the coal mostly gone, the area was fighting for cash, and a lot of people were moving away. She wasn't going down without a fight. At least not until she turned eighteen and could join the Army. Her cousin, Ronnie, had joined and was stationed up near Lexington. Pike County was beautiful, but Lexington and the surrounding areas were booming with technology, service businesses, and horse farm dollars. The city was flooding the area and full of prosperity. The Army would give her focus and teach her what she needed to know in life. She was going to succeed.

After cutting away patch after patch of thorns, Eleanor Marie came upon a clearing. There had not been a clearing here a year before when she wandered this area. She was cautious and a moment later came upon tight cables wrapped through the brush. She stopped and traced the cables until she found a small cellular box and a series of bells. She followed the line and was impressed that it had been run so only larger animals would set it off, most likely people. Sure, there were deer and elk in the area, and the occasional boar came through, but the normal coons and dogs would climb under if they could get here at all. She turned and reviewed her path. The thorns had been planted, and this thicket was built up to dissuade anyone from coming close, animal or man. After all, there was usually nothing here but brush, so who would care?

With patient ease, Eleanor Marie worked her way over the cables and watched for more. She was careful and didn't touch anything. Shine was legal now; in fact, there were Shine bars in areas close to them. Sure, the county was dry, but Pikeville allowed liquor sales, so she doubted it would be moonshine or similar. She also didn't think there would be much chance it was meth up here. It would be too hard to get in and out. No roads, no easy paths, just a lot of hills and wildlife. She worked up a short hill and looked out over a field.

The field was covered by netting and was partially shaded, but the sun was clear and crisp on the plants below. Pink and white flowers bloomed, and there was a significant amount, as far as her eyes could see. She was unfamiliar with the plant, but it was not something she normally would see here. There were irrigation lines running everywhere, and she knew this was a grow operation. She had seen several. For a long time, weed was one of Kentucky's biggest cash crops, but with the advent of legalization all over the country, this was being stifled and would soon become a commercial product in Kentucky. Eleanor Marie was glad. Her family had grown on State land, and their patch had been found and burned. It nearly put them out on the streets. She was not happy to break the law, but she was not happy about starving, either.

She picked a flower and put it in her pocket. Her dad would know what this was, and she would find out tonight. Turning, she worked her way back down the hill. As she made her way down, she watched for tripwires and anything out of the ordinary. She heard a whir and looked up, realizing she was now on a trail cam.

"Damnit," Eleanor Marie barked out loud as she doubled her speed. There was no way to get to the camera even though she could see the antenna. Someone would know soon. It was probable they already did. The area was not that big, she would be found, or worse, her family would be found.

Eleanor Marie cut a path through the thorns and pulled many of them closed behind her. The path would still show, but someone would have to have gloves as thick as hers to get through with any speed. Once off the hills, she came to her ATV. She considered for a moment. If they were close, they would hear the engine, and she would be an easy target. If they were farther away, she might have some time, and the ATV would get her quite a distance, maybe even allow her to evade the whole situation. Maybe the lens was blocked, maybe the leaves were in the way, maybe it was low resolution. Maybe.

"Damnit, girl, you got this," Eleanor Marie repeated to herself. She got on the big Honda and pressed start, the engine roared to life, and she took off in a cloud of dust heading towards home.

That was when she heard the whir. She pulled over after only 100 yards and killed the engine. The ATV coasted, and she could hear the whine of something in the air. She coasted next to a huge oak tree hoping the tree would give enough camouflage that whatever was up there would pass over. She waited. The buzzing was close then far, close then far.

Eleanor Marie jumped on the back of the ATV and hopped on a tree branch. She worked her way up several branches with her backpack on until she could see some of the sky above. She steadied herself and pulled out a smaller pack from her backpack. Opening it, she assembled a Ruger 10/22 takedown and, with a single motion, twisted it into a full rifle.

She then took a magazine from her pack and put it in the rifle and chambered a .22 round.

The buzzing continued. Eleanor Marie was watching. A few minutes later, she saw the large black drone sweep over the tree in an arc. It was moving very fast, and she didn't think whoever was driving it could have seen her, but then a second passed overhead, going across the line of the first. There were two, and they were searching with great vigor.

Eleanor Marie was concerned. She had seen drones and even flown one that her brother got in Louisville. She knew they could see a lot better than people. The one her brother had was HD and saw very well. She kept still and waited. She heard the drones swing back and saw one stop in the open area above her. She could see the camera twisting back and forth and then saw it focus on her. At the same time, she heard the second drone and turned around, seeing it only a few dozen feet to her right, hovering even with her. It was decision time.

Eleanor Marie turned to the high drone and aimed the rifle. She fired five shots in rapid succession. She was sure several hit as the drone began to fall. The second drone buzzed faster as it pulled away, trying to escape, but Eleanor Marie was faster. She turned and shot the drone four times. It fell to the ground a few feet from her ATV. She worked her way down the tree and jumped off the ATV. She put the rifle on the handlebars of the ATV and wrapped a cord over it.

Eleanor Marie could now hear other ATVs in the distance. She grabbed the drone and threw it on the back of the ATV, surprised at how big it was up close. She then jumped on, started the ATV, and headed out as fast as she could. There was a new sound now; she knew it well. Coon dogs were heading her way. She twisted the handle hard to get as much speed as possible and came out on the dirt road at the end of the hollow. Dust flew, and she slid, but she held control. She had been riding since about the time she could walk.

One hundred yards ahead, she could see the shape of a man waiting for her. He put up his hand and motioned her to stop. She didn't. He screamed, "Stop!" She could hear it only a little but knew that stopping would be the end of her, one way or another. People were tossed in hollows a lot, and she would not be found.

She was getting close now, and she saw the pistol being drawn by the man. She didn't recognize him. He was big, like her brother, but had a long black beard and dark glasses. His red short-sleeve shit was cut off to be shorter and was covered with stains. Eleanor Marie grabbed the rifle. It caught for a moment in the cord she had wrapped it with. She pulled harder, and it was free.

The man yelled stop again. She was only 100 feet from him now. He was aiming almost at her. Eleanor Marie aimed the rifle from the hip, like her daddy had taught her, and fired. The rifle was only a .22, but she saw it hit. The man looked surprised. She fired three more shots, and the man fell backwards. She passed by him on the dirt road and twisted to the south.

Where to go?

Eleanor Marie headed down the street to the abandoned Nichols farm. It was at least a mile, but she would make it. She could not hear the other ATVs or the dogs now, but she knew they would have heard her shots and probably had more drones. She hoped not, but they always had more in the movies. The road came into view, and she turned hard onto the driveway; it was only a short run to potential safety. A few dozen yards later, an old barn came into view. She saw the opening and shot into the mouth of the barn as she killed the engine. She pushed the ATV into a stall and got her pack and the rifle. Inside her pack was a sling for the rifle, and she put it on. She checked the 25-round magazine. She had ten shots left. She had one more but decided it was better to evade than to try to fight. She wasn't afraid, but she was outnumbered. Eleanor Marie then grabbed the drone and looked at it. It was not flashing or blinking, and she realized her shot had broken the battery packs. She was careful not to touch them. Her daddy always told her to keep her distance from open batteries. She looked over the drone, found a slot, and opened it. Inside was a small memory card. She took it and wiped the drone down the best she could. She put the card in her pack.

Eleanor Marie pulled off her bandana and reached into the front pocket of her pack. Inside was a bottle of red powder. She poured it on the bandana and threw it onto the ground. She reached into her pack, pulled out her phone, and took a picture of the drone. A moment later, she headed out the back of the barn and across a small field.

She looked at her phone as she entered the deep woods on the edge of the Nichol's farm. There was no signal. The farm was low in the valley, and signals bounced a lot out there. A few feet from now, she could have a signal. She walked for a while and checked again. She had one bar, and one bar of battery left. Neither could be counted on for long.

Behind her, Eleanor Marie heard gunfire. The dogs were barking and, a moment later, started whining. Eleanor Marie smiled, knowing they had gotten a full whiff of Cayenne and Ghost pepper. They would not be trailing her soon. Stopping for a moment, she scrolled through her phone's contact list until she came to a number. She dialed. Her cousin's voice came on the phone, "This is Ronnie Comer; leave me a message."

"Cousin Ronnie, this is Eleanor Marie. I am in some trouble, and I didn't know who to call. They are comin' for me. I need yer help. Call my daddy, call somebody, but I know you will find someone to help me." Shots were fired, and Eleanor Marie half shouted, "Got to go," and hung up.

Eleanor Marie ran and was soon deep in the woods. The shots kept firing, and the dogs kept wailing, but they were further and further behind her. She pressed further into the deep woods.

Chapter 5

The morning passed quickly as the team met and discussed the pile of paperwork Alex had before him. It made sense to Ronnie that the entire team was in the gym for his sparring match earlier. The team was there to determine their next steps and how they would be divided up. Occasionally there were larger jobs that required all of them to be involved, but lately, a lot of the work they did was on a much smaller scale. The new administration was always budget-conscious, and general Tarkington worked hard to show his team was a constant value.

Alex spent a considerable amount of time trying to sort through and decide what was best based on the skills of his team. In reality, they were a very low-budget group usually. It was only on the larger jobs that they sometimes ran into issues or had to spend on either equipment or transportation.

General Samuel Tarkington ran the team, and for the most part, they were off the books. Only a few people had working knowledge of the team's purpose and their actual work. Tarkington had originally taken and resolved issues that other agencies could not easily do, off the record and using whatever means necessary. The current team was built when a CIA operative went rogue and, in the process, uncovered an ex-assassin and tried to kill them. The situation didn't work out for the agent.

Tarkington recognized the unique bond of the team Alex Brown had created, and focused on items that were partially incomplete or needed resolving. Many of these involved the ex-assassin Jonathon Michael Masterson and the considerable tasks he took on while contracted by Tarkington.

Recently, they found that Masterson had also worked for a covert organization that dealt justice to those who "got away with it." The existence of such an organization had interested certain government agencies. The team was recently involved with a group that had gone rogue, and that made certain people worry.

"We are fully funded for two years, but the more we can do to extend that funding, the better for the team and us. I have been going through a series of open and unsolved cases in other agencies at the request of the General, and I would like your input. He may override us at any time, but in the end, we will have some downtime and can use that to further our value." Alex was serious and pointed in his approach. He handed out a single sheet of paper to everyone.

Alex scanned the room. Terry nodded and looked at the paper. Ronnie took the paper and held it in front of him. His lips moved a little as he read. Barbara took the paper and glanced at it. Sarena studied the paper and didn't look up at Alex. Rachel didn't look at the paper while Jim folded it into a paper airplane and threw it at Rachel.

"Or we could retire," Jim grumbled as he leaned back in his chair. "I was enjoying retirement before you pulled me back in here. I mean, I like you guys, and the team is good, but I was done. I had put in my twenty and was tired of saving Tarkington before we started saving Tarkington."

Alex considered. "Do you want out then?"

"Well, maybe," Jim said, "We have had some fun, but we have taken some beatings. Your face was nearly pounded to death, and the luck train runs out someday."

"What about the skill train?" Alex asked.

"I am just a dumb ol' country boy from Kentucky; we ain't got no skills," Jim retorted.

"Maybe it is best if he goes," Sarena was stern in her voice. "If he doesn't want to be here, maybe he puts us at risk."

Rachel threw a stapler at Jim, and he caught it midair.

"That solves the skill part," Rachel looked to Sarena. "Jim will save any one of us easily, including you. I feel pretty good about him having my back." Rachel paused and looked around, "Til I get my twenty in, at least."

Everyone laughed.

"In or out?" Alex asked Jim.

"I guess I am in," Jim said. "Too many ex-wives anyway. I don't want to find another. The mess feeds me, Rachel keeps me in shape, and I am sure Sarena will teach me how to shoot."

"What about me?" Ronnie asked.

"I need someone to outsmart me from time to time; you are it!" Jim grinned.

"Now that we've established that, let's get some work done," Alex moved to the front of the group. "In front of each of you is a sheet of paper with a series of case numbers. I put a short description with each one to give you a reference of what it is. I would like each of you to review these and give me your opinion on our direction. I have a call today to discuss something we may be pushed into, but I doubt it will take long. With that in mind, we have the resources available in this team to do almost anything. Each of you has a say, to an extent. We are still a military-run operation, but Tarkington has given us leeway because of our successes. My expectation is that we will have the freedom to choose some of our work as I've already said. If you would rather, I choose for us, I can do that, as well."

"Do you really want us to look this over without the background you've already collected?" Jim asked as he unfolded his paper airplane. "If you have a reasonable idea, I am more than willing to follow your lead. After all, you're the reason I'm here. That, and that Tarkington drafted me when Masterson came out of hiding."

"As I said, that's an option. If everyone agrees, I have no issue choosing for us all. I will ensure that we get the best possible jobs to improve us individually and our team," Alex was looking over several papers diligently as he spoke.

"I think I would rather do it that way," Sarena looked up from her papers; "After all, I would choose something someone else might not like. After Indianapolis, I'm here to learn from all of you."

"Wherever you want me to go, I will be there," Ronnie was direct and humble. "I'm here to serve, and this is the best opportunity I have ever had."

"Barbara and I'll fly you anywhere," Terry stated, "and will be there to fight whenever you need us."

"Hell," Rachel leaned back in her chair as she talked, "you just keep giving me people to be in the middle of, and I'll be happy. I'm not one for all this paper pushing and would rather be in the middle of an all-out fight in Venezuela than trying to figure out where our next job will be."

"See, boss," Jim stated, "that was pretty easy. We're like a group of finely aimed missiles. You aim us, and we'll take care of it."

"Okay," Alex said. "Dismissed then. Don't forget to pick up your phones."

"Oh yeah," Jim said; "this no phone rule in the meetings is for the birds. I could have caught up on a few games of Angry Birds during this discussion."

"That's exactly why the rule is there," Alex glared.

Jim laughed.

They walked to the tables at the side, and Ronnie picked up his phone.

"Weird," Ronnie said. "I missed a call. No one ever calls me."

"People always call when you can't answer," Rachel laughed. "Don't worry, it's probably about your car warranty."

"My cousin called," Ronne stated as he hit the buttons and played the message. "Something's wrong. She sounds scared, and she is scared of nothing."

"Really?" Rachel asked. "I have to meet this cousin."

"Listen," Ronnie said as he replayed the message on speaker.

"Cousin Ronnie, this is Eleanor Marie. I am in some trouble, and I didn't know who to call. They are comin' for me. I need yer help. Call my daddy, call somebody, but I know you will find someone to help me. They are here. I got to go." There were sounds in the background.

"That was gunfire," Sarena said as she walked up. "Small arms, probably an older TEC9. They looked cool but were barely more than 9mm pistols. You can hear the mock suppressor."

"You can?" Jim asked. "I never heard a mock suppressor."

Sarena smirked at Jim. "Please," she said, "I am sure you have."

"Well," Jim laughed, "Maybe once."

Ronnie picked up the phone and called the number. He waited, "Straight to voicemail." He scrolled through his contacts and called another number. He waited, "Her daddy is straight to voicemail too."

"Police?" Sarena asked.

"Troopers are down there sometimes, and there are lots of Sheriffs, but I don't know anybody anymore." Ronnie stated.

"Let's make some calls," Jim was serious for a moment. "We can head there if we need to."

Ronnie shook his head, "I will go; this is my problem, not yours." Ronnie headed out the door and said, "I will pack my bag."

"Problem?" Alex asked.

"Ronnie's cousin seems to be in an issue in Pikeville or somewhere down there," Jim was solemn. "He is a bit concerned and wants to head down there alone."

"We may have a job to do," Alex said. "But we can take some time if we need to."

"I will head down with him," Rachel was pointed and a little protective. "I wanna meet the girl who has no fear. We can handle it or call if we need help."

"Might be better if I go," Jim said.

"Can it, Jim," Rachel was quick to reply. "I can deal with anything you can."

"I know," Jim raised an eyebrow. "I just don't want you losing your temper."

"I can be good," Rachel whined. "We will be fine;" she paused, "She is probably pregnant or something."

"Take gear in case, and one of the Suburbans," Alex was practical. "Call if you run into trouble. Don't react, call."

"Yes, Sir," Rachel said. "I will keep up with Ronnie."

"You do that," Alex said as Rachel headed to the locker rooms.

"She will be fine," Jim assured Alex.

"I am sure she will," Alex replied. "I don't like it being so close to Ivel."

"Didn't think of that," Jim thought out loud. "Maybe we can just call down and…"

Alex raised an eyebrow, "Shut up, Jim."

Jim laughed as the group left the room.

Chapter 6

General Samuel Tarkington sat at his desk looking at the computer screen. He wasn't really reading anything and instead was thinking about the events over the last year. He had been injured and could have been killed. He was saved by a team that should have been dysfunctional. Tarkington considered the woman he put in Gitmo and the man he put in prison. All of these people had some ties to his past and the work of Jonathan Michael Masterson. It would have been easier if Masterson had gone off-grid completely. If he was in Bora Bora or some Pacific Island with no name, perhaps some of this would have never happened. But after thinking about it, he knew that people always reacted. Well, most people reacted.

Coming back to reality, Tarkington saw an email from another agency. He got these on occasion when someone needed help, wanted to scream at him, or wanted to talk about old times. He looked at the email and read through it, realizing this was actually a little of all three. Another agency wanted to discuss a person of interest that, through previous actions, Tarkington had accidentally put into power.

Tarkington pressed a button on his desk.

"Sarah, could you come in here for a moment?" he asked.

The door swung open a mere moment later, and Tarkington's admin, Sarah Collins, walked into the room. "Yes, Sir." Sarah had been with Tarkington for a long time. They had seen major issues together, and Sarah was offered many promotions. She refused them all. For a government employee, this was often a bad thing. But Sarah was loyal to Tarkington and wanted to be sure she was there for him and his teams. Every day was an adventure, and Tarkington kept her on her toes and constantly interested in her job.

"I'm going to forward you an email. I'd like you to pull the file on the job associated with this email. It's likely to be redacted, and maybe the redacting has been redacted but see what we have." Tarkington stated. "After you do that, we'll arrange a call with Alex and try to determine if we want to be involved. I know Alex will be all in, but this is another issue that will pull us back into Masterson's world. We may want to consider taking a break on that." Tarkington was sullen.

"Is there another team you want me to contact?" Sarah asked. "We have two out in the field right now and a list of independents you can call on."

"Let's wait until I talk to Alex and see how this goes," Tarkington said.

"Anything else, Sir?" Sarah asked.

"No, not at this time," Tarkington busied himself at his desk. "Let's take this as it comes. I have a scheduled call with Alex. I want you in the room too."

"Yes, Sir," Sarah said as she left the room.

Tarkington looked at this desk then stood and walked across the floor of his rather spartan office. He paced for a few minutes and then returned to the computer and replied to the email with a simple line.

"We will look into it."

Chapter 7

Alex Brown was at his desk with Jim Simpson, waiting for a call. Sarah Collins, General Tarkington's assistant, called and told Jim and Alex to be ready. The two waited.

"I guess we wait," Jim pulled out his phone.

Alex was reading a report, "Yep." Alex turned the page in one of the folders. "You could help and review a few of these outstanding items."

"Why in the world would I want to do your job for you?" Jim laughed as he pressed buttons on the phone and leaned back a little. "It is what makes you who you are and defines your level of bureaucracy."

"Pardon me?" Alex looked up from the folder. "How about we reassign and let Jim handle it all?"

"Oh, Alex, if you do that, I will not do it the way you want it, and you will take it away from me in a matter of weeks. By then, I will have solved or thrown away half of the items you stress about, and you will cuss me for about six weeks, and then we will be sitting here again."

They both started laughing.

"You are so easy," Jim pressed a few more spaces on his phone. "You need to lighten up."

The office phone rang, and Alex hit a button, putting it on speaker.

"Hello," Alex opened.

"Hi, Jim," Sarah said, "Hang on, and I will get the General."

The phone was quiet for a moment. "Alex. Who is with you?"

"It is just Jim and me," Alex replied.

"I will send you a file shortly about new activity in Ukraine. It appears numerous entities are acting and reacting within state and local governments in the States, and we need to determine how to address it.

At the center of it all is Yuri Petrakov. We crossed paths when his father, Anton, was eliminated about four years ago. Yuri took over his father's affairs and created a bigger, more progressive group that has weaseled its way into countries across the globe. Yuri's brother, Gaston, is off-grid and not considered a threat anymore."

"Why us? Surely there are larger groups?" Alex asked.

"True, but you may get traction on some of this if you talk to someone," Tarkington replied.

"How so?" Alex said.

"Five years ago, someone was sent in to eliminate Anton. That person did extensive research to ensure that the target would be eliminated without causing any upheavals in the government. To do so, they interacted with a number of individuals on a cursory basis and spent weeks monitoring and learning the habits of Anton and his family. It was determined the best solution was for Anton to die after breakfast, when he usually took a nap after his daily bacon and ostrich eggs. A special weapon was designed that injected Anton with a non-standard poison. This weapon was utilized like a small paint gun under high pressure. I don't know all the science behind it. The result was that Anton died of natural causes, as far as the world knows. No one was aware of Yuri's tenacity and his ability to grow his father's empire. To ensure the elimination was kept under wraps, only two copies exist of the report. No surveillance report was filed, nor was any of the workup done to get close enough for a contact poison weapon. The work was extensive on Anton and the rest of the family, including Yuri."

"Okay, so how do we get this intel?" Alex asked.

"You visit my daughter and see if you can persuade her boyfriend to divulge what he learned," Tarkington replied. "I doubt he has records, but who knows? He is thorough and may have his own record systems."

"Michael?" Alex asked.

"Did this guy kill everyone, I have been wondering about my grandma, we thought she had a flare-up of old age, but now I think maybe she got a visit from the guy," Jim chortled.

"Michael was very successful for us. He had a knack for direct and indirect elimination methods and was very thorough. You should know that by now. When he was working, he was almost obsessed with his target and their weaknesses. When Congress got soft and told us to stop doing what we always did, it slowed him down, but he got creative. His resolutions were more creative and less dependent on firearms. What was unique is he was not trained by us, nor anyone else we could find," Tarkington noted.

"He was trained, though," Jim was serious for a moment. "When we sparred, he used a lot of advanced techniques in the short time we were fighting. These aren't learned from books."

"His father had something to do with that, but he doesn't talk about it. When I first met him, and he began working for us, he was in college, and he was almost the same then as he is now. Perhaps a little cockier, if you can believe that," Tarkington replied.

"That would be scary," Jim was relaxed again.

"Do you have an issue with this Alex?" Tarkington asked.

"No, why?" Alex countered.

"You are being very quiet. I am not used to your dumb, excuse me, I am not used to you being so non-communicative," Tarkington stuttered.

"President still has his leash on you?" Jim laughed.

"Alex, can you handle this?" Tarkington reiterated.

"Of course," Alex began. "We have no ill will between Michael and the team. I am pretty sure he helped us recently in Venezuela, even though we didn't discuss it. That being said, each time we become involved with him, we run the risk of a pile of bodies in the wake."

"We never talked about it, but Michael was there in Venezuela," Tarkington said.

How do you know?" Jim asked.

"Classified, but it had to do with the target's death. The DEA is still in chaos over Miz. Samples and her refusal to step down or admit she did anything wrong. Justice would like her removed, but she did indirectly get results even though her goal was to capture a drug lord, and all she got was a dead drug lord."

"Classified?" Jim asked. "I think we know just about everything about this guy, and a lot of top-secret items do come our way."

"We'll talk about it over a beer next time I am in Kentucky," Tarkington said, "Until then, engage with Michael, determine a course of action, and get back to me. This could be a red herring, or at least not as important as it's being made out to be, but it could be a problem, as well. I expect to be kept in the loop if anything outside the States is necessary."

Sir," Alex broke in, "What is on the table here? If we discover Yuri is interfering with state or local governments, how are we to act?"

"You don't need to act," Tarkington replied. "Bring me the proof, and I will take it upstream for a decision. If you get involved in something, act how you think you should. Your ultimate job is to protect this country. Right?"

"Yes, sir," Alex said.

"He is so uptight," Jim laughed.

"It would be nice if you had a little respect," Tarkington snarked.

"I do have a little respect. I respect a good steak and a nice beer."

"Smartass," Tarkington replied.

"Oh, I am gonna tell," Jim laughed.

"You do that," Tarkington replied. "I am about tired of this little charade that was placed on me anyway. Maybe I need to go off, and either end this or get someone in a big white house to understand what I have to go through daily."

"I getcha," Jim laughed again, "I would not have been able to make it a day."

"Brown," Tarkington shifted the subject; "Let me know if you need anything or work via Sarah, and she will keep me apprised. I want weekly updates or as necessary."

"Will do, Sir," Alex replied.

The line went dead.

"We get to go play with Michael again," Jim laughed as though he was spinning a nursery rhyme, "that didn't turn out so well last time I went to his house."

"Get us a car, get Sarena, and the three of us will head to Ivel," Alex ordered.

"How do we know he is in Ivel?" Jim replied.

"Well, we don't," Alex stated. "We don't exactly have a phone number."

"Send Rachel and Ronnie over. They are close," Jim said. "We can go down after."

"Good idea, but it isn't that far we can't drive down," Alex said. "It will give us a chance to get out of the base for a while.

"Okay," Jim was obviously scheming, "but I get to drive."

"I can deal with that," Alex rolled his eyes. "Make it happen."

"You do know I was hoping Rachel could spar with Michael this time. I was sore for days after the last time," Jim smirked.

"You do know she would love that," Alex laughed.

"Yeah, she would," Jim replied and headed out the door.

The computer beeped, and Alex clicked his email: a file from Sarah. Alex opened the file and looked over the contents. He printed the file out so they could review it on the long drive. It took several minutes and finally was complete. Alex carefully stacked the papers, put them in a file folder, and turned off his light.

Always a new challenge.

Chapter 8

Eleanor Marie Comer had made good time into the deep woods. She kept working south, knowing that 881 was along a south route, but she was mindful that the dogs would be coming again. The pepper trick could not last for long. Eleanor Marie checked her phone, and the battery was nearly dead. She got a signal a few times, but when she tried to send anything, it failed. She didn't have a flashlight with her, so when she could not see, she was forced to use her phone as a flashlight, further draining the battery. As she got closer to the main roads, she might be able to find a place to charge. There were a few churches and a few houses, but not many.

Eleanor Marie knew how to start a fire and would have done so if not for the chance of being tracked. The warm Kentucky summer was not an issue, but the cold damp of the night was harsh and made her sore at every turn. Still, Eleanor Marie pushed forward. She had to hit a road in a few miles or less; there just wasn't that much free space in the area without roads. She figured she was in about 3,000 acres of trees, hills, hollows, deer, squirrel, and other animals at the moment. She just needed to get through a few hours. Someone in her family would come; she had counties of kin that could help.

What if they couldn't? The darkness tried to creep into her soul. She walked through the woods with as much stealth as possible. "If no one can help me, I will fix it myself," she said as she walked. Her cousin taught her that. She thought the world of Ronnie and wanted to understand. One day she and her ATV were stuck in the mud, and Ronnie came upon her, just sitting there.

****

"What are you waiting for, girl?" Ronnie had asked.

"I can't get it going," she said.

"Well, what are you waiting for?" Ronnie asked again.

"Someone to come help," she replied.

"You mean if I hadn't come along, you would have been sittin' here tomorrow when I got here?" Ronnie asked.

"No Sir," she said and started thinking.

"You know how to fix the problem. You know how to do it, so do it." Ronnie said. "I'll be off to the Army soon; who's gonna save you when ya need savin' then? You need to remember if no one can help you, then you can help you, right?"

"But I..." she started.

"You have a big butt there," Ronnie said. "Fraid yer gonna get dirty?" Ronnie picked up a wad of mud and flung it on her, getting her covered.

"Momma's gonna..." she yelled.

"Momma's gonna do nothing if you can't get home," Ronnie said, throwing more mud at her. As Eleanor Marie jumped off the ATV and she and her boots sank in the mud. She reached down and grabbed some mud and slung it at Ronnie.

"That's not gonna get you out," he laughed.

She looked at him with her head turned.

"Don't look at me like that," he pushed, "Solve the problem."

She looked at the tires, and one was dug in while the other road high. She dug around and grabbed sticks and brush from everywhere while Ronnie watched. She put them in front and in back of the tires and kept filling the muddy area. Then she jumped on the ATV and started it. She backed a little, then forward, then back, then forward, and she gained enough momentum to pull out of the muddy patch. She jumped off the ATV and yelled, "I did it."

"Who did it?" Ronnie asked louder.

"I did it," She yelled again.

"Feels good, doesn't it?" Ronnie said.

Smiling, she jumped on the ATV and began the ride home. Ronnie walked into the woods, and as she turned, he wasn't there anymore. They never talked about it again.

****

She wished Cousin Ronnie were here now. He would take care of this. She had no idea who was chasing her or why, but she had maybe killed a man now, or at least hurt him really bad. "Stop it," she said out loud. "No fear can grow where there are no worries."

She continued making her way through the woods. Her phone rang.

She looked at it; it was Ronnie. "Hello," she answered.

"Are you Okay, Elma?" Ronnie asked on the phone.

"You know I hate when you call me that," Eleanor Marie said.

"Are you okay?" Ronnie asked again.

"My phone's almost dead. I am in the hills, I think, about a mile or two from 881 to the south. I got turned around a little in the dark. I left the ATV at the Nichols farm, pretty sure they found it."

"Who are they?" Ronnie said.

"Don't rightly know," she replied. "I found a field full of flowers; it was wired like a still field or a pot field but had a canopy over it too. Then they just started chasing me. Tried to shoot me too, but I shot back."

"You find someplace and lay low, find a way to charge your phone but turn it off until 10:00 AM," Ronnie said, "You got that? Turn it off after you hang up til 10:00 AM."

"I will," Eleanor Marie said, "I got a charger in my pack, just got to find a plug."

"You do that," Ronnie said, "I am heading that way."

"Thank you," Eleanor Marie was relieved. "I knew you would come."

"I will try to get your family on the drive, they must be worried about you," Ronnie said.

"Naw," Eleanor was more relaxed now. "I sleep outside a lot in the summer. They won't miss me for a while."

"Well, I will get in touch with them anyway," Ronnie replied. "I will call you at 10:00AM sharp. You got that?"

"Yes, Sir," Eleanor shouted with a military snap.

"Bye," Ronnie hung up.

Eleanor felt good knowing he was coming; Ronnie would know what to do. As she worked through the brush, she saw a distant light pass. It was a car, no more than half a mile from her. She made sure to turn her phone completely off. She then stowed it in her backpack in an inside compartment. She didn't want to lose it now. As she worked her way down towards where she saw the light, she was very careful. There were no streetlights or any other telltales, and this time of night, she doubted there would be another car for a while. The darkness made moving very slow. As she came down the road, she was surprised to see a light. Below her was a house, and she could now work her way towards the light.

Coming to the street, she looked out both ways, and the road was clear. In front of her was a small house, then a larger building off to the side. She moved towards the larger building that was quiet and realized it was a school. She found her way around the larger building and looked all over the walls until she found an outside outlet.

Eleanor pulled her charger and phone from her backpack and plugged them into the outlet. She was excited when she saw the screen show a battery and begin pulsing. She followed the building a few feet further, and there was a series of decorative bushes. Walking back to her phone, she hid it under the edge of the school, then tucked herself behind the bushes. It was not comfortable, but not as bad as some of the places she had slept. She leaned back and soon was asleep.

Chapter 9

Ronnie drove from Richmond to Pikeville in just over three hours. Rachel forced him to let her come with him, and Alex was good with that.

"Maybe you two can keep each other out of trouble," Alex said.

"Maybe I should go," Jim added.

"Wow, maybe not," Alex laughed. "It may not be a big deal at all."

Ronnie tried to call everyone he knew in the area with little luck, and when the time got away from him, he tried Eleanor one last time. She answered, and he knew he had to leave then. It was 2:00 AM when he left, and normally the drive would have been just under four hours. Ronnie watched the sunrise and woke Rachel as they came into the city. The big Black Suburban was well suited for the area and would climb a mountain if necessary.

Alex gave orders that if there was trouble to call, the team could be there in short order and land at the small airport in Pikeville. Ronnie knew it would be fine.

As Rachel yawned, Ronnie put on his headset and dialed Harv Comer.

"Hello," came the voice.

"Harv," Ronnie said; "This is Ronnie."

"Ronnie boy," Harv replied in a split second; "What are you doing calling? That could get you in trouble with those Army dudes, right?"

"Harv, I am here in Pikeville. Elma called me last night and said there was trouble," Ronnie stated.

"You know she hates it when you call her that," Harv replied. "Let me see if she is here."

"Harv," Ronnie interupted; "She is in the woods."

Ronnie heard Harv yelling for her and then voices in the background. He waited, knowing the phone could not be heard at the moment. Then he heard shuffling, and a voice came back, "She ain't answering Ronnie. I will have her call you." Then the line went dead.

Ronnie looked frustrated and dialed the phone again. "Hello," came the voice.

"Harv, don't hang up on me," Ronnie said, trying to remain calm.

"No, I don't want no insurance for my car. You people best be calling some other folk and not bothering me." The phone went dead.

"Something's wrong," Ronnie said.

Rachel was awake immediately. "What?"

"My uncle just told me not to talk about insurance," Ronnie replied, "Someone must be there."

"Well, what are you waiting for?" Rachel said. "Let's go!"

"It ain't that easy," Ronnie began, "He is up in the hills. If we drive in, there is only one way in or out, and we would be sitting ducks. We would have to park somewhere in the distance and make our way over the hills to avoid being seen."

"That works, too," Rachel laughed. "What's your problem? We have done that in worse places."

"My uncle, well, he is a bit of a prepper. There could be traps everywhere."

"Ronnie, we have been in worse than that, I am sure," Rachel replied. "Get us somewhere so we can find out what the hell is going on and get back."

Ronnie put the Suburban in gear and headed out. Pikeville is a beautiful town and transitions from city to country in an instant. The city faded into the background, and they were heading up a hill, then down another, and repeated this for miles. With virtually no warning, Ronnie pulled over and parked on the side of the road.

"Okay," Ronnie pointed, "It is over that hill and down a bit, we can get there easily from here."

"This is like that Red River stuff you took me on, right? Billy goat style?" Rachel stated.

"You said it was no issue. I am taking you at your word," Ronnie laughed; "And we did the zip lines later, so you were happy too."

"Yeah yeah," Rachel grumbled. "Too much silliness first. We could have done them twice. Let's rock this."

Both of them got out of the car and pulled packs from the back, Rachel began to pull her M16, Ronnie said, "We may not need that."

"We might, though," she was adamant, "What if we do and leave them here?"

Ronnie considered, "I know you are right. I just don't feel good about going on my uncle's property loaded for anything."

"Ronnie," Rachel continued, "For someone so damn smart, you are stupid sometimes. Your uncle all but told you something bad was going on, and you still want to give whatever is bad the advantage? How about we don't?"

Ronnie lowered his head. "Family does that to you."

"Yeah, and if there is nothing wrong and your uncle has a screw loose, well, we will show him the shiny big guns and laugh about it later."

"You're right, Rachel," Ronnie admitted.

"Ah hell," Rachel laughed, "Say it again!"

Ronnie pulled out a flak vest and, setting down his pack, put on the vest, then cinched it. He put his pack on his back and adjusted the strap on his weapon, so it was in front of him. Pulling it up, he checked his rounds, made sure one was chambered, then put the safety on. "Ready."

"That's what I'm talking about," Rachel laughed. She did the same and put on a pair of fingerless leather gloves.

"Why do you like trouble so much?" Ronnie asked as he locked the Suburban.

"Who says I like trouble?" Rachel questioned.

"You rush in all the time and are always ready for trouble," Ronnie stated.

"I would rather rush into trouble than have trouble rush into me. If I am pushing, I control how we engage rather than playing defense."

"Well, isn't that why Jim beats you?" Ronnie asked.

Rachel stopped and looked at Ronnie for a second. "Maybe," she began, "but maybe I need to push the envelope for both of us. Jim fights very defensively; I don't, but it works for both of us. Ever notice we don't play to win anymore."

"Yeah, since the first time you fought, and he made you mad."

"I learned something that day," Rachel seemed thoughtful for a moment. "I am not always going to be the best, but I am also not going to be anyone else. I will never be able to fight like Jim, it would make me crazy, and he rarely fights like me. When we go at it, we are the best we can be for how we fight. I mean, you remember Bruce Lee, right? He didn't teach people to fight only one way; he taught them to fight the best way they could. He knew more about fighting than most people ever would, but he died early. I read his book, *Striking Thoughts*, and he was that way with his brain too. Open your mind and be the best you can be, not the best that someone can make you."

"Wow, Rachel," Ronnie said as he climbed the hillside, "You never talk this much."

"I think Jim is rubbing off on me," Rachel laughed. "We talk about crap like this all the time. He wants me to think through things more, and I keep barreling in. Last time a fat guy jumped on me, remember?"

Ronnie picked up the pace. They were heading up the hill in short order. As they came to the top, Ronnie stopped and looked out over the hills and the much higher mountainsides.

"One more hill," Ronnie said as they ran down the current one. As they reached the bottom, Ronnie began going back up and stopped.

"Watch your step." He pointed to a tripwire with a camera on it. They both stepped over. As he worked his way up the next hill. There were fifteen more traps in various areas, including two claymore mines. "I am not sure where he gets these mines; they are military only."

"Sure, you don't know," Rachel giggled.

"I would never," Ronnie was indignant.

"I know that. I was kidding." Rachel giggled more. "Your body would catch fire if you ever stole anything."

Ronnie turned red as they reached the crest of the next hill. He crouched and then lay in the thick grass overlooking an older white house. The house was not falling apart or in terrible shape, but the wood slat siding and faded paint said it was at least fifty years old. There were barrels and pallets in the yard and an older Chevy truck with grass growing up around it. Ronnie pulled out a monocular and scanned the area.

"There are two men on the porch I don't know," Ronnie said. "They both have side holsters." He handed the monocular to Rachel.

"Yeah, one car, two men. You know they are driving the black Ford Focus."

Ronnie took back the monocular and looked again, "Yeah, my uncle sure doesn't have one of those."

"Can we sneak up on them?" Rachel asked.

"Maybe, but we will have to work our way around and hope they are not walking the area," Ronnie said.

"Are you expecting them to be military up here?" Rachel asked.

"Well," Ronnie said, "No, but you know how some people are."

"Wow," Rachel said, "I guess I do. Let's work down from the back and come out on both sides. I will cover you at twenty yards as we go downhill."

"Yes, Sir" Ronnie said.

"What?" Rachel laughed.

"Force of habit," Ronnie said as they worked their way to the back of the house. Ronnie began the crawl downhill, staying in the grass as much as possible. Rachel watched the area and saw no movement. After Ronnie was about twenty yards out, she started her descent and stopped every few yards to watch over him. Ronnie reached the bottom and rushed to the back of the house. There was only one window on the back of the house, and it was up high for the back bathroom, so no one could see them unless they were in the line of sight.

Rachel was down next to Ronnie in a matter of moments. "You ready?" she asked.

"Yeah," Ronnie said, pulling his weapon to ready and turning his black ball cap around.

Rachel walked to the other side of the back of the house and peeked around; it was clear. She looked at Ronnie and then put up her hand for five seconds. She turned the corner and walked to the front of the house. She was sure Ronnie was doing the same. Three, two, one. Rachel swung around the front with her weapon aimed at the two men just as Ronnie did the same.

"Hands," Rachel said.

The two men raised their hands up in a very slow progression. "Who are you?" The lead man asked.

Rachel sized him up. His accent was European. He had dark hair, almost black. His dark brown eyes were piercing, and right now, they were angry. He wore a black dress shirt and jeans with expensive cowboy boots. A silver belt buckle on his belt made him look like he just exited a rodeo.

"Welcome wagon," Rachel smiled.

"Where's my uncle?" Ronnie asked.

A big man walked out of the house and looked at Ronnie, then at Rachel.

66

"Tell them to lower their weapons," the man in black said.

"The hell I will," Harv said, hitting the man in the face, knocking him to the ground. The second man reached for his weapon, but Ronnie hit him with the butt of his rifle and stepped over the top of him, pointing the M16 at his face.

The man in black started to draw his weapon. Rachel said, "No, no, I would hate to ruin that pretty face of yours."

He held his hand at his holster. "You are bluffing," he said. "A soft American soldier. You will not kill me."

Rachel stared at him, and Ronnie jumped in. "Don't kill him, Rachel. Alex will have our hides."

"Not mine," Rachel said, her finger off the guard and on the trigger.

Harv walked down and pulled the man's weapon from him.

A gunshot fired, and a slug hit a few inches from Rachel. She glanced at the bullet hole and looked out, "Oh no, you didn't!" she yelled and began walking towards whoever was firing. A second shot came in at her feet, and Rachel began firing towards the area of the muzzle flash. The weapon was set in three burst rounds. Rachel fired until all thirty shots were spent. As she "duck walked" towards the earlier muzzle flash, dropped the magazine, then slapped in another and flipped the switch to full auto. Rachel began spraying the area where she had seen the muzzle flash and didn't stop walking. She guessed the shot was about 100 yards out, and there was no other return fire.

The man in black tried to get up. Ronnie swung the rifle over and shot him in the foot.

"Ayyyy!" the man screamed and fell to the ground. Harv pointed the 1911 at the man.

"It'll heal," Harv said. "Just shut up."

Rachel dropped another magazine and loaded again and kept spraying. At about twenty yards out, a man yelled, "Stop, I give up," in a European accent.

Rachel stopped firing and waited. The man stepped out, his arm was bleeding pretty bad, and he held it with his other hand.

"I need a doctor," the man wallowed.

"I need a Pepsi," Rachel replied. "Get your ass over here."

He walked to her. Rachel towered over him. "You shot at me?" She pushed him forward and walked him back to the house. As they walked, she slapped him on the head twice in frustration.

Ronnie looked at his uncle, "Who are these people?"

"I don't rightly know, Ronnie," Harv replied. "I've seen this guy; he calls himself Victor. He has been at the bar downtown wearing a big black cowboy hat. I'd never seen the others until the middle of the night last night. They came into the house and punched me in the face. They were looking for Eleanor."

"Have you seen her?" Ronnie asked.

"No," she was out again. "She sleeps in those damn hills all the time now."

Rachel zip-tied the man whose arm was bleeding and knocked him to the ground. She then walked to the man in black. "Howdy Victor," she laughed and easily picked him up with one arm. Victor reached to his side and pulled out a knife, but Rachel let her rifle dangle in front of her and grabbed his knife hand. Victor pushed the knife. It was working its way toward her chest. "Oh no," Rachel said in a girly voice. She turned the knife, and with biceps flexing, pushed the blade all the way to Victor's throat. "I am sure you didn't mean to treat me with a lack of respect, Victor. Should I shove this blade through your damn neck, or are you ready to cool your jets?" Victor still struggled, but Rachel smiled. The tip of the blade began to pierce his skin.

"Okay," he surrendered. As Rachel backed off her hold, he let loose the knife.

Rachel twisted his arm behind him, then grabbed his other arm and zip-tied them together. She pulled him back to her. "Bad move, little man."

"You do not know who you are interfering with," Victor seethed.

Rachel grabbed Victor by his zip-tied arms and lifted him off the ground. He groaned and tried to twist.

"Maybe it is you that don't know who you are dealing with," Rachel said in his ear. "I would be really pissed if you had hurt Uncle Harv here. I might have had to rip your arms off." She threw him down.

"This your girl?" Harv laughed. "I like her." The two men on the ground looked up at them. The third man under Ronnie was still prone. Ronnie stepped off him and pulled him up. Rachel zip-tied his hands tight and threw him with the other two.

"Any more?" Rachel asked.

Harv shrugged. "I only saw the two. The third must have been dropped off. Name's Harv." He put out his hand. Rachel took his hand and shook it firmly.

"Rachel, Rachel Brown," she said, "I work with Ronnie."

"I thought maybe you were Ronnie's girlfriend," Harv grinned.

"Uncle Harv," Ronnie broke in, "she is just a friend."

"I know, I know. You told me all about Rachel," Harv said. "Ronnie's told me all about you, Rachel."

Rachel raised an eyebrow and looked at Ronnie, then knelt down to the three men. She picked up Victor's knife. "Boy, the ideas this gives me. What are you three doing here?"

"Having tea," Victor said.

"I'm gonna ask you again," Rachel replied. "What are you three doing here?"

"Rachel, these are civilians," Ronnie warned.

Victor looked at Ronnie, then back at Rachel, "We were having tea."

Rachel slammed the blade of the knife into Victor's femur. The blade stuck fast in the bone.

Victor Twisted his head and spit. "I want some more tea."

She left the knife and stood up. "Harv, what did they want?"

Harv looked down at the knife and smiled as Rachel put her foot on the man's leg. "They just wanted Eleanor. They said she took something that was theirs."

"That right, Vic?" Rachel asked as she leaned down and started pulling the knife. "Damn, this is stuck good." She started wiggling the blade back and forth while Victor winced. Eventually, she pulled it out. "Did the girl steal from you?"

"Yes," Victor said. "We wanted to discuss it over tea."

"We'll see," Rachel chided and slapped Victor, knocking him over. "Ronnie, you wanna go find the girl, and I will stay here with these bozos. We can have some tea."

"I can take care of them," Harv said. "You can both go find Eleanor."

Ronnie looked down at the three men. "One of us can stay, and one can go. Can we put them in the house, though?"

"Damnit, Ronnie," Harv said. "Eleanor knows these hills better than anyone. You should both go."

Harv reached down and picked up one of the men. "We can put them on the couch so I can watch my shows."

"Whatcha gonna watch?" Rachel asked.

"*Days of Our Lives*," Harv said. "My retirement morning. I have a bunch on cable to catch up. The damn box is almost full. Gotta get rid of some of them to make space for the *Bachelor*."

"Well, fun," Rachel said, rolling her eyes.

It was 8:00 AM, and Ronnie looked at Rachel. "Two hours, we can join."

"I'll make you some breakfast," Harv was walking towards his kitchen.

"Yum," Rachel laughed. Ronnie scanned the outside as Harv and Rachel took the men into the house and deposited them on the couch. It was a big area. He wanted to know where Eleanor was, and he knew it needed to happen now.

Chapter 10

Eleanor Marie woke with a start. There were people close, and she slowly sat up and looked around. She heard cars in the area and the droning sound of a number of people talking. Eleanor scurried to where she plugged in her phone, unplugged it all, and checked the phone charge. It was at 100%. She checked her watch and had an hour before she needed to call Ronnie. She put the phone in her pack, put her hood up, and began walking down to the road.

It was a sunny Kentucky day. The blue skies were spotted with only a few puffy white clouds, and the early morning breeze was cool and refreshing. The mountain air was filled with scents of the plants around them. The crisp smell of pine, mint, and a dozen other smells assailed Eleanor as she walked. She was hungry and pulled out a *Powerbar* from her pack, then went to the unmarked trail on the next hill. She had some time and just wanted to be out of the way.

Finding a large tree, she sat down and thought about the previous night. It had been tense, and she began to overthink the moments. She shot a man, and she was on the run. She pulled out the flower she found. She had not seen it in the area and was sure it was not a good flower. Ronnie would be here already; Ronnie would know what to do. Feeling impatient, Eleanor put away the flower, found her phone, and turned it on. It took a few moments to come online, but she had a signal and wanted to get moving. Eleanor dialed Ronnie.

The phone rang only once, "Elma?"

"I hate it when you call me that," Eleanor noted. "We discussed that last night."

"You're early. Where are you?" Ronnie asked.

From her vantage point, she could see the building below, and watched two black BMWs pull up and park. Four men got out of each car and began to look around.

"Ronnie," she whispered; "They are here. I am going back into the woods and turning off my phone. I am right on 881 now, at the school with the church next to it. I will go in deep and try to watch for you."

The men were holding a small device and moving it around.

"Just stay put; I will be there in five minutes," Ronnie said, and she heard an engine whine over the phone.

"I can't," Eleanor said. "They have some box, and they are looking this way; I have to go." Eleanor turned off the phone and put it away. She put on her pack and began climbing the hill with as much stealth and speed as she could muster.

She could hear the beep of horns behind her and looked back for a second to see several of the men coming across for her. She felt some relief as she saw the man she shot in the distance with a sling, but then regretted it and wondered how she missed. The hill was steep in areas, and she was careful not to slip. The loose rock occasionally ground between her shoes and threatened to take away her footing, but she held fast. She could hear rustling below her, too close for her liking. Eleanor picked up her pace. The hill was challenging, but Eleanor was used to the embankments and began running up the hill.

The sounds behind her started to fall back. She heard a large rustle, then scream; someone fell. She didn't stop; instead, she moved even faster. Eleanor didn't give an inch and was soon at the top of the hill. She looked down; the building was now small, and the cars were tiny from this distance. She went down the short slope and began climbing the next hill.

As she reached a few dozen feet up, a man broke out behind her, about 200 yards back, and she saw him pull a gun and fire at her. It was odd that he would shoot at her as he could not have a clear shot nor see her easily, but she wasn't waiting to see if he could get lucky. She moved faster up the second half of the hill. She heard another shot and ducked but could not see the man anymore. Realizing he may be trying to slow her down, she worked her way up, then began walking down the hollow of the next hill. She made good time and had her choice of where she should go next. This time, she went due north. This angled her up a hill.

She made sure to walk on as much rock and wood as she could so as not to leave a trail or tracks. She heard a crashing behind her and slipped behind a big Oak tree. As she peered around the edge, Eleanor saw that one of the men had lost his footing and fallen. They were far behind her now, but even at this distance, she could see the blood pouring off his head as another man helped him up. Both were looking around, and she was sure she was out of site. They began to work their way up as the bigger man helped the man who was bleeding.

Eleanor knew this was not a reprieve. She worked her way up the hill to the north and found a spot to rest for a moment. As she sat on a limestone outcropping, she heard buzzing. She knew instantly what it meant; the drones were coming again.

Eleanor got up and ran under the cover of the trees. She listened and watched and kept working her way to the north. The hills she was on now were higher and would take her longer. She kept her eyes glued to the sky as the cover thinned as she got higher up. Fortunately, the drones were moving more east and west, following the edges of the road, most likely. Their flaw was they didn't think she would go back into the woods. Her advantage was she could live in the woods almost indefinitely.

She saw a mark in the trees. It was a simple set of lines, but she knew the mark and knew she could follow those marks to a shelter. She and her older friends had marked many areas so they could play Army in the woods. Her friends had grown up, got jobs, got pregnant, gone to college, or moved to big cities. She was the youngest and a few years away. Using the tree as a sight, she looked for the next one and found it about thirty yards away. She worked her way to the next tree and then duplicated the process again, finding another tree about thirty-five yards away. The drones were nonexistent overhead now. Either the woods became too thick to hear them, or they were searching in other areas.

Another tree led her to a small door hidden in brush over a limestone cave. This was the realm of the other team. If she had followed the marks the other way, she would have found her old home base. She went inside and pulled the door closed. Eleanor reached into her pack and pulled out a Zippo lighter. In the cave no one could see, so she lit it and looked around. A small oil lantern hung on the wall.

Eleanor opened the lantern and found it still had fuel. She closed it up and lit it, then turned it down fairly low. The old base was about ten feet wide and snaked backward for a while. She knew it could go far back or only a few feet. Only the first ten feet or so were cleared. Several other lanterns were on the wall, a flag for their team, and a series of boxes hung from the roof of the cave.

As Eleanor stood, she could open the boxes to see inside. The first box had food in it. Old Army MREs in plastic bags, candy bars, and a small bag of Twinkies. She remembered how both teams said to use Twinkies because they would never go bad. Looking at the Twinkie, they may have been right, but as she pulled one out, she realized it was no longer spongy. She laughed and looked at the date; it expired over three years ago.

"Might wait on that," she spoke out loud and grinned at the echo.

She went through another box that contained old knives and BBs for their BB guns. These would not help her much, so she closed the box. The next box had several boxes of 22LR ammunition and an older Ruger Mark 1 pistol. She took the pistol out and checked it. It had some rust on the sights but otherwise looked clean. Eleanor checked the magazine. It was full. She ejected a live round from the slide. She wasn't sure whose pistol this was, but it might be useful now. In the box was a cloth and gun oil as well. She didn't see a cleaning kit, so she did the best she could with what she had available and cleaned the sleek black pistol the best she could. She checked the bore, and it looked clear as well.

"Lucky me," Eleanor was excited about the find.

She checked the cartridges in the magazine by removing them all. As sometimes happens, the top one was crimped over time. She left the slightly crimped cartridge in the box and reloaded the magazine. Eleanor then chambered a round, engaged the safety, then stowed the pistol in the front of her backpack.

The next box contained multiple lighters; she took two so she would have them if necessary. Various other items, like a compass, and clamps, were in the box as well. She didn't need those and left them. She made sure all the boxes were closed. It was good to know there were MREs if necessary, but she didn't need them yet.

Eleanor felt silly for a moment and reached into her backpack and grabbed her phone. She sighed when it showed no signal. She walked to the door area and, with great care, moved the door. She heard nothing. Her phone still showed no signal, so she opened the door a small amount and stepped outside. There was no sound; she could not hear the drones or any people; just the birds, the animals, and the rustling of the breeze. She checked the phone as she scanned the area. There was a little signal.

Eleanor dialed Ronnie. As she did, the phone beeped and was out of range. She ventured a little further from the cave, and there was a little more signal. She dialed again.

The phone rang once, and clicked on, "Elma, where are you?"

"Ronnie," Eleanor was irritated, "I don't like that name. I am at one of the forts in the high woods."

"We just got to the church. There are people all over," Ronnie reported.

"They were in cars, Ronnie," Eleanor whispered. "They were chasing me; they have drones and all." Eleanor heard crashing in the distance, "Someone is coming. I have to go."

The phone hung up.

Ronnie would find her. She would be fine.

Chapter 11

Ronnie and Rachel arrived at the small church area. There was a hustle and bustle that was unexpected, given the size of the area. Rachel jumped out of the Suburban and looked around. Two men stood in front of two black BMWs to one side of the parking lot. One was talking on the phone. As Ronnie got out of the big vehicle, Rachel walked towards the two men.

Ronnie hurried his pace. He knew Rachel was decisive and would not be too hasty, but he also knew that he needed to find his cousin more than roust a few men that might or might not be involved. Rachel was twenty yards away from the men when the man on the phone closed his phone and spoke. He wore a black leather jacket over blue jeans and a T-shirt.

"May I help you?" the man asked in a thick accent.

"Yeah," Rachel pleaded in an exaggerated Southern accent, "I am looking for my little sister. She is a girl about this tall." Rachel moved her hand up and down a little, not stopping at any one height. "She called and said some bad men were chasing her, and I was hoping you nice gentlemen could help me and my poor brother find her. He is a little touched, you know. Have either of you seen a young girl running from some bad men?"

The two looked at each other, "No, we have seen nothing."

"Okay then," Rachel said in her exaggerated voice. She turned and walked back towards Ronnie.

As Ronnie walked towards her, Rachel reached him and grabbed his shoulders. "What are they doing?" she whispered.

Ronnie glanced over her shoulder by getting on his tiptoes. "The one you were talking to is on the phone gesturing towards you."

"Good," Rachel said. "Now keep watching."

"There, there," Rachel shouted in her over the top Southern accent; she turned a little towards the men again. "He is just so torn up. I have to take him back to the looney bin later today."

"Looney bin?" Ronnie exclaimed in a whisper, "What am I, the dumb brother?"

"Well, yeah," Rachel laughed a little facing him again. "I wasn't gonna be the dumb lookout. You pay attention better anyway." She reached into his shoulder rig and unlatched the pistol lock in the rig. "What are they doing?"

"They are talking, and the man you talked to is really irritated; they are both looking at us. He is reaching into his coat; he has a gun."

Rachel was already moving. She pulled Ronnie's M9 out and spun on her heel. The man was arcing his pistol up as she yelled, "Drop it." He didn't. His eyes widened as Rachel shot twice. His body flew back with the impact of the two slugs in his chest. The second man began to draw his weapon but stopped as he saw his partner fall to the ground. Rachel rushed up to him and pressed the weapon to his forehead noting the man pull back as the hot barrel burned. "Ronnie, check the other one," Rachel yelled.

Ronnie rushed to the second man lying on the ground. His chest was covered in blood, and two holes were dead center in his body. Ronnie checked the pulse in his neck. "He's gone."

"You killed him," the man Ronnie held said with virtually no emotion. "Why?"

"Don't ya'll know to never pull a gun on a Southern girl?" Rachel said in her exaggerated Southern drawl.

"You are not from here," the man remarked.

"Ya'll don't know that," Rachel declared in her southern accent. "What's yer name?"

"I am John," the man looked away as he spoke.

"Well, hiya John," Rachel said, noticing the few people walking out of the buildings and looking their way.

"One of ya'll call the police," Rachel yelled and saw a woman scurry away.

"Yes, the police will be good," John said. "My poor friend is dead, and you killed him for no good reason."

"Aww, you sayin' we are gonna get in trouble?" Rachel said as Ronnie stood next to her.

"We have deal with city. You will go to jail," John replied.

"Can't have that can we? I may as well kill ya'll too," Rachel laughed a little, "Then I can make up my own story."

John's eyes widened but only for a moment. "You are from America; you are not a killer."

Ronnie actually started laughing. It began as a small giggler and erupted into a belly laugh, then a roar. Rachel turned and looked at him. "What are you laughing at?"

Ronnie motioned to John, "Him, you just killed his friend, and I think you have," Ronnie paused, "what, twenty confirmed kills in the last month. Hell, you beat that guy to death in Michigan; that wasn't too long ago." Ronnie paused again, "Plus, this guy has been messing with my cousin. I think I want to kill him."

John was looking from side to side as Rachel replied, "Well, we could take him back to your uncle's and see what he knows."

"Too late," Ronnie said, "Police are probably on the way."

"We need to kill him then?" Rachel said.

"No," John said, "I can help you."

"You just said you were gonna turn us in," Rachel said as she turned back to John.

"I was wrong," John replied, "I will tell the police all is well."

"Your friend is dead," Rachel looked at the body and kicked it once. "Dead bodies are not exactly looked at as positives." Rachel scanned the crowd; several were using their phones to record the incident. She doubted they could hear voice, but they would see anything that happened. "Ronnie, start shooting at the hills," she whispered.

Ronnie took his gun from Rachel as she drew her sidearm and started firing at the hills. Rachel watched the group swing their phones to the hills and focus; as they did, she shot John in the head. He fell fast.

Rachel then began shooting at the hill as well. As she scanned, all attention was on the hills, and everyone was looking for the new target. She stopped and ducked down. "Get down, everyone," she yelled. People scattered, and as they hid behind cars, two police cars drove into the lot. Rachel looked up as the officers got out. She pulled out her ID and held it up, "Federal agent, there are shooters in the hill."

The officers dropped down and moved behind the cover of their cars. The first car had two officers, and the second only one. The Eastern Pike Regional Police Department officers opened back doors and pulled out two Ruger Mini-14 Police edition rifles. All three were wearing body armor and were focused on the hill.

Ronnie was focused on the hill, looking up and back, then hiding behind the car.

"What now?" he whispered to Rachel.

"We will be fine," Rachel was quick to reply. "No witnesses, no issues. We need to find this niece of yours."

Rachel heard radios clicking. She hunched down and ran to the nearest police vehicle. As she got close, the officer looked over at her. She pulled out her ID. "Rachel Brown, I work for an investigative unit in the Army."

"Phil," the officer said, "Phil Comer."

"Comer?" Rachel said, "Related to Ronnie?"

"Yeah, he is my cousin," Phil said.

Rachel smiled, "Well, he is sitting right behind that car over there."

Phil looked at her, then the car, "Rockhead, you over there?"

"Fillup? Is that you?" Ronnie peeked over the car.

"Damn boy, what are you doin' back here?" Phil laughed. "'Cept shooting up my mountain."

"Tryin' ta find Elma," Ronnie yelled back.

"Elma with you?"

"No, she has gone off in the hills up there, being chased by some guys. Two of 'em are laying dead over here."

"You makin' paperwork for me, boy?" Phil giggled a little as he said this.

"Might be," Ronnie laughed.

"When they shoot last?" Phil asked Rachel.

"Been a few," Rachel replied.

Three more cars pulled onto the lot. Lights flashed, but no sirens were on. Five men jumped out and got behind the cars. Each pulled out an M16 and focused on the hill.

Phil stood up, "Helmets."

All five pulled on helmets with long visors.

"We had shooting from up the hill," Phil ordered, "Run 'em down."

"Yes, Sir," the men stated in unison and began moving forward. The two others who came with Phil moved up to the cars that had just arrived and aimed at the hill from opposite sides of the vehicles. In a moment, the men were in the woods, out of sight.

The radio began to chatter, and Ronnie made his way over to the car. He held out his hand to his cousin. Phil didn't take it but instead grabbed him and hugged Ronnie. "Why didn't ya call?"

"Yeah, why didn't ya call?" Rachel asked.

"Elma called and I didn't know if you were still with the force." Ronnie sighed.

"Ya know she hates that name," Phil laughed, "You always did get under her skin."

"I did?" Ronnie asked in a concerned voice.

"She never told ya because she thinks you are Superman," Phil laughed.

"Nothin' up here, boss," came a voice over the radio, "Tracks head up into the kills. A size nine followed by a bunch larger looks like four or five men up there after someone else. Woman or kid. Tracks are fresh, rained, so only new stuff showin'. Couple of deer up here too."

Phil spoke into his microphone on his shoulder, "Sweep the area, make sure there ain't no watchers, then get back here."

The other men turned and walked to Phil, who was standing up. "Where is Ellie, and who was shot?"

Ronnie turned towards the other car. "They drew on us first, we were talkin' to one of them when we convinced him not to shoot us, but then It all went crazy, and he got shot too."

They walked to the cars where the two men lay dead. "Well, that one's name is John. He and some others moved here about a year ago. They have a few small businesses and live in the city. Someone's got money. They have been reported for a few items, but nothing we can pin to them hard."

"They had guns," Rachel said.

"Welcome to Pike County; everyone has guns, so what?" Phil said. "Ronnie, I can have my men find Elma. You can head back to the big city."

"Naw," Ronnie said, "I am gonna visit with Uncle Harv for a spell. Oh, and how come you get to call her that."

"She's not around, is she? Suit yourself," Phil said. "Just don't be getting' in our way."

"Ha," Ronnie said.

"We'll take care of this," Phil looked at the men. "Where you stayin?"

"Probably back at the house," Ronnie said.

"Your ma will be happy to see you," Phil said. "Let's do some food this week."

"Yeah," Ronnie said, "I'll give ya a call."

"You do that," Phil said. "You do that."

The men came back out of the woods and walked to their cars. Ronnie and Rachel walked back to theirs and got in.

"What do we do now?" Ronnie asked.

"Is there another place we can park and get up in those hills?" Rachel replied.

"Sure," Ronnie thought about it for a moment, "but it won't be close."

"You think she's close?" Rachel asked.

"No, you are right," Ronnie looked at the mountains. "We can work our way up from the other side."

"Then get us movin'," Rachel barked. "We don't need any more of your family showin' up."

Ronnie put the Suburban in gear, pulled out of the parking lot, heading out on the country road.

Chapter 12

The drive to the Pikeville area was relatively straightforward, except there was no good direct route to Pikeville from Lexington. Like many areas in the mountains of Kentucky, there were a dozen ways to get to the location, but none of them were as direct as they could be.

"Do you remember that TV show, *Justified* years ago?" Jim asked as they drove.

"Yeah, why?" Alex asked.

"Well, I always wondered how they could get from Lexington to Hazard in fifteen minutes, maybe a half hour. It was a magic car, I bet?" Jim laughed.

"It wouldn't have been an hour show if they had done it right," Alex replied.

"They lost me when they pronounced Louisville like it had a 's' in it," Jim giggled.

"It does have an 's' in it," Alex proclaimed.

"You know it is silent, right?" Jim was serious for a moment.

"Yeah, but not everyone does," Alex teased.

The cars passed from the front window to the rear window as Jim drove and replied, "Then they shouldn't have made a show about it."

Alex laughed. Sarena sat in the backseat and was silent for some time.

There were more jabs at other shows that tried to depict Kentucky life.

"What about *Next of Kin*," Jim chided.

"Well, I liked it," Alex said, "but I don't know how you can get to Chicago that fast."

"That's what I mean," Jim said. "When they talk about Kentucky, there just doesn't seem to be any realism in time. I mean, look at us driving along, and the roads are good, a whole lot better than a lot of other states, but they just don't have as many. If it wasn't for the Interstates, we might be sunk."

"I thought we were talking movies," Alex laughed.

The siren was loud and sudden. The lights flashed behind them and lit up the inside of the suburban. Jim looked in the rearview mirror and laughed. "Ooops," he said.

"How bad?" Alex was serious.

"90 in a 55," Sarena said. "It is usually good for a visit to the courthouse."

"That'll be fun," Jim almost giggled.

"Are you going to pull over?" Alex asked.

As he said it, they heard the bullhorn from the officer behind them, "Pull over."

"Oh, I guess," Jim said. "I bet I could outrun him."

"Maybe," Sarena interjected, "but you can't outrun the radio. Also, many Kentucky trooper vehicles have been enhanced. Some boast well over 500 horsepower and will outrun this monster without shifting gears."

"Wow," Jim laughed as he pulled over, "she is a regular encyclopedia."

"You're showing your age," Sarena remarked. "Not many people even know what an encyclopedia is anymore. They use sites on the Internet."

"Turn off the vehicle," came a voice from behind them.

Jim turned off the Suburban and rolled down the window. The trooper got out of the car, and Jim watched him unclip the safety strap on his weapon. "Uh oh," Jim said, "he's going huntin'." Jim giggled again.

"Put your hands out of the window," the trooper ordered. As he got closer, he peered into the Suburban and could barely make out people in the back.

Jim was laughing, then he stopped. "Federal agent, we are armed."

The trooper ducked down a little and backed up with great caution.

"Let's see some ID," the trooper said, "Get out of the car showing your hands and face front, then walk backward to me."

Jim started to put his hand in to open the door, and the trooper yelled, "Hands out of the car!"

"Umm, how do I open the door?" Jim said.

"Open it using the outside handle," the trooper replied.

"It's locked," Jim said.

"Unlock it," the trooper yelled back.

"How can I do that without putting my hand in the car?" Jim laughed.

"Put your hand in, unlock it, then put your hands back out and open the door so I can see your hands," the trooper said.

Jim did as he was told. As Jim stepped out of the car, he worked his way around the door and bumped it closed. His hands were still up as he began walking backward.

"Can I get my ID?" Jim asked.

"Step back to me," the trooper replied.

Jim kept walking backward until he was at the back of the black Suburban.

"How about now?" Jim asked.

"Okay," the trooper said, "Slowly."

Jim reached into his back pocket and pulled out his wallet, opened it, and held it up.

"Take the ID out of the plastic," the trooper said.

Jim reached up, took the ID out of the plastic, and dropped the contents of his wallet on his head. "Damnit all," he said.

"Don't you use that language around me. I don't care who you are," the trooper replied.

Jim laughed.

"Are you laughing at me?" the trooper asked.

"Well," Jim started, "no, but yes. I am a little amused by the theatrics."

"You were doing 88 in a 55. I could run you in for that," the trooper said.

"You were wrong Sarena, it was 88, not 90," Jim laughed.

"You think it is funny?" the trooper said. "Turn around."

Jim turned. The man before him couldn't be more than twenty-four. He was a textbook trooper. Fresh out of school and clean cut to a high degree. His trooper uniform was pressed and perfect, and his hat was placed in a perfect manner, making him look like the ultimate expression of the law. He was tan but not overly tan, and his dark eyes were seething. Jim knew he was the cause of the frustration. Jim's hands were still up. "Can I lower my hands?"

The trooper had his ID and was looking at it, "Army huh?"

"Yeah, I was redrafted to run around the country being a janitor," Jim said.

"A janitor?" the trooper replied. "Why would that make you drive so fast? Where's the fire?"

"Alex," Jim yelled, "he wants to know why I was driving fast."

Inside the suburban, Alex put his face in his palm. "Tell him," Alex yelled back.

The trooper looked at the Suburban and then at Jim. "Yeah, tell me."

"Okay," Jim said, "We are on our way to Ivel, Kentucky, to find an informant living in the hills who may know something about a militant group that the government has been tracking that may have found a new way to get drugs into the country. We are doing it in association with the DEA, and it has a bit of urgency associated with it. I could have driven a little slower, but I have to admit, I like to drive fast and if I was in my car, I would have been going a lot faster. I also have to admit I considered trying to outrun you, but our little ex-FBI agent said your car could be a supercar. With that in mind, I pulled over so we could dance for a while and waste my time with our little escapade."

"Your ex-agent was right. I would have caught you and probably shot out your tire," the trooper said.

"Troopers don't shoot out tires," Jim said.

"Out here, we do what we have to do," the trooper replied. "You need to slow down. Not for me but for you. Coal is not mined as much out here, but it still is, and the coal trucks would smash that Suburban like it wasn't there." The trooper paused, "I will have to call this in and verify your credentials."

"Go ahead," Jim said, "Or talk to Alex; he has the stripes."

"I will call it in," the trooper said. "Wait here and keep your hands where I can see them."

Jim watched as the young man walked to the vehicle, reached in, and picked up a radio mic. He talked and waited for an answer, eyes on Jim the entire time. Jim heard the radio but could not make out any words and waited. The trooper nodded a few more times and put the mic back in the car. He walked to Jim holding his ID.

"You check out, but you don't have the necessary authorization to drive that fast out here. I am going to ask nicely for you to slow down," the trooper said.

Jim looked the man in the eyes, paused, blinked a few times, and said, "I will try."

"I would hate to have to tie you up in red tape for a few hours," the trooper said.

"Understood," Jim replied as the trooper handed back his ID. "This thing could have caught us?"

"Easy," the trooper replied, still showing no emotion.

"Okay," Jim laughed.

"So where is this informant?" the trooper asked.

"I would rather not pinpoint it too close," Jim said.

"Why is that?" the trooper said.

"He's best left alone," Jim said.

"Something I should worry about?" the trooper asked.

"No," Jim said. "He won't get in any trouble unless trouble comes for him."

"Really?" the trooper asked.

"Yeah," Jim said, "Problem is, trouble likes him."

"Really?" the trooper asked.

"Yes, Sir Trooper," Jim looked at his nametag. "Trooper Thorne?"

"Yep," Trooper Thorne replied, "That would be me."

"I will try to slow it down," Jim jested.

"I will try not to stop you again, but I won't guarantee anything," Trooper Thorne replied.

Jim laughed, "All I can ask."

The trooper smiled only a little for just a moment then it was gone. The trooper turned and walked back to the car, latching his pistol as he walked. As he got back in the car, he took off his hat with almost a ceremony and sat down in the car talking on the radio. Jim put his ID away then knelt and picked up the dropped contents from his wallet. Brushing his hands off Jim walked to the Suburban, and got in.

"That went better than I expected," Jim remarked.

"I called a friend I know in KSP and had him call down here. We can't afford the delays," Sarena moved forward closer to the two of them.

"Really?" Jim laughed.

"Pays to know people," Sarena leaned back in her seat.

"Always the quiet ones," Jim said.

Alex laughed. The three pulled out and kept driving while Trooper Thorne watched.

Jim accelerated, and soon they were up to 70. He checked the rearview mirror, and there was no car behind him. He wasn't going as fast, but he intended to poke a little at the trooper. Apparently, the trooper wasn't interested. As Jim cruised at 70 to keep Alex off his back, he saw the blue lights behind him. They were coming up fast, and Jim thought Trooper Thorne and he might have another discussion, but the trooper passed him as though he were sitting still.

"We must not be the only game in town," Sarena said. "He had to be doing over 130."

"I wonder if Rachel and Ronnie are the cause of this?" Alex asked.

"Rachel, I would believe, but not Ronnie," Jim laughed.

"I'm not so sure of that," Alex teased; "after all, he got serious laughs at your expense yesterday."

"I will give you that," Jim agreed. "It's nice when you see the kids grow up."

"I bet you weren't thinking that when he knocked you around the mat," Sarena laughed.

Jim turned around a little. "That reminds me, it's going to be your turn to pick between me and Rachel."

"I'm sure we can work something out," Sarena said; "after all, I haven't had a good workout since Indianapolis."

Alex began to laugh. "I never would have thought I would have a team that is not strictly by the book. I often wonder what I did wrong to deserve this."

"You never know," Jim laughed, "you may have done something right to deserve this team."

"You may be right," Alex laughed. "It is a good team."

Chapter 13

Eleanor waited.

Her patience evaporated on the hot Kentucky day. The foreign men roamed around the front of the cave entrance after she retreated to it. She was careful to cover her tracks, but the men were being thorough but not stealthy. For fifteen minutes, one of the men stood no further than twenty feet from her, smoking a cigarette and chattering at his companion as they kicked the brush. At one point, they kicked the bushes in front of the small cave but didn't see it, or if they did, they didn't venture into the darkness.

Eleanor was hungry, so she took out some of the candy she found in the ammo boxes. It was old, and she was worried, but as she bit into the Snickers bar, it tasted a little like heaven. She ate it slowly and drank some water to wash it down. Looking outside, she no longer saw any trace of anyone. It was clear, and the area was filled with the sounds of nature. She carefully stepped out of the cave, and her eyes adjusted to the bright light.

Eleanor's phone was in her pack. She got it out and turned it on. It took a few moments, but it came on; the battery was still fully charged. There was no signal yet. She moved forward until she got a signal, looked around the area, and dialed Ronnie. He answered on the third ring.

"Elma?" Ronnie asked.

"I really hate it when you call me that," Eleanor answered. "I know you do it just to make me feel like a kid."

"Sorry," Ronnie consoled. "Where are you?"

"Enemy fort," Eleanor proclaimed, "I have been hiding out. Two guys are up here looking for me, but they keep walking by and not seeing me. I thought about shooting them but only have a .22 and don't know how it will do."

"Shooting them?" Ronnie said to her on the call, stunned. "Why in the world would you shoot them?"

"Well, I thought it would get them off my back," Eleanor said. "The damn drones keep coming by too, makes it hard to get around."

"You get your butt in that cave, and we will come for you," Ronnie spoke in an authoritarian tone.

"Hell no," Eleanor said. "I am not a little girl anymore. I can take care of myself. I will head north until I hit the road. You be there when I get there."

"We are halfway around the mountain, we will be to the north, but you will need to call once you have a landmark," Ronnie said.

"I'm not stupid. I will find a place we can meet," Eleanor replied. "You've been gone too long, and I know these mountains better than you anyway. I think you've become a city boy and forgotten what it's like to be out here."

"Maybe so," Ronnie said, "but I've seen a sight more than you have, and I still don't know these mountains."

Eleanor hung up the phone and began working her way through the brush. It was slow going as she had to stop and listen often to make certain that she was not detected. As she continued through the brush, she considered the past two days and wondered why she was so important. The hills of Kentucky had been home to moonshine and marijuana for a long time. People often thought tobacco was the largest cash crop in Kentucky, but many were also of the mind that marijuana had taken over that spot long ago. Growers, making sure to avoid the police, often put their crops on Federal land instead of their own. That way, if the crops were found, the only prosecution was anyone found with it. If you were caught growing anything illegal on your property now, it was likely you would lose your property and do jail time.

Eleanor was pretty certain that she had stumbled upon opium. That was a crop that could be grown here as well, but it wasn't as common. The most common thing lately was meth labs, and even those were few and far between. Eleanor had never seen such a high-tech farm with all of the cameras and drones; a lot of money was involved. She knew that property for a long time, but people didn't go out in it is as much as they used to. It was easy to hide anything in the hills of Pikeville if you needed to hide it.

Eleanor wasn't an expert, but she also wondered why they cared. Lots of people went missing in the United States every year, but in Pikeville, Kentucky, there were a lot of close families. Messing with the wrong family could get you in a lot of trouble or even dead. Messing with the city in general or anyone in Appalachia was a risk, at minimum. With the coal mines slowing down and a lot of people moving away, there was a lot more to consider. People were greedy for any type of work, and those with money seemed to make the rules. New people were moving in. Eleanor heard about all of the different people from Europe. Normally she didn't care, but it seemed like these new people weren't exactly trying to do things aboveboard. Right now, it looked like they wanted her dead.

Eleanor ducked into another bush when a drone flew overhead. As it passed, she hoped it was just a camera and not some fancy infrared or other spy camera. Unconsciously she held her breath, wondering. When the drone was out of earshot, she exhaled heavily and breathed hard for a few seconds. It was probably silly, but she still felt safer for doing it.

Eleanor made her way even further and came over a rise. About 100 yards away was a cell tower at the top of the next hill. Eleanor texted Ronnie as she pulled up her map. She put in the GPS coordinates and hit send. She heard the drones again in the distance and ducked into another bush, then waited for a reply. Eleanor held her breath again as the drone flew over. She almost passed out, waiting to hear the sound fade into the distance. This time she coughed when she took a breath again.

She looked down at her phone and saw a text message. It was Ronnie. He said to hang on, stay there, and they were on their way. Moments later, she heard rustling in the bushes and stood up. She scanned the area. As she began to turn, she felt strong arms grab her from behind. Whoever it was had hold of her elbows and was holding her tight, too tight. Eleanor screamed and struggled the best she could but was held fast. She screamed again and heard a voice come back to her.

"Elma," Ronnie yelled, "Is that you?"

"Ronnie!" Eleanor yelled as a hand came over her mouth. She bit the hand and let out a shrill cry that could only be considered a wail. She was red with struggling and excessive anger.

"Elma!" Ronnie screamed. Eleanor could hear him running through the brush below her on the hill. There was a movement behind her, and she was pulled back into a chokehold while another man stepped in front of her. The man held a strange-looking gun that Eleanor had not seen before. He fired into the bushes, spraying bullets from side to side in the direction Ronnie was coming from. The bullets didn't appear to end. The man kept firing over and over.

"Kill her and let's get out of here," the man firing said as he stopped firing.

"No, we were told to bring her back to see who she has informed," the man holding Eleanor barked.

"We will figure it out on our own," the first man said and brought his weapon up to point at Eleanor.

"Elma," Eleanor heard a voice." Ronnie stepped out from the bush and fired once at the man pointing the weapon at her. Eleanor was immediately covered with a spray of blood from the man's face. He rapidly fell forward into both her and her captor. Eleanor tried to stand to get away, but her captor still held her arm. She was pinned and pulled back to him.

"I'm sorry, Eleanor," Ronnie said as he dropped to his knees. "I'm sorry."

Ronnie's shoulder was covered in blood, and his face was bloody on one side. He was wearing what Eleanor assumed to be a bulletproof jacket. There were multiple hits on that jacket and blood showing on the front. Ronnie held himself up by his rifle and started choking.

Eleanor's captor lifted her easily under his arm. She tried to squirm, but it was no use. He moved away rapidly. Eleanor was facing back and watched Ronnie fall to the ground and roll over face up. A woman dashed out of the bushes and knelt beside him while pointing a rifle forward. They locked eyes. The woman began to get up but heard Ronnie choking and stopped. She knelt down to Ronnie and unzipped his jacket. Eleanor was scared. She couldn't see either of them anymore as she was carried through more brush.

Eleanor began crying and stopped her squirming, realizing that she may have just lost her cousin.

Chapter 14

Rachel knelt by Ronnie's side. They had Eleanor, but if she pursued, she knew Ronnie would die right now. Ronnie closed his eyes, and Rachel slapped him hard.

"You stay awake, boy," Rachel ordered. "Don't make me keep beating you."

Ronnie gasped. There was pink lung blood dribbling from his mouth. Rachel remembered that she needed to figure out where his lung was punctured and keep it inflated, but she was no expert. She was not a doctor and was not trained in anything beyond the basics.

Rachel quickly got Ronnie's vest off and then quickly ripped open his shirt. She looked at the wounds and was thankful there was only one that got through the vest. She stopped and picked him up slightly to look at the exit wound. Rachel didn't get a look at the weapon that was fired, but it went straight through without destroying everything in the exit. It was still bad, really bad. She was pretty sure there were major problems with his right lung. His left leg was also messed up badly. She could tell that the bone was shattered, and that, too, could be an issue.

Rachel held back a tear as she pulled gauze from a pack and put it on his wound. She didn't know if there would be pressure or no pressure, but he was losing a lot of blood. Rachel pulled out her phone and dialed Alex.

"Hello," she heard.

"Ronnie's been shot, and he's hurt really bad," Rachel said. "I don't know where I am, and I can't carry him because I'll probably kill him. I need help, Alex. I need help right now."

Rachel heard Alex talking to Sarena and then told her that Sarena would find out where she was. Alex told her they would have a chopper heading that way from a local hospital.

"They won't have any good hospitals down here. He needs a doctor right now that can fix him!" Rachel yelled. "Where are you?"

"Sarena has your location, and it looks like we're about ten minutes out," Alex said; "Jim says five."

"You have to hurry," Rachel was almost frantic, "don't let this boy die."

"At this rate, we'll be there pretty fast," Alex said. "Listen for us."

"Rachel hung up the phone and set it to her side. "You stay with me. I can't have you dying on my watch."

"Ain't gonna die," Ronnie choked. "Find Elma and get that son of a bitch."

"I'm not leaving you," Rachel said, "and what the fuck did you mean getting so far ahead of me?"

"I know the hills better," Ronnie gasped, "I couldn't wait for you. They would have killed Elma if I hadn't made it."

"Damn it, boy, you know better than to go alone into a firefight," Rachel said. "I could have helped. I could have stopped you from getting hurt."

"You couldn't have stopped me any more than you could have on the mat," Ronnie coughed again, bubbling pink blood. "It hurts Rachel; it really hurts bad."

A tear welled up in Rachel's eyes. She reached into her pack and pulled out a small field syringe of morphine. They were told in training not to use it unless it was a last resort, and she hesitated but then looked at Ronnie writhing in pain. She put the small portable syringe into a vein on his arm and squeezed it in. "That'll help with the pain."

It wasn't very long before Ronnie said, "I can feel it working, but it burns."

"The burn will go away in a second," Rachel choked. "You stay with me, and don't you dare try and go to sleep."

"I ain't that tired," Ronnie said. "I'm ready to go kick some ass. Help me up so we can go get Elma." Ronnie tried to move, but Rachel held him down. He was still foaming, and it was obvious he wasn't going anywhere."

Rachel heard something rumbling in the distance, and she looked down the hill. Looking down, she could see brush and trees moving but couldn't see what was causing it. There was the sound of an engine straining, and then she saw the battered black suburban burst out of the woods into the small clearing. The front bumper was hanging off, and the grill was gone, and the hood was dented in several places. There were no mirrors on the suburban, and much of the paint was scraped off.

Three of the truck's doors slammed open, with the driver's door bending too far back as Jim pushed his way out and ran to her and Ronnie. Sarena came out of the back seat and drug a large first aid kit with her. Alex had his M16 out and was scanning the area, covering them.

Rachel looked at Alex first and said, "They're long gone."

Sarena was next to Ronnie now. She pulled off the gauze and examined the wounds. "Rachel was right; this is really bad. I'm worried about this lung shot, but it looks like the bone is shattered in his leg. If Rachel hadn't put this tourniquet on, he might already be dead. We need a trauma team now."

"Helicopter is inbound," Alex said as he dialed a number. "It should have been here already."

Jim looked up as he held Ronnie's head for a moment. "I hear it."

"I hear it too," Alex said.

The medivac helicopter came into view. There was no place for it to easily land, but Alex saw a man hook to an external line and lower himself down. It only took thirty seconds, and a paramedic was on the ground with him. The line went back up while the paramedic checked the wounds. It was hard to hear anything with the beating blades of the helicopter clamoring above them.

"Do you have any idea what did this?" the medic asked.

Rachel stood and ran to the man twenty feet away that Ronnie had shot. Next to the man was an AK 74. It was a Russian rifle, and she knew it quite well.

"5.45x39mm rifle." Rachel said as she made it back to the paramedic. "Where it hit the bone in his leg, it's pretty messed up. It looks like it went through his lung, but you're the expert."

A gurney was lowered from the helicopter hovering above them. It was silver, held a blanket, and the cables were now loose where they had given slack. The paramedic looked at Jim and said, "Help me get him on here, there's no way to easily stabilize him, and the faster we can get him to the hospital, the better." Jim nodded. On a three-count, they moved Ronnie as carefully as they could to the gurney, where the paramedic covered him up. He latched onto the gurney and put his thumb up towards the helicopter. The gurney, Ronnie, and the paramedic were rapidly brought up even as the helicopter began gaining altitude.

"I haven't seen them do that before," Rachel said as the helicopter continued to climb and move to the east. "He must be pretty bad."

"You already know he's pretty bad," Jim said. "I'm not going to go through this again. That boy is going to live."

All three of them were covered with blood, but it was Jim that walked over to the dead man and looked at his body. He went through his pockets and found a phone. He also pulled out his ID and found two other weapons on the man.

"Somebody's gonna pay for this," Jim choked. His eyes were moist with tears.

"Maybe we need to get another group in here," Sarena was pensive; "maybe we're too close to this now."

"You leave if you want to," Jim wiped his eyes, "I'm going to find Ronnie's cousin, and then I'm going to find the people who did this to Ronnie."

"Jim, you and I both know you need to calm down," Alex comforted.

"No Alex, you need to gear up," Jim was looking at the ground. "There are clear tracks going up this hill, and they're heavy because it looks like somebody was carrying a little too much weight, like a teenage girl. Rachel, you coming?"

"I'm right there with you," Rachel checked her rifle and vest, "nobody else is going to die today except whoever took that girl."

Alex looked at Sarena, "I'll stay with the truck and try to get it back down the hill. If you want to go with them, it works good by me. If you want, I'll go to, and they'll be four of us facing whatever, but somebody needs to deal with the local police and get in touch with Tarkington. It's better that's me. You stay in touch with me and help these two in every way you can."

"Jim!" Alex yelled.

Jim looked back, and Alex threw his M16 to him. Jim caught it and pulled back the slide making sure it was chambered. Rachel again checked her weapon as Sarena ran to the back of the truck, threw the first aid kit in, and pulled out her weapon. The three of them headed up the side of the mountain, following Jim and the tracks.

Chapter 15

Michael and Abby enjoyed running on their property in the Appalachian foothills. Appalachia, as a whole, was some of the most beautiful country in the United States. You could easily fall in love with different parts. The sky almost always seemed clear, and the air felt fresh and clean. There was an abundance of animals, and Michael enjoyed the predatory birds in the area. It was true you saw more Turkey buzzards than anything, but an occasional eagle or hawk was a treat during the sunrise.

Over time, Michael and Abby had cut a trail through the woods making it very easy to run. They had done so in Wyoming as well. It was a hot, humid day, and the dampness made Michael and Abby sweat more rapidly as they ran. Several places along the path had quick drops and a variety of challenges, but they were used to it and navigated the run easily. It always turned into a little bit of a race as both Abby and Michael were incredibly competitive.

They were panting as they ran. "Will we get the furniture today?" Abby asked as they jumped over a fallen tree in the path.

"I expect that we will. I'm a little frustrated that our short trip to get furniture turned into such a mess," Michael replied. "I will follow up when we get back to the house and make sure the truck is coming. David was pretty sure he would get to it this morning. He said he didn't need much help but would bring one of the boys along."

"It will be nice to have furniture again," Abby laughed as she slid deftly down the side of a hill. "Do you think we'll have to deal with anything from our furniture store visit?"

"I'm sure something will happen, but I'm not sure if we need to be involved," Michael replied. "It's not like anybody who works for Yuri to back down. I never really told you about my interaction with his father and with Yuri. It was when I was still dating Madison and wasn't sharing as much with you."

"It still makes me laugh that your college job took you all over the world assassinating people; seems counterproductive," Abby laughed.

The path widened for just a minute and Michael took the opportunity to take the lead back from Abby as they began the climb up the hill towards the house. "It made for a unique college education in many ways. I wonder how things would have gone if my mother had lived."

"Probably close to the same," Abby said as she jumped over a rock and took the lead back. "I think we are who we are, and we eventually become the person we were meant to become whether we like it or not."

Michael stopped dead in his tracks. Abby ran a few feet, then stopped as well and turned around. Michael was breathing harder but not under any type of strain. "Do you think I would be a killer no matter how my life would have worked out?"

"I don't see you as a killer," Abby assured Michael. "Sure, you've killed more people than I or anyone else could ever understand, but I don't think you were malicious, and I don't think you were a psychopath. I probably should end up on the Dr. Phil show just for saying it, but I think you're amazing."

"It would take me time to figure out how many terminations I have done," Michael was nonchalant about it. "I never really considered the number like so many do. It was just a task. Lately, I've thought more about it, but I still don't feel the same way so many others do. It was a job. If I hadn't done it, somebody else would have had to do it. I suppose the first time I considered it as anything more was when I looked through the scope and listened to a man who had deceived me into thinking his wife was a horrible person and deserved to die. At that point, I knew I had to do something morally correct. To your point, I have never thought about being anything else. I know we went to school for it, and I have my degree. I could go into economics, but I know it wouldn't challenge me."

"The biggest thing that challenges you is me," Abby laughed; "maybe you should spend more time running and less time talking." Abby was trying to lighten the mood and took off running up the hill again. Michael smiled and fell in behind as she set the pace. The hill was steep, and many people would have had difficulty, but Michael and Abby had run this trail often, recently and before the house was destroyed. As they reached the top of the bluff, the house came into view. It was secluded, and neither Michael nor Abby were ever concerned about visitors.

"We never seem to have anybody visit," Abby verified.

"The last time someone showed up, we ended up having to rebuild. Is there someone you want to invite so I can make sure the house is ready for it?" Michael laughed as they cooled down in the front area of the house.

"It would just be nice to have visitors from time to time," Abby said, "and not just visitors wanting to kill us or exact revenge on my father."

"I agree with you," Michael said, "but at the same time, I'm happy with you and I alone."

Michael grabbed Abby by the waist and picked her up. She put her arms around his neck. "I think we're both sweaty messes."

"But we're sweaty messes that are having fun," Michael laughed.

"That we are," Abby replied.

They walked to the door of the house. The door didn't swing on the standard hinges. The set system and lock inserted into the frame. The door was more like the door of a vault than a home door, and Michael's designs were after masses of testing and retesting. The resultant door would likely resist a tank, and the beams built around it were equally as strong. Where many homes had a secure door, but around the frame was very thin. The design of the entire house was built with the simple idea of protecting the inhabitants. Michael turned the special handle, and the door swung open upon itself.

As they walked into the house, the echo was deafening. There was minimal furniture in the house since it was newly built. The open design combined with the hardwood floors and vaulted hardwood ceilings gave the house a unique echo.

"We got the bedroom set. Why didn't we get everything else?" Abby asked.

"That is a very good question," Michael mused, "I guess we got distracted."

"We could always go back; Bob seemed very nice." Abby was full of smiles.

"We could, and maybe we should, but let's get our bedroom set first," Michael laughed as he walked to the bedroom. "I think a shower is on my agenda right now."

Abby ran down the hall after him, taking off her clothes as she went. "Me too," she hooted as they entered the bedroom. "Me too."

Chapter 16

General Samuel Tarkington was sitting at his desk when Sarah walked in rapidly. He didn't look up and continued reading a report sitting in front of him.

"You need to take this call, Sir," Sarah was imperative.

"Why do I need to take this call?" Tarkington asked.

"There's been an issue, Sir," Sarah's voice was evasive but firm.

Tarkington looked up and over at Sarah, who was obviously concerned. He looked at his phone and picked it up.

"Tarkington," he said.

"General, this is Alex. We've arrived at a situation in progress. Ronnie Comer has been shot. He has been airlifted out; his current status is unknown. Jim, Rachel, and Sarena are pursuing at least one hostile. We are unsure of the hostile's intentions, nor do we have a complete identity of the hostile. I have one dead hostile identified as Gornev Chibski, ID in hand, but this does not match anyone in the computer. Our transportation has been compromised, but it's still mobile. I will follow my team in once I have transportation in place."

"Alex," Tarkington sighed, "I think everyone down in Appalachia just loves to kick your ass, don't they."

"Yes sir, it appears that way," Alex replied.

"What's wrong with the vehicle?" Tarkington asked.

"Jim drove it up a mountain to get into an active fire situation and save Ronnie," Alex said; "in the process, the Suburban had an altercation with multiple trees, rocks, and who knows how many squirrels."

"Good for Jim," Tarkington said. "You need to be in there as quickly as possible. Your two team members, Jim and Rachel, will approach things in their own manner without proper guidance. Your newbie is highly unlikely to be able to control them even though she seems to have a clear frame of mind at all times. I need the status on Ronnie, and I will let Sarah take care of that."

"I intend to have the rest of the team here as quickly as possible," Alex said. "We need something to pivot out and have not been able to get to Masterson yet."

"I think you've gotten yourself into enough trouble without adding trouble that might just end you. I seriously doubt Masterson has anything to do with any of this, and it would probably anger him to no end if we suggested such. You have quite a bit on your plate right now. Engaging an assassin along the way doesn't seem like a good idea, now does it? Resolve the issue and then engage Masterson and see what you can find out about the rest of this mess."

"What if they're related?" Alex asked.

"I had considered that, and I'm glad you did as well. If you think there is anything that links what's going on with you with what I sent you there for, then get Masterson involved right away. He will know how to handle it. Hang on for one moment."

Sarah was waiting at the door while Tarkington was talking. "Get on the phone, find out where Ronnie Comer was taken and get me a status. If we need him sent somewhere else, let's get it done."

"Yes Sir," Sarah replied and left the room.

"Alex, this is complete bullshit, and you are responsible. You need to get your ass in gear and solve this problem, this family problem, that Ronnie got us into. I don't want to hear another damn thing about it. Sarah will take care of making sure Ronnie is okay if it's even possible. That team of yours has pulled off some pretty spectacular stunts to fall for a couple of people in the hills, and you've also pulled off quite a bit. Like I said, you had your ass handed to you last time you were there; it's time for you to start handing people their asses."

"On it," Alex said.

"You get Barbara and Terry down there in the jet and get some serious weaponry, if necessary, but you make this happen. I'm not losing another person to some podunk shit. If I have to, I'll nuke the entire city out of existence if they are part of the issue. I am completely and totally tired of being reactive, and it's time for you to be proactive. Do you get me?"

"A nuke, Sir?" Alex asked.

"Don't try fucking with me now," Tarkington said, "I don't want to explain another funeral. You know what I mean. Now get on it!"

Tarkington slammed the phone down. Sarah walked in a moment later. "He's currently in Pikeville Medical Center. Ronnie Comer is considered critical and not expected to live. I'm trying to get more information, but the doctors are working on him now. No one on staff seems to know what's happening except that he was shot."

"Find a way, Sarah," Tarkington barked. "You always find a way; now, find a way to see how this boy is."

"Will do, Sir," Sarah said as she left the room.

Sam Tarkington stood and walked over to a wall with pictures on it. He looked at the different pictures and thought about all the men he had lost over the years. It came with the territory. Sometimes you ordered people to do things, and bad things happened, but this was unexpected. This should have been routine, and now it was another complex situation. Tarkington considered getting on a plane and heading to Pikeville Kentucky but realized it would likely be all over by the time he got there. He probably would just cause more miscommunications than he would solutions. Tarkington realized a good leader was strong, but he knew when to trust his team and when to be involved. Right now, he needs to trust his team.

Sam Tarkington walked back to his chair. He opened the drawer of his desk, pulled out a small cell phone, and turned it on. With one click, he dialed a number and waited.

The phone answered. "Hello?"

"Abby, I know I never call anymore. This is hard for me to say, but I think I need your help," he said.

Chapter 17

Terry Drake and Barbara Stone were in the air within minutes of Alex calling. They filed flight plans quickly, and the total flight time would be less than fifteen minutes from Lexington's Bluegrass Field to the Pike Country Airport. If they needed to get Ronnie somewhere else, they would be on station to do so. They also carried their standard weaponry for Alex and the team. As they took off, Barbara looked over at Terry from the copilot seat.

"Do you think Ronnie's going to be okay?" she asked.

"He's a strong kid," Terry said. "I'm sure he'll pull through."

"Alex said it was really bad," Barbara lamented.

"You know Alex," Terry comforted, "everything is bad. Jim says he didn't used to be this way, but now he's almost always "glass half empty" even when he's trying to be glass completely full. It's like he's trying to prepare us for the worst, then fight for the best."

"You know I tease him a lot, but I shouldn't." Barbara began, "I really do like him, and he's so sweet to me all the time."

"Have you ever told him that?" Terry laughed.

"How could I tell him?" Barbara said. "I mean, he's three years younger than me, and I don't want to lead him on."

"I'm sure he would be happy to know that. Actually, I'm even more sure the three years means just about nothing. Ronnie is a full-grown man with a huge heart. Can you imagine anyone that would treat you better than him?"

"Well," Barbara paused, "no, not really."

"Have you ever had a boyfriend who would treat you as respectfully as Ronnie does right now?" Terry asked.

"Absolutely not," Barbara replied.

"Then why are you avoiding what both of you really want?" Terry queried. "I don't talk about my life much, but I would give my right arm to have somebody like him treating me the way he treats you."

"You mean you..." Barbara started to ask.

"No," Terry said, "that's not what I mean. I've been married twice, but maybe that is right. Ronnie treats me better than any of my wives ever did. I think he would do everything in his power to make you happy."

"You're probably right."

"You know I'm right," Terry reassured. "Name one thing that Ronnie wouldn't do for you. Think about how he looks at you. It almost makes me sick how much he worships the ground you walk on. All that, and you don't give him the time of day, and he still is over the top for you."

"I guess I never really thought about it that way."

"We're coming in for landing pretty soon, so I want you to listen close to me. If you and Ronnie were together, how much would those three years matter to you in forty years? How much would it really matter to you in ten? How much time have you lost when both of you could be incredibly happy? I hate to say this, but I've seen some of the guys you date, and I wouldn't waste a bullet on some of them."

"Hey," Barbara protested, "that's not very fair."

"It may not be very fair, but it's very true. How many times have you had to pick up the bill or pick up some deadbeat because his car broke down? You just don't seem to want to be happy. I think that's true with most men and women. For some reason, they get stuck with somebody who doesn't really care about them."

"Is that what happened to you?" Barbara asked.

"No," Terry confided. "In two marriages, I believed in my job more than I did my marriage. I don't blame any of them, and anyone that got into a relationship with me knew the job came first. Sure, I tried to treat them nice, but I'm not very good at it."

"I guess I've got a lot to think about," Barbara stared out the window.

"You may not have a lot of time; so if I were you, I would get to the hospital right now," Terry said.

The sleek plane landed like a feather at the Pikeville Regional Airport. As they landed, Barbara called Alex. Terry was busy with the tower and being told where to put the jet.

"We're at the airport now in Pikeville. We will secure a vehicle and head your way," Barbara said.

"One of you needs to stay with the plane, and one of you needs to get to the hospital and protect Ronnie. I want constant updates on how he is, and I want whoever goes to be fully armed and ready to protect him. I don't want anything to happen. I don't know how serious the police in this area will be. I will call whoever stays with the plane with more orders later. Don't let me down. Ronnie has to live."

The phone went dead.

"What did he say?" Terry asked.

"He said one of us needs to stay here, and one of us needs to protect Ronnie. Which do you want to do?" Barbara asked.

"I think we know who needs to do what. Am I just sitting here, or will I get a call?" Terry asked.

"Alex said he would call with more orders for whoever stayed with the plane," Barbara said.

"Good," Terry said. "Arm up and get your butt to the hospital. I'll stay here, and whenever Alex calls, I will head out."

"Terry," Barbara paused and looked at him, "thanks for telling me what I needed to hear. I appreciate it."

"It's no big deal," Terry smiled for a moment. "If ever anyone needed their eyes opened, it was you. Pay attention to how Ronnie looks at you. I think you'll be surprised."

"I know exactly what you are talking about," Barbara said as she put on a shoulder holster. "I've seen the way Ronnie looks at me, and I've taken it for granted. I'm not taking it for granted anymore."

"You know Alex may tell you that team dating is not allowed," Terry laughed.

Barbara punched Terri in the shoulder. She put two magazines in the magazine pouches opposite her M9. She grabbed a jacket and put it over the entire rig. She zipped this jacket only a little so it could be pulled apart easily, if necessary. Her mind drifted for a second, and she thought about how Ronnie had looked at her on their picnic together. She was such an idiot, she thought to herself. She thought about the small cross Ronnie got her for Christmas. Every gift and everything he did should've told her exactly how he felt.

"Good luck finding a car here," Terri teased.

"Sarah has already set it up," Barbara stuck her tongue out. "Sarah can find and set up anything, or haven't you figured that out yet."

"I sure have," Terri said as he sat in the cabin area of the sleek plane. "Be careful. Who knows how much trouble we are in."

"I'll be careful," Barbara reassured.

The door to the G650 was lowered, and Barbara stepped out onto the tarmac. She walked to the far side, where the tower and a small admin building waited, and walked into the door. A man was waiting with a sign that said, "Alex Brown Party." Barbara walked over to him and said, "I'm with the Alex Brown party."

The man looked at his clipboard and said, "Are you Barbara?" He was about six feet tall, wearing khaki pants, hush puppy shoes, a big green windbreaker with a Cadillac logo, and a hat that said, "Welcome to Pikeville."

"Yes, I'm Barbara Stone," she replied.

"Please sign here," the man showed her a clipboard.

Barbara signed on the bottom, and the man handed her a set of keys. "Which car?" she asked.

"Black Escalade sitting out front, they wanted a Suburban, but this is all I had," he replied.

"Did we get insurance, or do I need to sign anything else?' Barbara asked.

"I have no idea if you have insurance," the man said. "They bought the car. It's yours."

Barbara nodded to the man and headed out the door. A new black Escalade was waiting. Barbara clicked the key to open the door. The inside smelled new, and the leather was perfect. Barbara climbed inside, closed the door, and hit the start button. The Escalade roared to life. She took out her phone and plugged the hospital into the GPS. She clicked start, put the vehicle in drive, and sped out of the parking lot.

Chapter 18

Jim, Rachel, and Sarena continued tracking the man who had Eleanor. It was an easy trail to follow, and Jim was surprised the man hadn't knocked Eleanor out yet. Branches were broken, tree bark was scraped, leaves were pulled off, and leaves were left on a path with footprints leading back into the woods.

"On the other side of this hill is a school," Rachel was scanning as she talked. "We were there this morning and got into a gunfight. Some foreign guys, or at least guys with foreign accents. We also met one of Ronnie's cousins who runs the police force here. He kind of told us to back off and let them do their work, but obviously, we didn't listen.

"What happened?" Jim asked.

"I told you," Rachel pushed forward , "they were going to kill Eleanor, and Ronnie wasn't having it. When the first bullet hit him, I saw the blood spray, and he didn't even slow down. The only thing that slowed him at all was when it hit his leg, and I know it shattered bone, and that damn fool kept walking. I can't believe how stubborn he is."

"That's why I'm glad he's on our side," Jim said. "This isn't right, we were just coming up here to talk."

"No, they were full trying to kill Eleanor," Rachel said. "I'm not sure what she saw or what her curiosity got her into, but they weren't playing games. They wanted her dead."

"You sure they wanted her dead?" Sarena asked. "They could kill her pretty easily right now or earlier."

"Yeah, I'm sure," Rachel's voice was firm, "but when the men were talking, and they were about to off her, one man told the other that they had to figure out how much she told us. We're right back to what did her curiosity find?"

"Drugs, weapons, something else," Sarena replied. "It's all around here, but it's usually run by the families in this area. They don't like outsiders here, so this is kind of different."

114

"I'd say different is right," Jim was looking at the tracks and signs and forging ahead, "but it doesn't really matter. We're going to find the person who shot Ronnie, and the person who took Eleanor, and make them pay."

Rachel laughed. "The person who shot Ronnie is pretty much dead, but this guy's gotta go, too."

"I guess you can't get much more punished than dead," Jim smiled a little, "but whoever started all this has to go, too."

"You guys really don't know anything about due process, do you?" Sarena asked. "We really aren't supposed to be judge, jury, and executioner. We are supposed to represent the government. We're supposed to uphold the law. We're supposed to defend this country against enemies both foreign and domestic."

"Yeah, you're right," Jim said; "What's your point?"

"We should be arresting these people, not killing them," Sarena stated.

"Okay," Jim crowed, "You arrest them, and if they resist, then I'll kill them."

"With your skill, you could subdue almost anyone," Sarena quipped, "Why kill them?"

"Today, it's because I saw my friend nearly dead," Jim said sullenly.

Sarena considered for a moment. She thought about Ronnie and the team. Then she nodded her head. "I see your point. Still, our job is to uphold the law."

Sarena's phone rang. It was Alex.

"We're on the top of the hill," Sarena reported. "We're following a pretty clear trail, and we have to be catching up. He's still carrying her, but she's probably causing quite a ruckus. I expect we'll be close in the next five to ten minutes."

"I made it down the hill and am on the road. I had to rip the bumper off and put it in the back, but the Suburban actually drives straight. Tell Jim he didn't break the car. Terry and Barbara are here. Barbara is on her way to the hospital. I expect we'll start getting reports from her pretty soon," Alex was quick with his words and to the point.

"I would suggest that she be armed in case they try to clean up loose ends," Sarena suggested.

"Good suggestion," Alex said; "already been done. Barbara can take care of herself and Ronnie, too."

In front of them, shots were fired, and the three hit the deck as bullets whizzed by. Sarena pulled the phone to her ear, "I guess we have to go. They seem to have realized we're following them."

"Got it. I'll head around to the other side of the mountain and work my way up," she heard Alex shuffling.

Sarena hung up the phone.

Rachel and Jim were already moving. Sarena stayed low and watched as Jim worked his way around to the left and Rachel to the right. Sarena couldn't see any movement, so she drew her weapon and fired three rounds into the air. As she hit the deck again, gunfire rang out from in front of them. She waited.

"Small arms fire," Sarena stated the obvious, "9mm, the action is a bit off. If he fires a little more, I may be able to identify it."

"How about we get up closer and deal with this, and you can play with the weapon when you have it in your hand?" Rachel suggested.

"I was hoping I could identify the weapon, so I know how many shots he has before he reloads," Sarena said. "I'd rather not be a target and end up next to Ronnie."

"Good point," Jim considered the situation. "Let's work our way around. Rachel, take left, and I'll take right. Sarena, you stay here. If anyone gets a clear shot, fire one in the air. If he still has the girl, we don't want to take the chance of hitting her, but at least we'll know which direction is open. Once we're spread apart, if we can keep firing on one side, the flank will work their way around."

"Good plan," Sarena recognized how the team worked. "Once you have some distance, I'll fire one shot so they can focus on me. At the current time, there's only one shooter. Let's hope we keep it that way."

Jim and Rachel belly-crawled away from Sarena in opposite directions. Sarena could see both of them and kept a close eye on where they were. Once they had a reasonable distance, she fired a single shot in the air and was greeted with three shots back in her direction. She was now relatively certain this was a Glock17. Normally she would have recognized it right away, but whoever was shooting it probably modified the action, or it had a suppressor. She filed that away to look at the weapon afterward then realized she was probably being overly optimistic. As she started working her way forward, Sarena wondered about the team she joined. This seemed like a very good idea after the debacle she faced in her previous position, but it also seemed like this group pushed too fast and skirted the edge of the law. This was a problem to her, at least right now. She knew that the team did well together, and they dealt with some very difficult situations where other teams would have surely failed. Still, they were not a SEAL team, nor a Ranger team, nor a SWAT team. Instead, they were a semi-covert team, and she was not sure how she felt about that anymore.

Two shots hit close to her, and she realized her daydreaming would probably be the end of her. She needed to focus on getting the job done and stop worrying about what was being done. That realization opened her up to another possibility. The difference between the team she was on and the team she had been on was that this team focused on getting the job done.

Sarena's family had been in law enforcement for generations. She had a strong desire to do the right thing, but she had been tied up in red tape many times and was now considering that maybe the red tape was a problem as well. She knew Tarkington's reputation for solving difficult issues, but part of that solution had to be bending the law to ensure success. Even her addition to the team showed a bend in the process, and with that in mind, perhaps she needed to rethink her approach to law enforcement. She decided she needed to really start paying attention, or she was going to die right here and not be able to think about this anymore.

Normal magazine capacity of the Glock 17 was 17. She ran through the shots in her head and was reasonably certain he had shot eight, leaving nine shots left in a standard magazine. Sarena decided that it was unlikely that the Glock had an extended magazine, but it was a chance she had to take. She looked to the right, to a rock outcropping, and rolled to it. She fired one shot into the air. Three more reports followed as she rolled back to the left as far as she could and shot another into the air.

Sarena thought to herself about the bullets she was firing into the air and wondered what the possibilities were that they would strike someone. Where the projectile coming out of her weapon was traveling at an extreme rate of speed, around 1,100 feet per second, it would not return to earth at that high speed. Instead, it would slow to terminal velocity. Though it could cause damage, it was unlikely to hurt anyone, given the area.

Sarena fired into the air again and was rewarded with three more shots. In theory, just two shell casings were left in the pistol before a new magazine would be necessary. Sarena fired once more into the air, and this time only two shots came back. She was sure she heard the click of the slide locking into place with an empty magazine.

Sarena ran towards the outcropping, where she was relatively sure the shooter was located. She didn't look for Jim or Rachel but hoped they heard the same and understood the significance. Sarena was taking a big chance. In tactical courses, she could reload in under a second and empty a magazine in just a few seconds. It was obvious that whoever was firing had been trained. They were firing in three-round bursts and not just wildly emptying their magazine. Sarena was hoping that Eleanor was enough of a distraction to make it harder to reload. If she was not correct, she was about to die.

Sarena heard a struggle before her and a muffled scream. She ran around an outcropping of limestone and saw the man in a suit holding

Eleanor. The Glock 17 was still in his hand, and the slide was still locked back. The weapon was unloaded. Eleanor was struggling and twisting, trying to get away. The man only had hold of her hair in his other hand now. The man saw Sarena coming around the rock and let go of Eleanor. He reached inside his jacket, and Sarena knew he was going for another magazine. She swung her weapon up and was about to fire when she saw Rachel step up behind the man. Rachel grabbed the man by the arm and spun him. The man was probably seventy-five pounds heavier than Rachel, if not more, but it didn't matter. Rachel hit the man full force in the chest, and he fell back towards Sarena with his arms flailing wildly. The Glock 17 fell out of his hand, and a magazine fell out of his other hand to the ground. The man started to get up as he gasped for air, but Sarena put her pistol to his forehead.

"Time to stop moving," Rachel said.

Eleanor ran behind Sarena and watched.

Jim walked around the edge of the rock. "Maybe it's not time to stop moving."

Jim reached down, grabbed the man, and pulled him to his feet. The motion was so swift that the man was wide-eyed. Jim punched the man in the stomach, forcing him to double over. The man fell to the ground and vomited almost straight away.

"One of you shot our friend," Jim seemed calm but there was a terrifying reality in his voice. "I know you'll say it was our dead man, but I want to hear it coming out of your mouth."

"It doesn't matter what I say," the man choked in broken English. "I will be free before morning."

"You seem to think I'm part of a police force," Jim said as he knelt down in front of the man. "You need to give me something I can use, or things will get really bad right now for you."

"An idle threat," the man said in broken English again.

Jim grabbed the man by the index finger and pulled him up, then snaped the finger to the side, breaking it and putting it at an odd angle.

The man screamed.

"I have nine more chances for you to give me something on why you're here and why you were after this girl. My friend is in the hospital, and he may die. I'd like to know why." Jim spoke in an almost soothing voice.

The man was panting, and his face was covered with sweat from the pain, "Go ahead, kill me. I am not afraid to die."

"I've heard people say that before. It's a unique statement. I could say with almost complete certainty that you're not afraid to die, and we would both be right. Dying isn't your problem right now. You shouldn't ever be afraid of dying."

The man looked at Jim as he spoke with an indignant rage. He held his hand while standing on his knees.

"What you should be afraid of is how long you'll live. I think I could let you live a long time and every moment of that time you'll remember me and the decision you're about to make. I think you should strongly consider how each day in Guantanamo Bay will feel. I think you should strongly consider how you will feel being unable to use any of your limbs and feeling pain for the rest of your life. I think you should consider how the people I work for could keep you alive, perhaps into your 80s, screaming in pain every single minute. I know you're not afraid to die, but right now, your fear of me should be based on how long you're gonna live."

The man looked at Jim and then at his hand, "I had orders, and I followed them. I did not kill or shoot your friend; I was just told to take the girl. My comrade acted outside our orders, but I would have done the same. We were told to take the girl, and that's exactly what we would have done. People who get in the way are collateral damage."

"What's your name?" Jim asked softly.

"Boris," the man replied, "my name is Boris, and the man you killed is Igor."

Sarena sat by and watched all of this and realized that Jim had controlled the situation without killing the man. He was more brutal than most, and that was unexpected. Still, he got the information they needed and would surely get more if he asked. Sarena still struggled with the legality of it all, but this was a form of justice, and she was willing to live with it for now.

"You see," Jim beamed, "people can be reasonable if you convince them to."

"He said they were going to question me and then kill me," Eleanor said. "Where is Ronnie? How is he?"

"We'll find out in just a few minutes," Sarena said. "Let's get out of here."

Distracted for just a few moments, Boris took the opportunity to pull a knife from his side. Jim saw the knife and turned to him to defend himself, but Boris shoved the knife into his chest, directly over his heart and between his ribs. He gasped for a few moments and then fell forward, dead from shock.

"Well, that was nuts," Rachel said as Sarena turned Eleanor away from the scene.

"I guess he didn't want to tell us anything else," Jim quipped. "All we have to do now is figure out where Alex is."

"I don't think you're going to have to do that," Alex said as he walked up to the scene. "I caught the tail end of this and saw him kill himself from a distance. Not exactly the type of person you want to invite to Thanksgiving."

"He might have done well carving a turkey," Jim joked. "How far is the car?"

"Just over that hill," Alex replied. "I will lead you guys to it. Check for your weapons. We don't want to leave anything here. We'll let the local police take care of him." Alex took out his phone and marked the spot in the GPS. "I'll send this to them when we get back to the Suburban."

"Eleanor," Alex said, "my name is Alex; that's Jim over there, Rachel, and Sarena. We'll find out how Ronnie is as we head out okay? We're friends of Ronnie's."

"I know all of you," Eleanor said "Ronnie has written me about all of you and how awesome each of you are. He says that you're the best leader he's ever known, and Jim is the best fighter he has ever seen for real or on TV. He said Rachel would move the world to help a friend and Sarena knows more about guns and weapons than everybody in our family combined. He always talks about Barbara and how beautiful she is. Where is Barbara?"

"By now, she'll be at the hospital with Ronnie;" Alex said, "and you certainly do know us."

"It's good she will be with Ronnie. He thinks about her all the time," Eleanor said. "You know he talks to her a lot, but I know he thinks about her too. He never really dated anyone before, so he is a little silly about it."

"Silly?" Sarena asked.

"You know, guy silly? How guys get when they are always thinking about a girl?" Eleanor laughed, then cried just a little.

The hill was steep, but the group walked through the paths and worked their way around the dense foliage. It wasn't long before they could see the now well-worn Suburban.

"Oops," Jim laughed. "Did I do that?"

"Yes, you did," Alex kicked the tire as he walked up. "Fortunately, it is not as bad as it looks." They all looked at the Suburban then Alex added, "I am not sure anything can be that bad."

The small group reached the Suburban and began laughing.

Chapter 19

Barbara had been waiting for nearly ten minutes to get some type of status on Ronnie. Finally, she waited for someone to walk through the restricted doors and followed them back. As she walked back to the desk, a nurse looked up at her and told her, "You can't be back here. You need to wait out front."

"I've been waiting out front long enough," Barbara replied.

"I don't have a status for you right now," the nurse replied.

"Then get me a status," Barbara said.

"How am I supposed to do that?" the nurse replied, "I'm not the doctor."

"I know you're not the doctor, but you have access to where Ronnie is, and you can walk your ass back there and find out what's going on. I have a whole team of people who want to know what's happening. They're not going to want to wait ten more minutes or twenty more minutes, or even five more minutes. I need answers right now. I need to know if I need to get him on a plane to a real hospital."

"We are a real hospital," the nurse replied.

"Then prove it and get me a status," Barbara said.

A security guard came up behind Barbara. "Is everything okay here?" The man was tall and perhaps Hispanic, his blue pants were neat, and his white long-sleeve shirt was pressed and starched.

Barbara turned around and pulled out her ID. "Absolutely everything is okay here," Barbara calm and dry. "I'm trying to get the status of one of my team members and someone I care about an awful lot, and nobody here seems to want to give me a status. If I seem a little irritated, it's because of exactly that. I was given a task by my team leader, and I am unable to complete that task at this time because people are sitting on their butts when they could be doing something."

The security guard looked around Barbara. "Molly are you okay?" He then looked at Barbara's ID, "Army?" he asked. "What's the army doing here?"

"I'm sorry," Barbara replied, "that's classified. The rest of my team may be here soon. If it's necessary, they will explain to you what's going on. I can't do that." Barbara looked at the man's picture ID hanging from his crisp white shirt and read the name "Edward." "Edward, if you would like me to give you a phone number to call, I will."

It was Molly who spoke next. "I don't think that will be necessary. Edward, it's okay. Let me go see if I can get some answers."

Molly walked around the counter and down a short hallway until she reached another door. That door also required a card, and as Molly walked through the door, she put on a mask. The silver doors swung closed rapidly and with a finality that Barbara didn't like. Barbara looked around the room and saw Edward sauntering down the hallway in the opposite direction. Barbara stayed at the counter and was rapidly becoming impatient again after about five minutes. No one came in or out of the silver doors.

Barbara jumped when her phone buzzed. She looked down and saw she had received a text from Jim. The text was one word, "Status." Barbara typed; "Had to rattle cages, actively waiting for status." "Understood," Jim texted back. "Keep us in the loop."

The nurse, Molly, walked back out of the twin steel doors and took off her mask. She waited until she was completely behind the counter before she looked up at Barbara. "He is still in surgery. The doctor was reluctant to say much. There was extensive damage to his leg. They have managed to stabilize him while they continue to work on it. They don't know how much longer it will be."

Barbara nodded and somehow managed to keep her demeanor crisp and unemotional. "I will pass that on. I'd appreciate it if you occasionally let me know how things are going so I can pass it forward."

"I will do what I can," Molly replied.

Barbara took out her phone again and sent a message to Jim with the status. It was only a few moments later that she got a reply. "Keep eyes open."

Barbara knew that if Ronnie was a specific target the hospital was an easy place to get to him. With that in mind, she pulled up a map of the hospital on her telephone and reviewed her surroundings. There were only two ways in and out of the surgical area. As Barbara looked at the map, she noted that the most defensible position was the waiting room she was in previously. From there, she could see the hall that opened to the back entrance and the front entrance from one location. Barbara returned to the waiting room and moved a chair where she could watch both directions easily.

She took her phone out and sent a text to Jim. "In position watching both entrances. Hospital is quiet. Will advise further as necessary."

Barbara considered all that she had been through and sent another text to Terry, "You're right."

A few seconds later, a reply came only from Terry. "I wish my ex-wife would've known that."

Barbara smiled to herself and got comfortable. As she waited, the security guard, Edward, walked up to her.

"Sorry for your man," he said. "I was in for twenty years; it never gets easier."

"No," Barbara replied, "It never does."

"I miss it sometimes, then I think about all the bad memories I have. It wears on you every day, doesn't it?" Edward continued.

"Sometimes it does, but it's not something you expect on US soil," Barbara said as she stared forward.

"It happens everywhere," Edward said. "People just sweep it under the rug. Nobody wants to see it, so everybody thinks it doesn't exist. It's out here. Every day is some kind of war, even out here in the middle of nowhere, in Pikeville. I spent my time fighting for this dream. I came home and will fight for it here, too."

Barbara was quiet for a moment, not sure what to say. She knew he was right; a security guard in Pikeville, Kentucky, understood that sometimes the fight came home, and we all had to live with that. Barbara thought about Lisa. Lisa was her friend and a valued member of their team. She was gunned down next to the plane where Barbara stood. "It never gets easier," Barbara said to the man standing next to her. "Whether it's here or there, it never gets easier."

Chapter 20

The Suburban was a mess. It looked like it had been taken to a junkyard, picked up by a giant scrap arm, and thrown around the junkyard a few times. There may have been one spot on top of the roof that was not dented or crushed, but it would be difficult to find that spot. The doors were intact, but the back passenger door was bent so much that there was no way to open it. The group climbed inside the truck, and surprisingly, the inside was still quite pristine except for some spilled coffee, and none of the airbags had gone off.

"Nice ride," Jim laughed as the group piled into the car.

"Used to be." Alex started the vehicle with no issue and put the Suburban in drive. With his foot still on the brake, he turned and said, "Seatbelts."

Jim started laughing. "I have to cut my airbag out before I can put on the seatbelt."

Alex smiled and drove out into the road.

It was a testament to the vehicle's durability that it still drove okay. In spite of the cosmetic destruction, the vehicle was still quite drivable and more than a little comfortable. Alex was driving, Jim was in the passenger seat, Rachel, Sarena, and Eleanor were in the back.

"We should go back to Uncle Harv's," Rachel suggested. "We left a few hostages there, and he's just one old man."

"Not sure how we get there. Do you have an address?" Alex asked.

"I do," Eleanor piped in, "I live there, he's my dad." Eleanor gave Alex the address, and he put it into the Suburban's GPS system.

"Eleanor, you seem like the center of all this attention. Can you give me any clue about what's going on?" Alex asked.

Eleanor paused for a second. Normally she wouldn't talk to outsiders, but she felt like she knew these people. These were Ronnie's friends, and Ronnie trusted them, so maybe she should. "Well, Sir, I'm not

100% sure. I like to go hiking and explore. I know kids my age are usually hanging around playing video games and playing on their phones, but I want to know about the world. So, I was hiking two days ago and came across a plateau full of flowers. It was kind of covered but kind of open so the flowers would grow. I'm pretty sure it was opium. I'm pretty sure those people are trying to kill me because I found their field. I've been chased by drones, shot at, I shot one man, but I saw him, and he is okay. I've been chased through fields, and I've been thrown under the arm of a man who treated me like a rag doll. It's pretty much all because of me seeing that field."

"Was there anything special about the field?" Sarena asked.

"I don't know," Eleanor said. "I was curious, but I didn't go in very far because I saw the cameras and then heard the drones. All I got to see was the edge of it."

"All this trouble is over something you really don't know anything about?" Alex asked.

"I would say yes," Eleanor began. "I mean, it's not like it was anybody's land in particular. I'm pretty sure that area is all owned by the State or the government. I wish I could tell you more. The men who chased me all had an accent, but I don't know what kind, maybe Russia. They sound a lot like those Russians did on TV, but I never met anybody from Russia before."

"It doesn't give them the right to hunt her down and try to kill her," Rachel said, "and it didn't give them the right to shoot Ronnie."

"I'm not saying it did," Alex stated. "It just means there's more going on here than meets the eye."

"The question is, do we go to that field after we go see Uncle Harv, or do we go see our mutual friend?" Jim asked. "Barbara can take care of the hospital, and maybe it's time to get Terry to come stay with the uncle."

Alex picked up his phone and dialed a number. The phone rang on the Suburban's hands-free.

"Hello?" the voice said.

"Terry," Alex said, "I'm going to send you an address. Get a car and head to that address. We may be there, or we may have moved on. There will be at least two people you need to protect, and perhaps a few to control. I will advise further when we arrive."

"On my way," Terry replied and hung up.

"He is a man of few words," Jim laughed.

"Yes, he is," Alex replied.

"I don't think either of you wanna be in his crosshairs now, do you?" Rachel smirked. "Not all of us can be amazing conversationalists."

"You're right, Rachel, there are very few people I would rather have on the hill behind me," Jim noted. "It might be better if I shut up a little more often. Sometimes it's better to listen than flap your jaw."

The GPS was talking the entire time, and it seemed every turn led to another turn until they came to the driveway. As they drove up, they came to a closed metal gate. "Was this closed when you were here, Rachel?"

"We came over the hill and didn't come up the driveway," Rachel said.

"Why would you have come up the hill instead?" Jim asked.

"When Ronnie called, Uncle Harv blew him off like he was some type of salesman. Ronnie knew something was wrong, so we went over the hill and caught a few guys by surprise," Rachel stated.

"When were you going to tell me this?" Alex looked over the seat.

"It's not like we've had a lot of time," Rachel replied. "I mean, there's been a lot going on, and I've had a lot more target shooting today than I've had in the last few months. By the way, I really like Uncle Harv."

"Is there anything else we need to worry about?" Alex asked.

"No, I think that's the only thing you don't know about. We came to Uncle Harv's to talk to Eleanor, got into a firefight next to a school, talked to Ronnie's cousin who's apparently on the police force, and then Ronnie got shot, and you were there. I don't think I left anything out."

Jim got out of the car and walked up to the gate. He examined the gate and found a tripwire. He traced the tripwire to a pair of wires and clipped it so it wouldn't go off. Then he opened the gate, and Alex drove through. Jim closed the gate and reset the tripwire, just in case.

As Jim got back into the car, Alex asked, "What was that?"

"Looks like a simple tripwire; probably beeps in the house or blows us up, one of the two," Jim said.

"It beeps at the house," Eleanor said. "It's been set up a long time so that we know if somebody's coming. We don't have many visitors out here except family; they know how to reset it. With Ronnie gone, there aren't very many people coming around. Seems like people grow up here in Pikeville just so they can move away and make a living. Then they come back and get old at their old family place. There's a lot more opportunity in Lexington and Louisville than there ever would be here in Pikeville."

"What do you intend on doing?" Sarena said.

"Soon as I turn eighteen, I'm joining the Army like Ronnie did," Eleanor replied. "Ronnie's been showing everybody here how to do it and has told us all that Rachel and Melody are his heroes. He says that Rachel can whoop just about anybody, and that Melody is one of the smartest people he's ever known."

"Sounds like a good goal," Sarena assured Eleanor.

As they pulled up in front of the house, Harv walked out onto the front porch. Eleanor got out of the car, ran up to him, and hugged him. Rachel, Jim, Alex, and Sarena were right behind her.

"Looks like you boys have been having some car problems," Harv noted as he looked over the well-worn vehicle.

"We ran into a bit of an issue," Alex said. "I don't know how to say this, so I will just say it. Ronnie is down at the hospital. He's been shot, and it's not good. The last status I received said he was still in surgery, but he stabilized. We got Eleanor back, but several men died in the process. Rachel says you still have some men here?"

"Ronnie's a strong boy," Harv said as he choked back a tear, "God willing, he'll make it through, but we always have to pay a price. I'm glad this day to have Eleanor here and not to have lost her. I know. God willing I will not lose my Ronnie. Yeah, I got them three boys tied up in here. They aren't much into talking, but I've been throwing little peanuts at 'em and laughing a lot while I watch my soap operas."

Jim smiled, "I hope you're watching the good ones."

"Yes, Sir; I do," Harv replied. "You must be Jim; Ronnie has written to me about what a fine man you are and what good guidance you have given him and taught him about defending himself." Harv looked at Alex. "You, Sir, must be Alex; Ronnie says you are the best leader that anyone could ever have and that you would never have your men do anything that you wouldn't do. He beams with pride in these letters, and when I talk to him. All of you are welcome here and welcome to take these men wherever you need to."

"I appreciate that a lot, and thank you for the kind words," Alex said. "I would love for a chance to talk to these men. I have a man coming to sit with you and make sure you and Eleanor are okay."

"That'll be just fine," Harv replied, "as long as they like soap operas, they're fine by me."

"Terry will be here soon, and I'm sure you'll like him," Alex said.

"The pilot," Harv said. "Where is that girl pilot that Ronnie is so tore up about? Every time I talk to him, he rattles on and on about how pretty she is. I can't imagine her being prettier than Rachel."

"Barbara is at the hospital making sure Ronnie is safe," Alex replied. "She'll guard him with her life and make sure we know what's going on."

"That sounds really good," Harv replied. "Can you drop Eleanor off somewhere? I'm not sure I want her around these men. They had their minds set on taking her, and I'd rather not give them that opportunity. If you could take her to one of her cousins or drop her off at the hospital, they'll make sure she's okay. Her aunt works at one of the desks at the hospital, and she's let Eleanor stay there before."

"You know I'm not a child anymore," Eleanor said.

"You need to let some of us old folks decide this. Your damn curiosity keeps writing checks you can't cash. Let us handle it and keep you safe, and don't give us no sass. I don't know what I'd do if I lost you. Everybody's either moving away or dying on me now."

"Yes, Sir," Eleanor conceded.

"We'll take her with us and make sure she gets somewhere safe. We've gotta swing over to Ivel to have a discussion with someone who might know what's going on." Alex said as they reached the door.

"She's got a cousin by Ivel too, just drop her off there, and it'll be fine," Harv said.

"I'm going to sit out here for a second while you talk to these men," Harv said.

Alex and Jim walked into the room; Rachel stood outside. Sarena stood at the door and listened.

"Which one of the three of you is the leader?" Alex asked.

"We are all leader," a man said.

Rachel walked in. "He calls himself Victor; he was the one doing all the talking with me."

"Your girl, she put a knife in my leg," Victor said.

"Is that all?" Jim asked, then looked at Rachel. "That's all you did to him?"

"You are Americans; you have your rules. Why have I not gone to the police station where I can file charges against you?" Victor asked.

"That's a real good question," Alex said. "Has anyone called the police?"

"Not me," said Rachel.

"Not me," Jim echoed.

"Not me," Sarena said.

"It must have slipped everyone's minds. I'm sure your friends will be coming looking for you soon, so you better tell me where to find them." Alex noted.

"I have no friends. I just met these fine gentlemen today. We were out taking a walk, and your people killed one of our friends and have kidnapped the three of us." Victor said.

"I hate it when that happens," Jim said. "Do we want to take the time to figure this out with them or go try our other way?"

"This could take a while," Alex said. "It could never give us anything. Let's try the other way."

"What is your other way?" Victor asked.

Jim slapped Victor on the side of the face several times like a child. "Don't you worry your pretty little head about it. You aren't the only game in town."

Everyone went outside. The entire group gathered a few feet from the door of the house. Alex looked back at the house and considered for a moment. "Terry will be here soon, and we will decide if it's time to call the police. I have a feeling that we should go ahead and call someone that we know we can trust."

"I know someone on the police force," Harv began.

"We have a line on somebody that can't be corrupted. I'm not saying your family is corrupt, but I know whatever is going on here runs pretty deep. We'll figure it out. Jim, on the way out to the house, you can call our special friend." Jim nodded, letting Alex know that he understood.

"Harv, we will take your daughter someplace safe or keep her with us for a while. Either way, I'll make sure she doesn't get in any trouble."

"I appreciate that, Sir," Harv replied. "Ronnie says you are a good man, and I believe Ronnie is right."

"Alright, everybody, let's load up and get this done," Alex said.

"You sure you don't wanna take my truck?" Harv said "Your vehicle looks like it's seen much better days."

"It's still working," Alex laughed, "that's gotta be worth something."

"Y'all take care now," Harv said.

"We will," Alex said as everyone got into the Suburban. "We'll make sure the gate's closed too."

As they started driving away, Jim was looking through his phone. He found a number and dialed.

"Dispatch, please," Jim said and waited for a few moments. "Good afternoon; my name is Jim Simpson. I met one of your fine troopers this morning, trooper Thorne in Pikeville, Kentucky. I was wondering if I could get in touch with him somehow? A cell phone number would be nice, but I will take anything you can get, or you can get him a message?" Jim waited. "Yes, please have him call me. He has my number. Tell him he took it this morning when he pulled me over. Thank you."

"Well, we'll see if he calls," Alex said.

"He will call," Jim replied. "His curiosity will get the better of him."

Jim got out and opened the gate again, making sure to be careful with the triggers. He reset the gate after they had gone through, and Alex put a new address into their GPS. As they started to drive, Alex turned around and looked at Eleanor for a moment.

"Eleanor, for the moment, I think you're safer with us; but if I start feeling that you're in any type of danger, I will make sure you get someplace safe. We're going to see someone we all know, and I'm really

134

gonna need you to stay in the background. There are people out here that you really shouldn't mess with, and I found that out the hard way. Can you do that for me?"

"Yeah, I can do that," Eleanor said. "Ronnie says you're awfully serious. I can understand that, and if I'm going to be any good as a soldier, I need to start listening."

"GPS says this is only going to be a twenty-five-minute drive from here. It's funny how it's fifteen miles and twenty-five minutes. I'd be willing to bet we will be going in some circles and up some hills. You remember when I picked you up from down here?" Jim asked.

"How could I forget," Alex said, "I just lost my whole team and had no one else to trust but you."

"It's nice to be loved, isn't it?" Jim said.

Eleanor laughed.

"They are pretty funny, aren't they?" Rachel said. "They're like two old women always bickering and making fun of each other. Can you imagine them wearing some of those floofy old dresses?"

Eleanor laughed again; this time, it was really hard.

"I didn't know when I joined this group that it was going to be a comedy show half the time," Sarena said. "I try not to laugh, but sometimes this crew has you giggling."

"They think we're comedy club," Jim said. "Well, maybe we are until it's time not to be."

"I am not part of a comedy club," Rachel said, "I am my own little club."

"Somebody needs to take a club to you," Jim said.

"Maybe you best try to take a club to me," Rachel smiled as she said it.

"I think I'd rather take you to a club," Jim said, "maybe we can go dancing again."

Eleanor was laughing as everyone went back and forth. They were giggling so hard that Eleanor snorted, making everyone in the car laugh even harder. It was a nice pause to the thoughts and worries about Ronnie.

"I can't believe Ronnie's cousin is part pig," Jim said as he snorted multiple times.

Alex started recognizing some of the area, including the Dollar General where he stopped after his ordeal. A quick turn and he was driving up the hill where the missiles killed his team. In the end, the entire situation was born out of revenge. It turned out the revenge was wrong simply because the person wanting to get revenge didn't know the whole story. Alex thought about why he was there and how it was all a farce, but in the end, started this team. A group of people no one would have thought to put together working towards a single goal.

They came to a dirt driveway. Alex turned in and drove to the top of the hill. As they reached the top, a car greeted them in the driveway, likely on its way out. It was Michael's Aston Martin DB9. The car stopped, and Michael opened the door and stepped out in a crouching position. Alex put the car in park and stepped out as well. Michael moved his hand, and Alex realized he was holstering his pistol. Jim got out of the car.

"You draw that pistol pretty fast," Jim said.

"Obviously, I don't fire as fast as I draw," Michael replied, "I choose my targets more carefully than that."

"I'll give you that," Jim said as he walked to Michael. Jim put out his hand, and Michael shook it. Abby got out of the car as everyone piled out of the Suburban. Everyone except Eleanor.

"It looks like you had some severe car problems," Michael said. "At this point, I think it's totaled."

"Everyone keeps picking on the car," Alex laughed, "but it's still nice inside and runs well."

"I guess that works as long as you don't want to blend in. That being said, almost every government issue vehicle is a Suburban. Chevy must get a huge kickback to get so many Suburbans in the motor pool."

"Of course, you're right," Alex said. "It looks like you're leaving."

"We need to find some furniture," Abby stated. "We have an empty house here, and we were running down to Pikeville to fill it up."

"I don't want to interfere, but I have a couple of questions for you, Michael," Alex said.

"Sam called us and told us you would be coming," Michael said; "He also said you had some problems, and one of your team was shot."

"Sam called you?" Alex said. "I'm betting that doesn't happen very often."

"You are betting correctly," Michael noted. "You think Yuri Petrikov is behind some of this? I suppose it is possible. I haven't seen Yuri in quite some time, but his father was in control of one of the largest syndicates in Ukraine. Sam told me you would like some information, but he also asked me to find out directly if it was Yuri, and politely ask him to leave."

"Why would Yuri listen to you?" Alex asked.

"At one time, we were friends. Well, not really friends but compatriots. I had research to do on Yuri's father, and along the way Yuri and I began talking. He had a lot of very conservative political views and was very against his father's socialist agenda. I often expected Yuri to liquidate the family business and run for office on a conservative platform after I dispatched his father. I checked and found that he continued in his father's footsteps and did some very bad things. It was none of my business, but it was a disappointing situation. He had such promise and could sway people very easily. I said that we weren't friends, and that was correct, but if he had asked me, I probably would have considered being his friend. When I left, it was under a shroud of mystery. His cousin had uncovered who I was and knew I killed Anton. I had to leave in a hurry, and unfortunately, I had to terminate his cousin."

"So why would he talk to you if you terminated his cousin," Jim asked.

"His cousin never appeared. I know for a fact they may never find a body."

"With that in mind, how should we proceed with the group that's here in Pikeville?" Alex asked.

"I would say carefully," Michael stated. "I will be leaving in the morning to head to Ukraine. As long as the men here are under orders, they will do whatever they can to protect their business and clean up any loose ends."

"We appear to have a few loose ends," Alex said; "One, of course, is Ronnie, and one is in the Suburban."

"Who is in the vehicle?" Michael asked.

"Ronnie's cousin," Alex said. "Apparently, she stumbled on opium fields, and they have been chasing her ever since. Several men have died, and we have three men captive with Eleanor's father."

"They won't stay captive for long," Michael said. "Anton's men were near fanatical. It is likely they will either find a way out, and kill everyone there, or kill themselves to prevent any potential leak."

"Yeah, we already had that happen once," Alex said. "It was pretty messy, too."

"It's expected," Michael said. "I'm not sure what else I can tell you that you don't already know."

"I can't believe you're gonna go over and talk to this man," Sarena said.

"I am being well paid," Michael replied, "but I would have done it for free. Don't tell Sam that. I need to close that part of my life up. It'll make me feel better. I also have some property over there I need to clean up. I will get it ready and have a company ship it out. In the end, it'll resolve a lot of issues."

"You seem to have a lot of property," Rachel noted "everywhere we go, you have a house. So do you have a house in Ukraine?"

"No, I don't have a house in Ukraine," Michael chuckled, "I have a warehouse in Ukraine. It was easier to work out of a warehouse and not quite as conspicuous. I was only going to be there for a short time, so I set it up. Because the job was over so quickly, I left quite a few things there. Mostly weapons, but I might as well make sure everything is emptied, and maybe the warehouse can be used for something."

"A warehouse," Rachel said; "I suppose it had an apartment on the top floor."

"Actually, it did," Michael broke in. "I had to have someplace to unwind after partying all the time with Yuri and his group. I'm sure I still have some decent clothes there, not that it matters. Anything I left over there I haven't needed for a long time, so I really don't know that I need it at all. Mostly what I will be doing is cleaning up the formalities."

"You did a great job rebuilding this house," Alex said. "It was kind of premature when you destroyed it."

"I did what I thought was necessary, and it got everybody off my back," Michael replied.

"Yeah, it was a weird situation," Alex said. "I really didn't like you very much back then, but at least I have respect for you now."

Abby was pacing. "Michael, should we go inside, or should we all go into the city? We're standing out in front of our house talking, and we have a perfectly good house, or there are several restaurants in Pikeville."

"Do you need anything additional?" Michael asked.

"No, I don't think so right now," Alex said.

Jim's phone rang, and he walked away for a moment as he answered.

"I appreciate you taking the time to talk to us," Alex said. "We'll get settled in a hotel and then address the issues tomorrow with whoever Yuri has here."

"Good luck with that," Michael said. "Perhaps by this time tomorrow or maybe a little later, a lot of this will go away. Yuri can be quite reasonable, or at least he used to be."

"I hope that works out," Michael said.

Jim walked over to the group. "Good news. Ronnie is out of surgery. He is in serious but stable condition. He's asleep right now, but Barbara will go in in a few minutes once he has a private room."

"That is good news," Michael said, "he always seemed like a very honest young man."

"Again, thank you for your time," Alex said. The group got back into the Suburban.

"You know, there is an auto repair shop in town, and a body shop and a Chevy dealer. Any one of those three will help this out," Michael said.

"Thanks for the recommendation," Alex said.

Once everyone was in the car, Alex turned around and went out the driveway. He was curious why Tarkington had involved Michael but knew he probably had his reasons. At the bottom of the driveway, Alex turned out while Jim put the hospital's address into the GPS.

Chapter 21

Barbara walked the hospital hall in front of the room where Ronnie would soon be. He was being moved to the private room for his protection, but the nurse noted that he would still have a hard time for a while. It wasn't much longer that she saw Ronnie coming down the hallway on a gurney. The three nurses bringing him in asked Barbara to step out of the way as they moved the multiple IVs to the stands in the room.

With skill, they lifted the sheet Ronnie was on over to the main bed, rocked him, and removed the sheet. Two of the nurses left with the gurney while the third busied herself hooking up Ronnie's monitors. Ronnie still had an oxygen mask on but was breathing on his own. The nurse then worked to hang Ronnie's leg a little higher in a sling. It was fairly straightforward, and she was very gentle as she worked with the very large cast.

The nurse called Barbara in.

"The worst has passed, but we will still pay very close attention through the night. One of his lungs was perforated, but it was clean, and there was no shrapnel or debris. They were able to close everything up and, for the most part, repaired the rib that was shattered as the bullet left. He's breathing on his own, but we need to watch for infection very closely. If he has problems breathing, and we're not in here, you need to call. His leg needs to be raised. The bullet that hit him in the leg shattered the bone but missed the artery. The surgeon thought it was a miracle that he didn't bleed out. They rebuilt the leg the best they could, but we have to make sure it begins to heal correctly over the next several days. Things have come a long way. Other than that, he had cuts and bruises. He's a strong young man."

"Will he walk again?" Barbara asked.

"Yes, he will walk again, but it's unlikely it will be pain-free. Over time it will get better, but a shattered femur isn't something we see often."

"When will he wake up?" Barbara asked.

"Give him time. The anesthesia will wear off soon, but his body's been through a lot, and the best thing for him is rest. We will check on him often. Keep your eyes open as well. If you see anything buzz for us."

"Is there anything I should be watching for?" Barbara asked.

"You should be watching for everything, but he will be okay as long as he gets his rest," the nurse replied.

The nurse left the room and closed the door to a crack. Barbara watched the monitors for a moment and saw the lines go up and down for his heart rate. She knew what normal should be, and Ronnie's was normal. Barbera walked to the bed next to Ronnie and looked at him. Ronnie was young, and they never really talked about his age, but he was only twenty-five. She touched his cheek and felt the stubble and the warmth. The mask covered his nose and mouth. She studied him for a few moments. Ronnie's hands were at his side. A monitor was on his finger, and an IV was in his arm. Barbara put her hand in his and squeezed. She knelt down and softly kissed Ronnie on the forehead. She lingered, and a tear fell down her cheek.

"I'm not going to lose another day," she said. "You need to come back to me, Ronnie. You need to come back because I was foolish. You're the one for me. You're the one I want to spend my days and my nights with. You're the one I want to have children with and grow old next to, and I never really knew it until today. I know things might be tough. I know I've made some bad decisions in my life. Still, I want to be there for you and be the best possible person for you that could ever be."

Barbara squeezed his hand again.

"I know maybe I'm not perfect; after all, it was you who told me that I deserve better than the men I've dated. Right now, I feel like I teased you and didn't realize how you saw me. Right now, I see you that same way. I don't ever wanna stop seeing you this way. You need to come back to me, Ronnie."

Barbara picked up his hand and kissed it, then laid his hand back down and walked over to the recliner a few feet away from his bed. She looked at the door and considered what Alex said. Reaching into her jacket, she checked her pistol and made sure the safety was on. She made sure that she still had the magazines under her other arm. She set her weapon down on the recliner and walked over to the door. She opened it a little and then looked both ways down the hallway. The hall was empty except for a few nurses, and the floor was quiet. Barbara walked into the bathroom right next to the door and looked at herself in the mirror. Her makeup was slightly mussed, and it was apparent that she had been crying. She did what she could to straighten her makeup and patted her face in the process. When she walked out of the bathroom, she made sure that Ronnie was okay, then walked over and sat in the recliner.

Barbara sent a text. "In private room, Ronnie stable."

She sat watching the door, reached over and touched Ronnie's arm. She did not glance at her phone, try to work, play games, or do anything but be the diligent guardian she needed to be. She looked back and forth between the door and Ronnie. It was going to be a long afternoon.

Chapter 22

Jim's phone rang. He didn't recognize the number. Alex looked over at him from the driver's seat, and Jim said, "I think it's time for me to get a new extended car warranty." Jim answered the telephone, "Hello."

"Yes, Sir," the voice came back, "this is Trooper Thorne; I was given a message to contact you."

"Thanks for calling, Sir," Jim tried to speak in a civil tone. "Do you remember me?"

"Of course, Sir," the Trooper replied. "How could I forget your amusing humor and excessive speed?"

Jim laughed for just a moment. "Well, there is that. This was a difficult call in some ways. I assume you are still in the Pikeville area."

"Yes, Sir, I'm in the Pikeville area. There have been a lot of interactions, and the State Police are getting involved. I was sent down to look into several shootings in the area."

"About that," Jim said, "apparently, those shootings involve us, and I called you simply because I don't know who I can trust in the area. Let me rephrase that; we don't know who to trust in the area. The last individual we found shoved a knife through his own chest rather than answer questions. There's something bigger going on, and somebody in the Pikeville area knows about it. Actually, I'm betting a lot of people in the Pikeville area know about it. As part of our interactions, we have detained three individuals at an independent location. I would like to turn them over to you so we can be certain they don't end up back on the street five minutes after they are arrested."

"And what would they be arrested for?" Trooper Thorne asked.

"There are numerous weapons charges, and all three of them attempted to kill two of our team," Jim began. "Earlier, one of our team was critically injured. I understand he is stable now, but several people were shot, and it all revolves around a young woman who stumbled upon an opium field. Somehow, I don't think it's just opium we're dealing with, and we'll work on getting to the bottom of that."

144

"With all due respect," the trooper interjected, "this may be a Kentucky matter, and the Kentucky State Police are fully capable of handling any of these issues. I understand you work for the government as well, but in my opinion, it would be better if you turned everything over to us and just left the area."

"How about we let the politicians decide that?" Jim retorted, "Are you in a position to assist with the three prisoners."

"I'll talk to my supervisors and call you back in less than five minutes." Thorne noted. "I don't want to commit to anything without guidance. I am new to the area and new to the force."

"Thank you," Jim replied, "We will talk to you soon."

Jim hung up the phone.

"You must be rubbing off on me," Jim was thoughtful as he spoke. "I may be reading too much in that conversation, but it always seems like it's us against the world. Thorne says he's gotta talk to his supervisors. He made a statement about KSP handling everything, and I'm wondering what's going on."

In front of them, two police cruisers blocked the road as cars were slowly filtered through a makeshift checkpoint. The lights flashed on the Pikeville police cars, and about ten cars were in line. One by one, they were filtering through. It didn't appear that there was anything too invasive about the checkpoint. There was one officer on each side of the car. One checked out the car while the officer on the driver's side talked to the driver for a moment. Alex could see that licenses were flashed, and then people moved on. What was strange was that two more men were at the backs of the two police cars watching the line go through. Under normal circumstances, this is only in the event of a potentially difficult situation, not a routine traffic check.

"Are you thinking this is from the shooting?" Jim asked. Sarena moved forward in her seat. "Do you think they're looking for us?"

"I suppose it's possible," Alex said. "We haven't checked in with local law enforcement. I'm not sure if Sarah has. Let's be proactive. Go

145

ahead and call Sarah and let her know we're at a checkpoint in Pikeville. See if she is already talked to the local PD."

"I'll call her," Sarena said, "you two should keep an eye on what's going on. Go back twenty-five yards into those hills. Do you see the two men in suits? The bulges in their jackets are not extra muscles."

"Good call Sarena," Alex said. "It could be nothing, but it might be a problem."

"Anything to get out of the back of this cramped car," Rachel said. "I'd rather be stuck in a firefight than still back here."

Alex watched as they were now five cars from the checkpoint. He noticed the two men standing in the back begin to move up. Their suits were out of place, and so were they. The two men worked their way up, and it was obvious they were looking at the beat-up Suburban. More importantly, Eleanor was still in this car, and that could be a major issue. Alex watched as another car moved forward, and they were number four now.

"Jim," Alex said.

"I see them," Jim noted.

"What are we thinking here?" Sarena asked. "There are lots of people behind it in front of us. They would have to move us off the road to cause problems or start any type of firefight. Right now, that's six versus four, and we do not have a good tactical advantage."

"We've seen worse odds," Rachel said, "but I'm not liking these at all."

"Do we have the ability to turn around?" Sarena said.

Alex looked at the road and how much turn radius he had. "Yeah, I think I could whip us around if we needed to, but that still would make us look like we're in the wrong," Alex replied.

"Yes, but it could give us an advantage in that we could put some distance between us and at least some of the attackers. On the other hand, there could be nothing going on here at all. We could drive through, and not a thing happens," Sarena said. "Either way, I'd rather not be in the middle of a six-weapon crossfire."

"Let's see how this plays out," Alex said. "Sarena's right; this could be nothing."

The five sat in the car, waiting as the line moved up. When they pulled up between the two police officers, Alex rolled down his window. "How can I help you, Sir?" Alex asked.

"Damn, this truck has taken a beating," the officer said. "I'm surprised it'll even move."

"It did take quite a beating, but I know a good body shop, and it's still nice on the inside," Alex was looking around at the car as he spoke.

"Where y'all headed?" the officer asked.

"Hospital," Alex replied, "we got a friend who's in right now. Had a bit of an accident; we need to make sure he's okay."

"Are you all from around here?" the officer asked. Alex glanced back and noted the two men in suits were stationary. They had actually backed off just a little. "No, Alex said, "we're actually from Richmond."

"Richmond, huh?" the officer replied, "that's where the KSP training center is. They do some damn good work there."

"I hear that all the time," Alex was honest about this. "What's going on here."

"There's been some trouble around here lately, more just trying to slow down the traffic. We want to make sure nobody gets hurt. There's also a couple of men missing, but you guys aren't from around here. I doubt you'd know anything about that."

"No, not really," Alex breathed a sigh of relief as he spoke, "just want to get to our friend at the hospital."

"Well, you all stay safe and get this damn car fixed," the officer said as he waved Alex forward.

They drove about fifty feet, and Alex looked back at Sarena for a moment. "You can say I told you so any time. I guess sometimes we overreact."

The GPS told them to turn, and Alex did. They had two miles before the next turn. "I may have been the one that's wrong," Sarena said. "Black van 200 yards back, closing fast. I believe it's the two men. I thought I saw them run off to the side after we went through the checkpoint. How much longer are we on country roads? I'm betting they'll try to cut us off before we get back into any type of city."

"You're probably right, as always," Alex said. "Let's see if we can outrun them."

The Suburban picked up speed quickly. Ninety miles an hour through the country roads was taxing, but the van was not closing. As Alex went around another corner, there was a small shutter. They all felt a slight wobble in the front.

"How's it handling?" Jim asked.

"It's sluggish. We haven't lost a tire, but we may have lost a bearing or about half a dozen other things. There's no telling with the beating we've given this poor truck," Alex said. "I'm worried if I push too hard, we may lose a wheel or worse."

"We don't know how many are in that van," Jim said, "we could always stop and fight."

"We don't know what's in that van," Sarena said. "As far as we know, there could be RPGs or, worse an M134."

"Well, aren't you a breath of fresh air," Jim sighed.

"We've been through worse," Rachel was ready for anything.

"You keep saying that Rachel," Jim noted. "It's not giving me any great satisfaction knowing how bad we've had it."

"I'm just saying," Rachel said; "I'd rather go out swinging than a steel duck in a shooting gallery."

Alex took a corner and accelerated.

"We aren't getting to the hospital anytime soon, so we might as well gear up and hope we can stop anything that's coming at us," Alex said. "Get Eleanor a vest."

Rachel flipped over the seat into the back and pulled up the storage area. It was a cramped fit, but she was able to pull out a tactical vest and hand it forward to Sarena. Sarena helped Eleanor get the vest on and tightened it up. Rachel handed two M16s up to Sarena next and kept one for herself. There were two more, and she held them.

"I have a clear shot sitting back here out the back window," Rachel said.

"I'm gonna slow down and see if they pass," Alex said. "I don't want us firing on them if they turn out to be civilians."

"You're gonna what?" Jim asked.

"We got past the checkpoint fine. Think about it; that could have been messy." Alex said as he pulled over to the side of the road. The van slowed down for just a moment and then went wide and around them. "You see, this could have been much worse."

The van's side door slid open, and a single man with an AK-74 opened fire on them. Bullets bounced off of the bullet-resistant glass, and the engine almost instantly started smoking.

"You were saying?" Jim said as he opened his door.

The magazine of the assailant was spent. It dropped, and he began to put in another. Jim exited the van with his 9mm and began firing a stream of bullets at the assailant. Alex exited the driver's side of the vehicle and began firing as well. The man ducked behind the wall, which normally wouldn't be able to stop a bullet but apparently, it was reinforced. A moment later, the tip of the barrel came out and started spraying bullets at the Suburban again.

Sarena was behind Alex, with her M16. She began firing at the van. She slowed her fire, and Alex saw a very small grouping of shots.

Using the M16, she hit a very small spot over and over until a small hole formed.

"Better than a power drill," Jim said.

At the front of the van, a second man stepped out and began firing with another AK 74. Jim and Alex ducked down, and as the AK 74 emptied, they began firing at that side. Sarena stayed at the side to ensure that Eleanor was not hurt. Rachel opened the back door and disappeared into the woods. Sarena scanned the woods but could not see her anywhere. The smoke from the front of the Suburban was black and partially obscured the view.

Once again, there was a spray of bullets ricocheting off the Suburban from the two AK 74s. Sarena scanned the distance and saw some movement on the hill next to the front of the van. It was slight, but it was there. Through the smoke and through the woods, Sarena could see it.

"You have any great ideas?" Alex asked.

"Shoot straight?" Jim stated as he fired back at the van.

"Pay attention, you two," Sarena said. "Check right, thirty-eight degrees off center. Rachel had an idea."

Alex and Jim glanced off to the front of the van and saw Rachel working her way down the hill. Her weapon was behind her back, and she was thirty feet behind the lead man.

"Focus on the back shooter. Make it too noisy," Alex said.

All three of them open fire on the back part of the van. The man inside the door did not come out as bullets sprayed the area. The sound was deafening, with the three weapons firing like an unholy symphony of doom. As all three of them emptied their mags, Rachel reached the front man and, without much ceremony, smashed his head into the front of the vehicle. It was quiet.

"Jim, Sarena, secure the vehicle, watch our six and make sure Eleanor is okay," Alex said as he crept forward.

Rachel was on the far side of the van as Alex crept towards the open door. As he reached the open door, he noted the shell casings everywhere. Alex kept to the side of the open door while Rachel glanced inside the driver's door up front. She did not linger but whipped around, glanced in again, this time, for a little longer, and nodded to Alex. Alex quickly slid around the side where nothing moved.

Although the van may have been bullet resistant, the onslaught of the M16s was relentless. The man inside the van lay still. Multiple gunshots pierced him, and Alex could see light come through the other side of the van. Still, Alex reached in and pulled the man's weapon out onto the ground, ensuring he could not use it again. Rachel opened the front door, looked around, and noted all clear.

Sirens were coming. Alex yelled to Rachel to come back to the Suburban. Everyone put their weapons on the ground and waited. Eleanor fidgeted in the flak vest. "This is crazy," she said.

"You aren't wrong," Sarena stated, "You don't see this in the news, but it happens all the time."

Two local police cars pulled up and screeched at an angle as officers rolled out and pointed their weapons at the team. The entire group had their hands in the air, including Eleanor. The local officers advanced slowly, and Alex held his ID high.

"Who's in charge?" he asked.

"Doesn't matter," one of the officers said as they advanced. "Keep your hands where we can see them."

"I guess this is going to be fun to unravel," Jim said.

"Quiet," another officer said; "No talking."

Sirens still approached in the distance. Alex could hear at least three more vehicles heading their way. It seemed unlikely for such a small town to have so many officers.

"What should we do?" one of the officers asked another.

"Just let me think for a minute," the other officer said.

"These men tried to ambush us, and we just defended ourselves," Alex said.

"If you don't shut up, you're about to get shot," the first officer said. His gun was shaking, and he was obviously nervous.

"What the hell?" Jim whispered. "What have we gotten ourselves into?"

The first officer swung his weapon from Alex to Jim. "You both want to get shot; is that what you want? This is such a mess."

Jim could see several cars coming down the road. "Holster your weapon," the second officer said. "Everyone is about to be here."

There was a news truck in the distance now, and Alex recognized the antenna boom on the roof of the van.

"We need to get out of here," the second officer said. The two other officers in the other car got into the vehicle and backed it to the side of the road. The first two officers who rushed forward holstered their weapons and got back to their car. The first officer got inside and drove the car to the side of the road as well. Then, they stood waiting for the other cars to get there.

A marked police car pulled up to the front, and Rachel recognized Phil Comer as he got out of the car. He looked angry and surveyed the area looking at the smoking Suburban and the battle-torn van. He saw Rachel and walked forward with obvious purpose.

"What the hell is going on here?" Phil barked. "Where is Ronnie?"

"Ronnie's in the hospital," Rachel said, "a couple men shot him up pretty bad. We got a call that he is stable, but he went through surgery, and it isn't all that good. Something that Eleanor saw started all this. We were ambushed after your police blockade a few miles back. We tried to avoid it but couldn't, and all this was the result."

"I'm sure we can work all this out," Alex stated, "we didn't expect a firefight, but we weren't going to just be random targets."

"Who's this guy?" Phil looked at Rachel.

"This is my CO, Alex Brown. The members of my team, Jim Simpson, and Sarena Prince. We also have Ronnie, who is being guarded by Barbara at the hospital. One more of our team is at Uncle Harv's making sure he is safe," Rachel said.

"Safe?" Phil asked. "Y'all just shot up more ammo than last year's whole hunting season, and you're talking about being safe?" I've got more brass than we can easily count and weapons all over the ground. I'm assuming I have a couple of dead guys in the van."

"Either that or very sleepy," Jim said.

Phil looked at Jim, irritated.

"What am I supposed to do here," Phil said.

Trooper Thorne walked up to the small group. "There's a team headed this way, and we will be involved. There's also another trooper at Harv Comer's right now and a wagon on the way to take possession of the three men there. The men aren't talking, but we'll find out what's going on."

"Oh great," Phil said, "now we get to deal with KSP as well?"

"We didn't know who to trust," Alex said.

"What is that supposed to mean?" Phil barked; "We are a fine, upstanding force and above any ridiculousness that you might see in your big cities."

"What about the two cars and four men? They pulled us over and were trying to decide whether they were going to kill us or not?" Jim asked.

"What the hell are you talking about?" Phil asked.

Jim pointed to where the two cars were parked on the side, but in the confusion, they were no longer there. "The two cars that were here when you arrived," Jim quipped. "There were four men inside, and they had guns drawn on us, and we're shaking like leaves trying to decide whether or not to shoot us. They were talking crazy, asking each other what to do. One of them was at the roadblock we went through, talked about how beat up our car was."

"Are you trying to tell me that four of my officers set up an illegal roadblock, and we're here after this firefight?" Phil asked.

"That's exactly what we're saying," Sarena said. "Your people, or at least someone impersonating your people, are involved here."

"We'll make short work of this," Phil said as he pulled out a cell phone. He dialed a number and waited. "Jenny, send me the link to all of our officer's pictures. You know, the one that the PR company put together. It's on our website. Thanks."

Phil hung up the phone. "This won't take long because all you gotta do is identify one, and I'll know who the others are for sure. We heard that somebody got shot and was airlifted into the hospital, but with everything that you and Ronnie did this morning and all the chaos on the side of the hill, we weren't able to get to the hospital yet. The doctors there had to report it as a shooting, and it's our standard op to do a report after any potential shooting. There should be an officer going there anytime. I think we need to go somewhere and figure out what Eleanor saw and where she saw it so we can start unraveling this mess."

"That sounds like the best idea yet," Alex said. "We have a problem, though; our car isn't going anywhere."

"Yeah, that car is a bit of a mess now," Phil replied.

"I will take the girl to your facility," Trooper Thorne said.

"Actually, how about she rides with me?" Phil replied.

Eleanor slid behind Sarena, "I want to ride with them."

"Little lady, they don't have a car," Phil stated, "and I don't know what we're going to do with them. I'm not sure I can charge them, but I'm not sure I want them involved as this is getting out of hand, and I don't need my town shot up."

From the back of the line of cars, a black Cadillac Escalade pulled to the front. Terry got out of the driver's side and then walked over to the small group after being stopped by no less than four different officers. Each time he flashed his ID and then moved forward.

"I thought you might need a ride," Terri said. "They've taken the men from Uncle Harv's, and I heard them talking about the shooting and firefight here. I expected your vehicle to be in bad shape, but that's a little worse than I could have imagined."

"It looks like we have a solution," Alex said. "We can follow you down to the station and bring Eleanor with us until we get this worked out."

"I'm not sure that's a good idea," Trooper Thorne said. "It certainly is outside of normal operating procedure. Any witnesses should be under the control of the KSP."

"You gotta step outside your procedure right now," Jim said; "welcome to the wonderful world of espionage and intrigue."

"We don't have any idea of the scope of this at this moment, and I'm not sure I can just take your word for anything," Trooper Thorne said.

"These are friends of my family, and their word is good," Phil said; "that's the end of it."

The trooper was obviously upset but said nothing. Multiple officers were at the van and at the Suburban marking different areas. The entire scene had been roped off by yellow tape, and now two news crews battled for position to try to get a picture. People gathered all around and were hungrily chattering about what was happening. The van and the Suburban were both smoking, and two ambulances were on site. Stretchers were at the van. A medical examiner's car was also at the edge of the scene, and a man, likely the coroner, was reviewing everything. This was big news for the area but not the type of news they wanted.

Chapter 23

Michael and Abby arrived at the furniture store they shopped just a day before. Walking into the store, they noted everything was pristine, and it obviously didn't look anything like the mess they left for Bob to clean up yesterday. The couch the men were sitting on was gone, probably burned, as though the University of Kentucky had just won another basketball championship. A new couch was in the front with plush leather and a nice divan over to the side. Michael surveyed the area and wondered where Bob was, or who else might be running the store today.

They waited for a few moments as Abby looked around. Michael touched his back where his FN 57 was holstered. Furniture stores always seemed to have people begging for sales, and to Michael, the emptiness today seemed strange. Abby noticed that Michael was on guard and looked around as well. To the far-left side of the entrance, they heard a door click and the flush of a toilet. A few seconds later, they saw Bob walking out and a door closing.

"I didn't expect you all back so soon," Bob said. "Like I told you, everything was taken care of. What brings you back to my store? After all, he said I'd never see you again."

"Well, about that," Abby said. "We have the two-bedroom sets, but we seem to be missing the living room and dining room. If you don't want us here, we can leave."

"No no," Bob said; "it's fine as frog's hair that you're here. I can help you put something together for you that works. After all, you're a brutal negotiator, and I want to make sure that I keep you happy so that when you furnish your baby's room or your new mancave, you'll come back here again."

Michael chuckled at the obviously salesy idea. "A true salesman through and through," Michael said.

"We all have our skills," Bob laughed. "I like to talk to people. If I can sell them something along the way, it's all the better. By the way, before we start looking at everything, the boys policed your brass. Not sure if you want any of it or if you're worried about prints or anything like that. I told him to run it through the brass tumbler to clean it up. I hope that's okay."

"There were no prints, and its fine that they cleaned it up. Not sure if they have something to shoot it if they reload it, but everything on it's clean," Michael said.

"That's good, really good. Those boys seem to have more guns than they do common sense sometimes, but they were always very safe, and I trust them. The other issue was removed as well. I won't tell you anymore 'cause you don't need to know. Ain't had no one else show up, which is a good thing, but I'm being a little more careful now and keeping my eyes open now that I know they wanted me dead," Bob said. "You want to step over here and look at couches and a living room set, or do you want to look at the dining room or kitchen first?"

Michael chuckled again. "It's all up to her. She's the brains of decorating the house."

They started in the kitchen area, and Abby chose an oak table set. It was similar to what they had previously. She then picked out a hutch to go with it and moved over to the living room sets. Michael was asked to sit in just about every couch until they decided on a leather sectional, a Lay-Z-Boy that matched, and a set up in tables and coffee a table. As they were walking around, Abby picked up numerous decorations. Many of them were also close to what was at the original house, and Michael was very happy about how Abby understood decorating but still honored his ideas. The bill would be large, but it would be worth it. They wouldn't have to go to Lexington or Charleston to get furniture. Michael thought about it for a second and realized they could have also gone to Huntington or Ashland, but he didn't go there very often.

Abby continued looking around and added additional items to the order, including two bookshelves for the bedroom. As they were talking, Abby asked Bob about linens. They didn't have sheets, towels, and had been living out of suitcases until the furniture arrived earlier. They had very few clothes and needed to stock the house at least a little.

Bob recommended a small store down the street that carried fine linens. He stated they would have good sheets and towels, and although he had sheet sets, theirs would be far better. Abby finalized the sale and again negotiated brutally. Both Abby and Bob were laughing at the end of it all, and Bob called Abby "quite the horse trader" as he set up the invoice. Abby had the necessary cash on hand and paid Bob.

"You should bring all your friends here," Bob said; "you've made this a really good week."

"As I'm sure you can guess," Michael said, "we don't do much entertaining."

"I reckon so," Bob said, "but I'd be proud to call you friend. There aren't many people I owe my life to."

Michael and Bob shook hands again as they left the store. The linen shop was only a few doors down, so Michael and Abby walked. The store was well stocked. Abby picked out neutral colors, and they spent a little money. All in all, it would be a good day. Michael would leave tomorrow to see Yuri.

As they walked back to the DB9, Michael said, "I will be gone for just a few days. Normally I would take you with me. I'm not sure how this is gonna go. Obviously, some time has passed since Yuri and I were acquaintances. Still, I'm hoping for a positive result and to just walk away without issue. Your father probably wants me to eliminate the situation, but I may be able to eliminate the situation without killing Yuri."

"That's different for you, Michael," Abby said. "You must have really liked this guy because with most people, you wouldn't invest this much thought."

Michael stopped on the street. He considered what Abby said. "You know, you're probably right. Under normal circumstances, I would not have a second thought about this. Maybe I need to step away and let somebody else go."

"I don't think it's that drastic, but the Michael I know, and love is always prepared and won't let anything get in his way," Abby said. "If Yuri is the person, you think he is, you will do the right thing. If he has become worse, you will still do the right thing. I know you well inside and out, and you won't hesitate either way."

Abby and Michael continued walking. Michael noticed the black BMW next to the DB9. He opened the trunk of the DB9 and quickly put the linens in the back. "Wait here for a second," Michael said as he walked back to the furniture store. The front door was held, and Michael pulled it back rapidly. A young man in a black suit fell backward out of the door and clambered to the ground. Abby walked up to the man as he reached into his coat pocket and stepped on his arm. He looked up and saw her. She shook her head slowly as she pointed a pistol at his head.

Michael walked into the store where Bob was sitting, in a Lay-Z Boy, with two men standing next to him. One man had just hit Bob across the face as the second looked back to Michael. Bob's face was bloody, and his eye was partially swollen. There was a gun on the floor that Michael assumed to be Bob's.

The man standing partially behind the Lay-Z Boy reached into his coat. Michael drew his FN 57 with practiced speed and aimed at the man. His hand stopped.

"I guess you're going to make this a habit," Bob choked. "Sorry for the fuss. I probably owe that girl of yours another discount."

"I think we're fine," Michael said, pointing to the man who still had his hand in his coat. "Finish. Two fingers only, nothing too fast." The man behind the Lay-Z Boy pulled out a Glock 17. "Drop it." The man dropped the pistol to the floor. He glanced at the other man who's back was to Michael. In the blink of an eye, that man spun, and drew his pistol. Michael shot him between the eyes. He fell back over the top of the Lay-Z Boy, and Bob tumbled onto the ground with the body.

"After this week, I'm clearly going to be deaf," Bob muttered as he tried to get the body off of him.

The man behind the Lay-Z Boy slowly put his hands up and then pushed them down rapidly as Michael turned sideways, seeing the glint of the sleeve pistol. He fired and shot between the man between the eyes.

"Anymore?" Michael asked Bob.

"As far as I know, it's just the three of them," Bob said as he tried to stand.

As if on cue, Abby pushed the third man through the door, holding her pistol at the nape of his neck. The man looked at the two others lying on the floor dead, then looked at Michael.

"You will suffer for this," he said in broken English; "dis insult will not be tolerated."

"I seem to hear that a lot lately," Michael let out a breath and grinned just a little. "Why is it that everybody thinks that I'm going to get in trouble? After all, if there are no witnesses, there's no trouble, right? Why are you here?"

"You must know I will tell you nothing," he said.

"That's fine," Michael said. "I don't want to make Bob deaf so, sorry." The man didn't see the knife draw. It didn't really matter. The blade spun across the room and embedded into his eye. He was dead before he hit the ground. Abby stepped back like a ballerina dancing out of the way of his fall.

"Sorry, Bob," Michael said. "I guess we made a mess again."

Abby walked over to the counter and pulled up several Kleenexes. She went over to Bob and dabbed his face, trying to clean up the blood. "You're going to need stitches or at least some tight butterflies."

"Yeah, he hit me with my own pistol," Bob said. "I guess I don't draw as fast as I used to. I hoped it was another good sale coming in until I heard their accents. You just can't trust people as much as you want to anymore."

"Why is this store so important to them?" Michael asked. "They could have just opened their own store. There are several empty stores in the are. What makes yours different?"

"I don't know, Sir," Bob replied, "I mean, we get more shipments than everybody, but that's because our stuff is bigger. We do have a double semi loading dock. We're the only one on the strip that has it, but that is not a big deal. There's still an empty K-Mart that has an empty loading dock. There's an old bomb shelter from the 50s underneath us, but I don't think anybody knows about that. I just don't know why they would want my business so bad."

"We must be missing something," Michael said. "Did they say anything or do anything in all the times you've interacted with them that gave you a clue as to what they wanted?"

"No, Sir," Bob replied. "We're just an old store that's been around for a long time. We don't have deep pockets, but they're not thin, either. We sell enough furniture to get by. We do some repair work and have an upholstery crew that comes in and refinishes some of the old stuff. There's not much to it. I thought they just wanted furniture because before they started trying to buy me, they bought a bunch of furniture. You know, two living room sets, three bedrooms sets, kind of like what you did."

"Did they pay cash?" Michael asked.

"Now that you think of it, I don't think so. I think they paid with a card 'cause I remember them saying something about the card and me telling them they would get lots of points for it." Bob replied.

"Bob, are you okay?" Abby said, still holding the Kleenexes to his forehead. Do you have a first aid kit? Do you want me to try to patch you up for a moment?"

"You're awful nice, ma'am," Bob stated, "I think I'll be fine. When the boys come over, I'll have them patch me up, or I'll get a friend to come over and deal with it. I'll clean this up again. They have to be running out of men by now. I appreciate you not shooting again; my ears are still ringing from the other day. Now they are really ringing."

"That's why I used the knife," Michael said. "You really need to get some of these noise-canceling inserts."

"I really need to retire, or you really need to get a silencer," Bob said as he tried to get up again. He finally stood and held himself up on the Lay-Z-Boy. I need to get on the phone and get some people here to take care of this mess. I guess I'll use some of the money I just made to have a guard for a while. It's my fault for thinking I could take care of it myself. I'm getting old, and I just need to let others do the work of young men."

"Lock the door on our way out," Michael said.

"Yeah, I'll get the door," Bob replied.

Michael and Abby walked out the door and heard the click behind them. Michael was shaking his head. "Maybe we should have gone shopping in Lexington."

Abby laughed as she opened her door. "Do you think we should tell him about the car out here?"

"He took care of the last one. I guess he is becoming quite the cleaner," Michael replied.

"Michael, I know this has been a strange day, but thank you for all you do for me. I needed to go shopping, and it felt good to be with you. It always feels good to be with you. What is better is I feel safe. Sure, I can take care of myself and probably quite a few others, but it's nice to know that someone has your back." Abby reached over and hugged Michael.

"I feel the same way," Michael said.

"I wonder what's happening with Alex and his crew? They seem to get in as much trouble as we do, if not more."

"I'm sure they're doing fine," Abby said. "We should pick up some food on the way home."

"That's a really good idea," Michael smiled, "I'm starving. I guess shopping makes me hungry. Maybe it's spending lots of money that makes me hungry. Or maybe it's having international thugs beat up an old man that I have to deal with that makes me hungry. Either way, I'm hungry."

"I'm hungry too," Abby laughed. "Why don't we pick up Italian on the way back to the house? Remember eating at that little place?"

"We can get it to go," Michael said as he backed onto the street and drove away.

Chapter 24

Barbara was watching the door when she heard Ronnie's weak voice, "Elma?"

Ronnie had pulled the oxygen away from his face and opened his eyes slightly, looking around the room.

"She's not here," Barbara said, "but she's safe."

"What happened?" Ronnie said slowly. "How did you get here, Barbara?" Ronnie coughed and winced hard in obvious pain.

Barbara pressed the call button for the nurse to come. His being awake was a major issue.

A nurse walked in right away. She took Ronnie's hand away from the oxygen mask and placed it back on his face. "Let's leave that here for now. You'll have plenty of time to talk later."

"Noo," Ronnie said as the plastic facemask steamed from his voice, "I have to protect Elma."

A doctor walked into the room, and the two were checking Ronnie's vitals. Ronnie was struggling a little, trying to get free. The doctor walked over and unlocked the cabinet. He pulled out a small vial and a syringe. He filled the syringe to a mark, walked over to Ronnie's IV, and injected the syringe into the IV. Ronnie began to quiet down, and, in a few moments, he was asleep.

The doctor looked at Barbara. "I gave him a mild sedative, so he doesn't hurt himself. He's obviously very worked up and needs to sleep more than anything. We'll come back and check on him in a little while."

"Thank you, Doctor," Barbara said. Ronnie was still tossing and turning just a little, but Barbara returned to his bedside and held his hand. Ronnie squeezed a little, and she looked at him, hoping to see those eyes looking back at her. Instead, his eyes remained closed, and Barbara was alone with her thoughts.

"You know Ronnie, if you wake up, we're going to have a serious talk. I'm not getting any younger, and pretty much, you're the best thing that's ever happened to me. Nobody has ever put me on a pedestal like you have. Sure, there are guys who treated me nice, but we both know what they wanted, and they were probably mad when I didn't give it to them. You, you were always different."

"I know it seems like a line, but I really think I messed up by not being with you sooner. If you wake up, we can talk about this, and maybe find a way. I know I'm not perfect, but I know how I feel."

"Excuse me, ma'am," a man walked into the room. He was wearing white pants, black tennis shoes, and wore a nurse's jacket with a stethoscope around his neck. His voice had a slight accent, but Barbara wasn't sure where he was from. "I need to update this man's medication. Would you like to wait outside?"

"No, I'll be staying," Barbara said.

"It really would be better if you waited outside; he could have a reaction from the medication," the man said.

"You need to see the doctor before you give him any medication. He's just been given a sedative," Barbara said.

"I must insist you leave the room so I can administer the medicine," the man replied.

"Actually, I must insist you leave the room now," Barbara said. "If you want to do anything, bring back the nurse that was here or the doctor."

"I will have to call security on you," the man was getting anxious.

"Call them," Barbara said. "In fact, why don't we go find them together right now?"

The man reached into his pocket and pulled out a syringe. He started forward to Barbara, but she drew her weapon faster. She pointed at his center mass and told him to drop the syringe. The man stood there for a moment, obviously trying to decide what to do. Barbara considered. She had no way to determine how far her bullet would go past the man, then saw the cinder block walls. She wouldn't shoot unless she absolutely had to in case the bullet bounced or hit a secondary target. Still, she couldn't let the man get to Ronnie or her with whatever was in that syringe.

"On the ground now, or I will put you on the ground," Barbara said.

The man glanced from side to side; he was three steps away from the door and four steps away from Ronnie. He was five steps away from Barbara.

"I know what you're thinking," Barbara said; "you think you can get by me because I'm a woman. I will have no problem kneecapping you and won't have to worry about ricochets or penetration problems. You, on the other hand, will have to worry about walking for the rest of your life. Drop the syringe now."

The man dropped the syringe. A second passed, and the door rolled open as the nurse who had been in minutes ago walked back into the room. Barbara didn't waver. The man grabbed the nurse and pushed her towards Barbara as he took advantage of the open door and slipped out.

"Don't leave Ronnie," Barbara said as she pulled the door open and zipped out, glancing from side to side. She saw nothing. The man was gone, and that was impossible. Barbara stepped back into the room and kept her weapon out. "Call security. See if you can pull this guy up on cameras or something. He was trying to give Ronnie whatever was in that syringe on the floor. Male, six-foot, dark hair, brown eyes, wearing white pants, a nurse's jacket, and black tennis shoes. I think they were Nike's. Looked about a size 11 or 12; he had big ol' feet. Did you know him?"

"I never saw him before in my life. I walked in here because I saw him walk in and didn't know who he was. I thought he was on the wrong floor."

"I think he knew exactly what he was doing," Barbara replied, "I think they were coming for Ronnie."

"Why would they have been coming for this young man?" the nurse asked.

"For the same reason why they shot him," Barbara replied. "Why does anybody do anything in this weird world? I know it won't be a popular statement, but I'm ready to get on a plane and fly to a desert island."

"I know what you mean," the nurse said. "I'm Nancy. I'm sorry I didn't introduce myself earlier."

"I'm Barbara," Barbara replied, "thanks for taking care of Ronnie; he's pretty important to me."

"Do you two work together?" Nancy asked.

"Yeah, we work together," Barbara said. "We've always had this kind of connection, but I'm not sure anymore. I always thought we were just friends, but now I wonder if there shouldn't be more. Ronnie is such a good guy. I'm not sure I would ever be good enough for him, but I'm willing to try."

"Oh, be careful," Nancy replied. "People who work together and then get into relationships have problems sometimes."

"I know," Barbara said, "it's one of the reasons that I've taken a step back so many times. I don't want to mess our perfect friendship up with an imperfect relationship, do you know what I mean?"

"I know exactly what you mean," Nancy replied as Edward walked into the room.

"Howdy Edward," Barbara said. "We just had an intruder up here that was gonna stab Ronnie with that syringe."

"I knew you were gonna make this difficult on me," Edward said as he pulled out his radio. "What are we looking for?"

It was Nancy who spoke up, "Male, six-foot, dark hair, brown eyes, wearing white pants, a nurse's jacket, and black tennis shoes. I think they were Nike's. He looked out of place, which is why I came into the room. I surprised him, and he pushed his way out."

"Do we need to assign somebody up here?" Edward asked.

"That's why I'm here," Barbara said. "I'll make sure Ronnie's okay, but it'd be nice if they didn't get past you."

Edward walked out the door. Barbara and Nancy could hear him talking in the hallway. He was chattering, and then the sound faded as he walked away.

"As I was saying, I got involved with one of the doctors here, and it was a mess. He was new, and I had been here a while. I found out he was married, and it really made things awkward. It took him a while, but then he left. I think moved to Bowling Green." Nancy related.

"I don't have to worry about that with Ronnie," Barbara said. "He's a good old country boy from right here. He doesn't drink, smoke, or do anything without thinking about whether he should do it. And he's a fighter, a good fighter. There's nothing he wouldn't do for somebody he cared about or his team. People underestimate him, but he is always watching and learning. I don't think anything could ever slow him down. Here I am, sitting next to him, and he could have died. I'm not sure what I would have done if something had happened to him, and I never told him how I felt."

"Let him rest, and you can tell him pretty soon," Nancy said. "Do you need anything?"

"No, I think I'm good," Barbera said. "I'm wide awake now and ready for a fight. Thanks for keeping an eye on us."

"It's my job," Nancy replied.

"Well, there is one thing," Barbara asked. "Can one of you take that syringe and find out what was in it?"

Nancy grabbed the syringe with a napkin. "Should we wait for the police?"

"If they get here, we'll share what it is with them," Barbara said.

"I'll find out," Nancy replied and left the room.

Barbara sat down in her chair and resumed watching the doorway.

Chapter 25

Phil Comer looked at the troopers who were standing in front of him. "What do you mean you let them go?" he demanded.

"They said they had diplomatic immunity and showed the right credentials. We called first and verified that's what we were supposed to do," Trooper Thorne said.

"Diplomatic immunity," Phil yelled; "In Pikeville? doesn't that seem just a little weird?"

"They had the right credentials," Trooper Thorne said. "The law is the law."

"How long ago where they released?" Alex asked.

"It couldn't have been more than fifteen minutes," Trooper Thorne said. "They said they were heading to the consulate in Washington DC, but first, I had to stop by the hospital since they were treated improperly. They also said they would be pressing charges against the young man and woman who attacked them at the Comer residence."

"And you believed all that?" Phil Comer was shaking his head.

"I do believe they're probably going to the hospital," Jim said, "that would give them the opportunity to eliminate Ronnie and potentially Barbara. I doubt they know Barbara from anyone, but I'm sure they were updated that Ronnie was shot. We have a lot of bodies, but they obviously have a large workforce. We need to get to the hospital right now."

"I'm afraid I can't let you do that," Trooper Thorne said, "I have been asked to detain you until they are outside of the State to avoid a potential international incident."

"You can't be serious," Rachel said. "There is no way in hell we are not going to be at that hospital as fast as that car will take us."

"Ma'am," Trooper Thorne said: "There are seven State Troopers here, and if you attempt to leave, we will have no choice but to use force to stop you. We will not be the starting point of an international war."

"Did somebody give you those words? Rachel asked; "Any war is international."

"Not the Civil War," Sarena said.

"Actually, I think you're wrong," Jim replied, "although the civil war was between the north and the south, there were numerous players on an international level. Even in today's wars, inside countries are usually funded by external countries. Because of this, Rachel is probably right. Every war is international, but it would be nice if it wasn't." Jim was slowly moving towards the door as he talked to Rachel and Sarena. He turned to the Troopers, "I'm sure that Alex is going to make a phone call in just a minute, and whoever talked to you will crawl into their hole, but at this point, we don't have much time to debate. Our friends are in potential danger, and you're keeping us from getting to them. If you attempt to stop us, we may have to use force to detain you."

The trooper's hands went to their weapons, and one of them unlatched the buckle on his crisp leather holster. The seven troopers were near perfect. It was obvious that each of them had picked a different target, and all of them were ready to use lethal force, if necessary. Each one scanned the room and focused on one specific person. What they didn't see was that Terry wasn't noticed at all. Terry quietly moved behind the seven troopers.

"Y'all better not shoot up my station," Phil said. "We need to tone it down a notch or two. I would hope that we're all on the same side."

"I think we are all on the same side," Alex said, "just some of us know when to follow orders and when to think." Alex was waiting as the phone rang, and he put it on speaker.

"Alex," Sarah said, "there's someone from the State Department in with the General right now. I can hear them screaming at each other from here. What is going on?"

"Easy," Alex said, "there are a group of Ukrainians here who have tried to kill several people, and they shot up Ronnie. Right now, three of them have been released, claiming diplomatic immunity. They were on their way to the hospital, where it just so happens Ronnie is located. Barbara is protecting him. As far as we know, there are only three, but I am assuming there are significantly more. Currently, we're in the middle of seven State Troopers, six Pikeville PD, five of us, and a room full of triggers and fingers. At this point, I'm expecting the Troopers, who are following orders to the letter, to stand down when the General lets them know what's really going on. If not, I expect we're going to have a local incident, an international incident, a state incident, and a lot of incidents in several of these guys' pants."

The Troopers were all looking very keyed up but professional. The Pikeville PD were equally as professional, and several were squared down on the State Troopers. Jim, Alex, and Sarena were all ready for anything. Terry had control of the situation at a glance.

"Hang on, Alex, Sam's coming out," Sarah said.

They could hear General Tarkington over the speakerphone. "Get me Brown on the phone."

"He's on the phone waiting for you right now," Sarah said.

"Alex," Tarkington said, "there are some games being played here. I need you to stand down until I call you back. I may have to have a discussion with the Secretary of State in the next few minutes. I have some little dipshit here that says you're starting a war with Ukraine, and we both know that isn't true. I also have some dumb ass who thinks he can order around State Troopers telling me there are troopers on the way there."

"They are here," Alex said, "and they can hear you."

"Tell those little shits that if they interfere with you, they likely will be out on their ass in the next four hours," Tarkington said. "At the same time, you are to stay put wherever you are, and there will be no government interference. The government can have no say in this until I talk to the Secretary of State."

172

"Sir," Alex said, "Barbara and Ronnie are at the hospital alone. Ronnie is incapacitated, and I know Barbara can take care of herself, but we have no idea of the force size."

"There will be phone calls coming in to a lot of people in the next few minutes. It's unlikely that any government agency will be involved in this. I'm sure that the security at the hospital will be able to handle it. Barbara also has a friend that may come visit. Their friend may have some insight into a solution."

"Understood, Sir," Alex said, "Is Sarah taking care of that?"

"It's already taken care of," Tarkington replied. "For the life of me, I'm not sure why they will continue down that path. It's not like Ronnie was in the middle of anything or saw something he shouldn't have. The fact that they've tried once is not normal. It is likely there's something else going on."

"Thank you, Sir,"

"For you Troopers and everyone else there," Tarkington said louder, "This is General Samuel Tarkington. At this point, you are to all stand down and stay in the facility where you are now. You are not to leave for any reason, including going home, getting lunch, getting dinner, seeing your child, let's just say, for no reason. If you leave the building for any reason, you will be prosecuted as a traitor to   the United States of America. Possible penalties include death. There is to be no communication unless it goes through Alex. Your superiors in Frankfort have been informed. You will also have to sign a confidentiality statement at the end of this exercise. Your involvement is appreciated but has caused additional confusion. Do you understand?"

"I'm sorry, Sir we have conflicting orders. Our orders come from Frankfort," Trooper Thorne said. "Given that we do not know who you are or have a point of reference, we will remain in charge of the situation."

"Alex," Tarkington said, "are you in charge of the situation?"

Alex nodded slightly. Behind the troopers, Terry chambered a round in his M16. The sound of the round chambering has a distinctive clink, and the troopers shrunk slightly understanding what was behind them. "Jim and Rachel, please disarm the troopers for the moment. Don't worry, gentlemen; we will keep your weapons in good order. Please don't make any sudden movements. No one would be killed, but it hurts like hell to be shot in a bulletproof vest at close range. Trust me, it hurts really bad."

"Sir, this is very irregular," Trooper Thorne said.

"This whole situation is irregular, Thorne," Alex said. "Don't make it any worse. We could have cooperated easily, and we probably will be in a very short time."

Trooper Thorne bowed his head for a moment. "Sir, we need to follow orders."

"Yes, you sure do," Jim said, "and I appreciate you because you follow orders. But as you can see, I have my orders too."

"Gentlemen, I'll be in touch soon," Tarkington said. "I will also assume the hospital is handled."

"I'm sure it is, sir. Thank you for that." Alex said, "and with no government-related individuals."

The phone disconnected.

Jim looked around the room at all the officers, "Anyone got a deck of cards?"

Chapter 26

The hospital doors slid open, and Michael and Abby walked in. Michael's arm was wrapped in a towel, and there was red around the edges of the towel. He immediately sat down in the front waiting room as Abby walked to the counter to check him in. Michael surveyed the front door and waiting room and constantly checked where Abby was with the counter nurse. They were given a number and told to wait.

Fifteen minutes later, three men in black suits walked in and looked at the front directory. A nice woman walked up to them in a different-colored outfit designated for volunteers and asked them if they needed assistance. One of the men said, "No we're looking for our friend." He continued to look at the directory. Michael noticed there was one security guard, and he seemed extra inquisitive.

"Think that's them?" Abby whispered as she bent over, patting Michael softly.

"It's likely, but if we can get a little closer, we can find out," Michael replied while rocking in his chair.

The two stood and walked together. Abby feigned that she was helping, and Michael shuffled a little as though he was in tremendous pain. They walked to the desk, which was relatively close to the directory.

"You will have to sit down and wait your turn unless this is an emergency," the nurse said.

"He's in such pain," Abby said as Michael watched the men.

"There will be no painkillers without a doctor examination," the nurse said; "We wouldn't want you to accidentally get hooked on an opioid if it wasn't necessary."

Michael nodded. The men began to walk down the hall, and Michael cursed in Ukrainian. He said several things that were unpleasant. One of the men turned around, looked, and then laughed with his two friends as they pointed backward.

"It's probably them," Michael said, "I doubt many others speak Ukrainian here."

"What do we need to do?" Abby asked.

"Is there any way I can convince you to stay down here," Michael replied.

"No," Abby said. "Do I need to just start following them?"

"We have an advantage," Michael said; "We know where they're going, and it's several floors up, so it's time to run the stairs."

Abby and Michael found the stairwell and began running upward. They reached the floor where Ronnie was currently held and walked out, heading for the room. The floor was empty except for a few nurses. There was no hustle and bustle of the morning surgeries. A few nurses were dotted around the hallways but no one else. Michael noted again the location of the elevators and walked towards Ronnie Comer's room. From a strategic perspective, it would be better to wait and take the three men by surprise, but there were a lot of things at play right now. The largest was the nurses that were on the floor. Michael had to determine who would try to fight and who would run away. This meant adapting tactics to the situation.

Sarah called Michael and Abby and explained the situation. Neither Alex nor any of the police could get involved now, as the men had claimed diplomatic immunity. Since Michael was off the books and the budgets of Tarkington's group were off normal record-keeping, Sarah was given permission to pay Michael to protect Ronnie and Barbara. At first, Michael protested, but then he realized that Ronnie was probably his biggest advocate. Michael interacted with Ronnie several times, and Ronnie was always polite and respectful. Ronnie's country roots in Pikeville, Kentucky, made him even more respectful. He avoided conflict if at all possible. Michael wished that had been true for him.

Michael decided to split and have Abby sit with Barbara, and he would come in from behind. Abby walked forward to the nurses at the nurse's station and asked them to move to Ronnie's room. At first, they protested, but Abby was forceful and charismatic, and they began moving. They moved a little faster when she pulled out her pistol and aimed it at the floor as they walked to the room.

Michael stepped behind the counter and found a white jacket on the back of a chair. He put the jacket on, but it didn't fit. He took it off and put it back on the chair, wondering who was that small. Michael moved to a small room where he could see the elevators easily. Michael looked at the elevator and the angles of sight and unwrapped the towel from his arm. Under the bulky towel was his P90. One of the advantages of the P90 was size. The oversized towel had hidden the weapon, even though it was a little wider than some. The top-mounted magazine eliminated what many other rifles had, a protruding area. The P90 also had the advantages of an M16 without the longer weapon length. Instead, the barrel went further back into the stock. This was called a bullpup design, and the unique setup made the weapon look futuristic.

Fortunately for Michael, the room he was in was unoccupied.

Abby entered the room with Barbara, Ronnie, and the nurses in front of her. Barbara stood and drew her weapon but then realized who Abby was and asked, "What is going on?"

"Your team has been told to stand down, Sarah called us to back you up, and we have company coming. Somehow, I don't think they're very polite, so we were told to hold the line here." Abby asked the nurse, "Can he be moved to another room?"

"No, not easily," the nurse said. "Is there someplace you can get to that is safe, and take Barbara with you?"

"It is possible," the nurse replied.

"I'm not leaving Ronnie," Barbara said, "he's my responsibility."

"Well, then it's two against anything that gets past Michael," Abby said. "Can we take those chairs and put them in the bathroom? This room is all cinder block walls; it should protect the two of you." Abby pointed to the nurses.

The two nurses grabbed two of the smaller chairs sitting to the side. The younger of the two nurses started crying. "Quiet girl," Nancy scolded," I don't want your babbling to get us killed."

The younger looked shocked but quieted immediately.

Once the two women were in the bathroom and were situated, Abby put her finger to her lips, and they nodded as she closed the door. The doors in the hospital were solid wood, the walls were cinder blocks, and it was unlikely that a firefight would hurt anyone except those in the direct line of fire. Michael explained this to Abby as they drove in. He noted that most hospitals were bomb shelters, tornado shelters, and just plain shelter shelters because they were self-sufficient and built to take a beating, even the most beautiful hospitals were reinforced, had steel beams, and were unlikely to allow penetration from small arms fire.

Abby and Barbara moved the bookshelf and dresser in front of the door.

"What about Michael?" Barbara asked.

"Michael can take care of himself, and there are only three of them," Abby said.

"He's not Superman," Barbara stated, "he can die just as easily as Ronnie."

"Michael would disagree with you," Abby said. "Ever since I learned about what he did, I also knew I had to trust him or go crazy every moment of every day. I decided to trust him and his skill."

"You're saying I should trust him too," Barbara said; "How's that supposed to work?"

"It doesn't matter if you trust him or not," Abby noted; "he's very good at this, and even though he wants to leave it behind, he is still probably one of the best-suited people for the job."

Barbara hung her head for a moment. "I wish I could do it as easily as you did, as you do. I'm sitting here wondering if Ronnie's gonna make it out of this alive, and I'm not sure if I can protect him. I know he would do everything in his power to protect me."

"I'm sure you're right," Abby said as she watched the door. "But that's a choice. Every day you could lose everything, and you can either worry about it or realize that you'll live with it, good or bad."

"That's some real fortune cookie talk," Barbara laughed; "Did you get that out of a fortune cookie?"

"No, I got that from my father, believe it or not," Abby replied. "In spite of everything, he did teach me some good adages and some great motivations. Michael's really good at it, too, but he didn't have anything that fit this situation. I think I'm the only thing he ever worries about. Every time he needed money, he just made more. He's lost his parents; he has no family and not a lot of friends. At least people he would consider friends. I would be willing to bet the closest friend he has right now is Jim, and that's only because no one else would spar with him, ever."

"That's pretty sad," Barbara said.

"Not really," Abby replied, "we have each other. We went furniture shopping today and had a nice lunch, and as we were heading home, we got the call from Sarah. How many people that you know really understand each other? I think my tastes are a little more froufrou than Michael's, but I don't think that stuff really matters to him. He just wants to be happy and enjoy staying alive."

"Then why is he involved in this?" Barbara asked.

"Michael has a moral code," Abby said.

"But he kills people," Barbara quipped.

"Sure, he kills people, but he is selective on how and who he kills. Believe it or not, he has rarely killed anyone who is innocent, even when working for the government," Abby said. "Of course, I don't know all of his kills, but I know enough. He gives every person a chance to do the right thing."

Abby and Barbara waited, watching the door closely and listening.

In another room, Michael was also watching carefully. The elevator had not opened, and Michael was questioning whether the men were who we thought they were. As Michael got ready to go to Ronnie's room, he saw the elevator open, and one man step off. The man looked down each hallway and carefully assessed the area. The door where Michael was hidden was closed enough there would be no clear view. As Michael watched in the distance, he saw a stairwell door open. The three men were much more measured than he had expected. Normally a team will stay together, allowing for cover of each other. In this case, they had opted to ensure that no one would get away, having one person come up the elevator and two others up the only active stairwells. This gave them an advantage of interlocking fields of vision and, subsequently, interlocking fields of fire.

The only advantage for Michael would be waiting until he could take them, one at a time. He was not aware of their capabilities nor their current firepower. Engaging early would likely be difficult for him Abby, and the others.

Michael kept his eye on the two men he could see. The third moved forward and was going down the back hall. The man closest to him was heading directly at Michael. He slowly drew out the Hibben knife and slung the P90 over his back. To have any chance at victory, he would have to eliminate at least one of the three before engaging the others. If he was lucky, he could be silent enough to avoid detection. The man walked to doors and opened each, checking for patients and nurses. Michael was hopeful this floor would have a minimal number of patients to keep potential casualties to a minimum.

The man walked into the room next to Michael, and Michael flattened himself behind the door. The man opened the door, and Michael saw the tip of the pistol swinging from side to side, surveying the room. Michael watched carefully as the man's grip relaxed, and he returned his finger to the outside of the trigger guard. Obviously, a professional and obviously careful. As his hands started to move backward and he started to turn, Michael pulled him inwards and slid his knife under his throat and into his brain. It was a bold move as the blade could have bounced off the skull, but Michael made it work, and the man fell silently with Michael's help.

One down.

Michael surveyed the outside hallways and saw no one. He wiped his blade on the man's suit and holstered it. Michael then moved into the hallway and carefully peeked around both ways. He saw no one. This likely meant that both men were inside rooms. Michael heard the click of silencer gunfire. Most people think a silencer is completely quiet. It is not. Instead, you hear a loud click or pop depending on the type of silencer. Michael knew this sound and knew someone had been shot. He was thankful it was not Abby or Barbara. If they had found them, there would have been live gunfire.

Michael waited and was patiently listening. His position was between the two hallways. He could be seen from the corners of either if they came around the corner, otherwise, he was invisible. He heard a door open to his right and slowly worked towards it, making no sound. He glanced around the edge of the corner and saw nothing but an open door, three down. He waited. There was nothing. A few moments later, he saw the second man leave the room deftly closing the door behind him. The man looked in all directions and somehow missed Michael. He walked into the next room.

Michael guessed he only had a few seconds and walked towards the room, watching all around him. He scanned behind and to the far edge of the hallway. There was nothing. Michael smiled to himself, remembering the feeling known as kenopsia. He thought he would never have used that word until today. Staying focused, he slipped into the room. The man was three feet in front of him. Michael pulled his Hibben with no sound at all. He grasped the man around the throat from behind and plunged the knife into his heart. It took only a moment, and there was no struggle. His gun clattered to the floor.

Michael knew the sound had given him away. The third man would be on guard and ready and was probably heading towards him now. For a fraction of a second, Michael considered his options, then, looking at the room, went to the far side of the bed and waited.

There were voices. Michael heard a knocking. "Are you in there? I can't get the door open?"

Michael knew those voices would change the course of the last man. He got up and headed to the door. He was met face-to-face with that very assassin. Michael had the Hibben in his hand. The man had his pistol pointed down. It was a matter of reflex. Michael pivoted as the man's hands came up and put the Hibben into the man's arm. The gun clattered to the floor, but Michael's knife was embedded in his fibula as the man pulled away.

The third man screamed in pain, grabbed the knife and pulled it out. He swung the knife at Michael, who leapt backward and pulled a second Hibben from its sheath. There was fury in the third man's eyes as he saw the body lying on the floor. He muttered something that Michael couldn't hear, then said, "You will join him," in Ukrainian.

Michael replied in Ukrainian, "Doubtful."

The surprise in the man's eyes gave Michael a fraction of a second advantage, and he slashed the man's wrist where he held the knife. Hibben's are a solid steel design with no handle beyond the steel. With his wrist cut, the man could not hold on, and the knife clattered to the floor.

"What are you hiding?" Michael asked in Ukrainian.

"You must know I won't tell you anything," the man bragged as he lunged for Michael.

Michael sidestepped and plunged the knife under his solar plexus and deep enough to hit the man's heart. He pulled the knife out, his blood pumped, and covered his hand. The man looked at Michael in disbelief and fell to the ground face down. His body jumped twice before becoming stationary.

Michael slipped out of the room and looked down the hallway. There was no one there. He walked carefully and quietly until he saw a large security guard around another corner.

"Excuse me," Michael whispered.

The security guard jumped, turned, and fumbled for a moment but drew his weapon with better-than-average proficiency.

"It's okay," Michael looked around as he spoke, "the three men have been neutralized."

"Neutralized?" Edward replied. "Who talks like that?"

"I guess I do," Michael replied. "Let them know I'm out here, and Abby will help open the door."

"I called the police, but they said they weren't coming right away," Edward replied. "Hey in there, there's a guy out here that says everything's okay."

"Michael?" came a voice from inside.

Michael stepped forward and said, "Yeah, it's me; we are all clear."

There was a rumbling in the room from furniture being moved, and then the door opened. Abby stepped out with her weapon still drawn. When she saw Michael, she holstered the weapon, walked to him, and held him. She got blood on her clothes. "Is that blood?" she asked.

"I'm afraid it is. It might stain," Michael replied.

"I'm sure it will stain," Abby smiled; "it's not yours, is it?"

"No, it's definitely not mine," Michael looked at the stain and smiled. "I got lucky."

"You always get lucky," Abby nodded.

The two nurses came out of the room, then Barbara looked around the edges. Michael had done his job, and everyone was safe. Michael looked at Abby and said, "Call Sarah and let her know."

Abby dialed the number as Michael took Edward aside and told him where the three bodies were. "It might be better to put them somewhere so they're not out in the open. I also heard the click of silenced gunfire, and I am concerned that they may have killed someone in their room."

"I'll check all the rooms," Edward replied.

"We can help," the nurses said. "I've seen bodies before."

"I'm sure you have," Michael said.

"I want to say thank you for saving us, but I'm not sure who the bad guy is right now," Nancy stated. "Are you a good guy, or are you a bad guy?"

"I'm sure there's debate about that often," Michael considered as he spoke, "for now, I'm the one who was called to save you. For the moment, I am a good guy, I guess."

"Thank you for that," Nancy thanked him as the other woman nodded. Edward, Nancy, and the other nurse walked around, checking rooms one at a time.

"Sarah said Alex is stuck at the police station. They are not allowed to leave yet. Something about diplomatic immunity and diplomatic issues."

"Yuri's men will be gone soon. Alex needs to get out and figure out what's going on. Either that or you and I need to figure this out. Why would they need a furniture store? Does it have something to do with the loading docks, the area, or something else completely? What did Ronnie's cousin find, and why was Ronnie shot? We only have partial information there, but it has something to do with his cousin. I wonder where the cousin is. Maybe we need to talk to Barbara and then have a quick call with Alex." Michael knew there were more questions than answers right now.

Chapter 27

Alex hung up the phone and looked around the room. The medium-sized boardroom was built to have meetings and acted as a multipurpose room for the Pikeville Police Department. The groups split up based on their area, with only a few mingling. Jim and Rachel traded barbs at each other while they played Gin Rummy. Jim tried to get a poker game going, but none of the officers wanted anything to do with it. Several State Troopers sat with their crisp uniforms and waited with their covers on their knees. Sentinels waiting for deployment.

"Alright, listen up, everybody," Alex said. "The hospital was attacked, and three attackers attempted to penetrate the room where Ronnie Comer is being held. All three attackers have been neutralized, but this may not be the last attack. If anyone knows anything about why they're going after Ronnie, now is the time to say it."

"What do you mean they were neutralized?" Trooper Thorne asked.

"That's a really good question?" Several of the Pikeville PD asked.

"It means that three men are dead," Alex said. "They were coming to kill people, and they were killed."

"Killed by whom?" Trooper Thorne asked.

"I'm not at liberty to say," Alex replied.

"You better find a way to be at liberty. You're in the process of turning my town into a war zone. I wanna know what I'm up against."

"You know exactly what you're up against," Alex said. "Someone in this room knows something. There is some type of operation in the area otherwise, this wouldn't have escalated so quickly. Of course, it's very possible I'm wrong, but every time there's a big operation like this, there is also someone on the take. You need to ask yourself which of you has bought a nice car or a better house. Which of you goes out to eat or runs to Lexington more often? Which of you had money problems up until a short time ago, and now everything seems alright? Groups like this do their research. They know who is vulnerable and leverage that vulnerability to work for them."

"That's mighty big talk from somebody who's not from around here," Phil Comer said; "You're insinuating that one of my men is a liar and a cheat. You're pretty much calling us out, and our families, right?"

"I'm not calling anybody out," Alex said, "I'm just telling you the facts. If you take it personally, maybe you're the one with the problem."

Eleanor looked at Sarena, "Are they always like this?"

Sarena smiled, "Pretty much, but they get the job done."

Two men from the Pikeville PD stood up and were ready for anything. The State Troopers stood up as well, all of them. "This is a mighty proud town for a reason," Phil said, "I don't like what you're gettin' at."

"Yeah, and I don't like that one of my men almost died in this little hellhole. If I hurt your itty-bitty feelings, you can deal with it, or we can bump this up a notch," Alex barked. "Since we're all stuck here, what are we going to do about it? If we're going to fight, let's do it because I'm tired of dealing with this crap. If we're going to do something, let's figure out what it is. You guys are the ones with two men trying to kill us; why?"

"You've got most of our force here," Phil said. "Do you see the people that tried to kill you? I bet not. Y'all better back up. You may be good with all those international assholes, but this is Pikeville, and we were built to scrap."

Jim stood up. "Woah, woah, woah. As much as I love it that Alex is out of character right now, and as much as I would love to see Rachel pound a few of your men into the concrete while I giggle and laugh, all you boys better remember we're on the same side. Alex is a little keyed up because we're the ones with a man down and with people trying to kill our own. As far as I know, right now, not one of you is down, and not one of you has to worry about the bullseye on your head. Why don't you all listen to Alex, and let's try to take this a little further? We know that two men tried to ambush us with police help or someone who looked like police. It's obvious it wasn't police, but where would they get uniforms, and how would they know what to do? It's not like this is a big city. Wouldn't somebody notice them if they had their little roadblock?" Jim paused, "I kind of like this being the voice of reason." He paused again. "Oh hell, who am I kidding? I hate being the voice of reason. You guys talk this out."

Phil moved up towards Alex, and the troopers sat back down. "We should have been looking through people." He looked at one of the men, "Go get the pictures of all the men for the past two years."

"That seems like an awesome idea," Alex said; "Rachel, go help him."

Rachel stood and nodded. She had been around Alex long enough to know his being tough was a way to force people in the corner to be nice. She went with the police officer into the other room.

"What I said was true," Alex said; "Does anyone fit that mold? Anyone got too much money, or the bills suddenly went away?"

Phil looked around at the men in the room with him, "I don't think so, but it's hard to know. We're a tight-knit group, but things can slip sometimes. We're not always sitting around being super honest with each other. A little too proud, I guess. That being said, I think somebody would've known something. I guess you boys see stuff like this all the time."

"Not really, no," Jim said; "usually, we're sent into the middle of nowhere to solve a problem that everybody else is afraid to deal with. Sometimes we deal with some tough people, and sometimes we deal with people who made bad choices."

The troopers remained quiet off to the side. Trooper Thorne stood up. "I'm not certain we really need to stay here. I've been considering our orders, and it seems we have a loophole. We are not to interfere with the men with diplomatic immunity, but it is possible those men are now dead. Perhaps we need to relocate to the hospital, or at least some of us, to determine if the three men who died are the three men we had in custody earlier. If they are dead, we have nothing to prevent us from getting back to work."

"That's actually really smart," Alex said. "Your men would be able to identify those three men?"

"As would I," Trooper Thorne said.

"Why don't you take a group over and get the hospital under control, then. If it turns out that the men are dead, we can move on and start trying to figure out why it all broke loose."

"Can I go?" Eleanor asked. "He is my cousin." She was ignored by the entire group.

"We'll do that. Am I expected to run into your mystery guest as well? There will be questions that have to be answered, and someone will have to pay for the crime," Trooper Thorne said.

"I doubt it," Alex replied, "it's likely they are long gone. I'm sure someone there will give you some inkling of the situation."

"This is very irregular," Trooper Thorne stated as he waved the other troopers forward.

"You're a young man," Alex said, "consider this all a good learning experience."

"I'm an experienced young man and a State Trooper for the Commonwealth of Kentucky. I think that's more than enough."

"I'm sure you're right," Alex said with a smile. "You go take care of the hospital and see if the men in suits are the people you arrested earlier."

"I should go too," Eleanor said, this time in a much louder voice. The room looked at her partially with astonishment and partially with newfound respect.

"You can stay here with us, and we will go as rapidly as possible," Alex looked at Eleanor. "Ronnie would want me to ensure your safety. The only way I can do that is if I keep you close. We'll know pretty soon and be able to verify that Ronnie is getting better."

Eleanor looked down. She knew he was right but it didn't make her feel any better. In her mind, she played over Ronnie limping up, coming after her after being shot multiple times.

"Eleanor, is that okay?" Alex asked.

Eleanor nodded and turned back towards Sarena.

All of the troopers filed out of the building. Jim looked at Alex. "He has a major problem with his butt."

"What do you mean?" Alex asked.

"There's something stuck up it," Jim proclaimed. "I mean, good God, you gotta learn when to cut your line."

"I thought he was just fine. I'm not sure what you're talking about. After all, he's following orders, at least, he thinks he is. I bet you think I'm just like Trooper Thorne sometimes."

"Sometimes you are just like Trooper Thorne. Sometimes you're a lot worse," Jim laughed. "So why are we staying here?"

"Let's call Tarkington before we head out. I would much rather the State Police get into a load of trouble than us. After all, things that the State Department gets involved in tend to get front page attention."

"Why you cagey little devil," Jim said. "You're testing the waters using them. That's a little risky, don't you think?"

"Why do you think that? Alex asked.

"Easy," Jim laughed, "if they get in trouble, they will be mad at you. If they don't get in trouble, they'll come out the heroes and get all the glory. Either way, you lose."

"Not really," Alex commented. "When we dealt with the issue in San Antonio, we got zero media coverage. We dealt with Washington, DC, and stopped a lunatic in our offices, zero media coverage. We dealt with a group of rabid militia men in Michigan, and that was swept so far under the rug that no one will ever know they existed. We dealt with a major issue in Indianapolis involving freelance assassins running a corporation; I think that one missed the papers too. Oh, and we ended up fighting for our lives in Venezuela with kidnapped kids and crazy parents. That one didn't even make the National Enquirer. Is there some reason that I should think if we solve some type of drug ring in Pikeville, Kentucky, that anyone will care about us any more than they already do?"

"You have a point there," Jim laughed.

"Actually, I'll care," Phil interjected as he walked up, "I don't care who gets the credit; I just want to do what's right."

"See," Alex pointed at Phil to Jim, "Phil actually gets it. We're not in this to be famous; we're in this to do the right thing. Are you with me on that?" Alex was direct in his question.

"Yeah, I suppose," Jim laughed. "But you have to buy me dinner somewhere nice."

"We got all the pictures of anybody that's been here; care to take a look?" Phil pointed to the wall. The group walked over to a monitor on the wall, and a younger man walked in with a computer.

"This is Nick," Phil said, "he's an intern here, and he's been working with our systems. He has everything pulled up on a screen and will project it in here."

"Thanks, Nick," Jim said.

Nick was a young man of about twenty. He was six foot, very thin, and couldn't have weighed more than 140 pounds. He wore a white shirt with a loose tie and black slacks with a non-descript logo on them. The funny thing was that he was wearing chucks which gave him the appearance everyone expected for a computer technician. Nick sat down and plugged the cable into the side of the computer while he tapped on the keys rather noisily. After a moment, the screen was filled with men. There were only nine on the screen, but Jim pointed to two right away.

"#3 and #5," Jim excaimed. "Those were the two that were firing on us. They were also the ones running the roadblock."

"Deacon and Freddie Taylor," Phil said. "They were released last year after an issue was uncovered with their speed traps. Normally we don't have much problem with speeders around here, but these two boys set up a speed trap and were letting people off if they paid them half-price in cash. They admitted to $10,000 and paid it back, but estimates are it was probably closer to $50,000. There's just no easy way to know for sure. They were bad boys in town but seemed like good cops for quite a while. It would be easy to coerce them. They are less than, let's just say, they are less than perfect."

"How do we find them?" Alex asked.

"Should be pretty easy," Phil said. "Finding them is not going to be the issue. Convincing them to come in or arresting them might prove a little more difficult. Both of them like their guns and their women. They are probably off-grid with a few girls holed up in some shack or loaded for bear, ready to shoot us if we come for them."

Rachel walked back into the room. "Well, that sounds like fun. I'm in."

"Do you boys just like walking into trouble?" Phil asked.

"No, not really," Jim said, "but we are really damn good at it."

"Why don't you let me and my boys take care of this?" Phil said. "Maybe if it's just us, they'll still come peacefully."

Alex's phone rang and he picked it up in a hurry. "Sarah?"

There was a pause while Jim and Phil watched Alex listen. Alex then said, "Understood."

"We are free and clear," Alex said as he hung up the phone. "Jim let's get everybody together and get rolling over to the hospital. Maybe we can get some clue from Eleanor about what we're dealing with and then deal with it."

"You know you're going to have a stack of troopers over there," Jim noted.

"Yeah, a stack of troopers that don't like you very much," Phil added.

"Can't be helped, let's get it done," Alex said. "You take care of your Taylor problem, and we'll see what we can find out. I'll let you know where we're heading. As much as I would like to go after you're two guys, we have orders to figure out the bigger picture. Maybe together, we can figure out what the hell is going on?"

"I'm not expecting a lot out of those boys," Phil noted; "I thought they'd be good officers, but they're a few cylinders shy of a V8. Actually, they're a few cylinders shy of just about everything."

Rachel, Serena, Jim, Terry, and Alex nodded at each other, and the team headed out to the Escalade with Eleanor.

"I do have one question?" Phil asked.

Alex turned for a moment and looked at him. "What's that?"

"That Suburban of yours is in my impound. Where do you want me to take it to get it fixed?" Phil asked.

"They can fix that?" Rachel laughed.

"I'm sure they can fix anything," Sarena said in a dry voice.

"Anywhere you want," Alex said.

"Alright," Phil said; "you said anywhere, so it's not really a conflict of interest, but I have a cousin who does great work, and he'll get you back on the road."

"I'll believe it when I see it," Alex said. The group turned around and headed out the door.

Chapter 28

Ronnie opened his eyes and looked around. His vision was blurry. The room was sterile, white, and fuzzy. He looked down at his hand and saw the IV and felt the mask on his face. He felt the urge to cough and stopped himself. There was pain, but he had felt worse, a lot worse. As the room started to come into focus, he saw Barbara and wondered how she got there. He started thinking about how he got here. Remembering brought him back to being shot and the man carrying Eleanor away. Standing next to Barbara was a nurse, and Ronnie wondered how bad he was. He remembered getting shot and how it hadn't hurt as bad as he thought it would. Then he remembered his leg and reached down, feeling the thick cast around it.

The feeling in his throat was getting worse, and he coughed just a little. Then he coughed a little more. He was having a hard time getting his breath, so he coughed again and, this time was rewarded with some relief.

The nurse was by his side before he was even aware of it, and he felt Barbara squeeze his hand on the other side. The nurse checked everything, and Ronnie started taking off the mask.

"Leave the mask on," Nancy said, "it's a little too early to be taking it off. You're lucky you're not on a ventilator. You'll need to take it easy for several months."

"Hurts," Ronnie choked out.

"You were shot," Barbara said. "You're lucky to be alive."

"I remember," Ronnie said. "Tell me what happened."

"Why don't we wait for the doctor?" Nancy asked.

"Tell me now. I need to know," Ronnie said again.

Nancy looked at Barbara, and Barbara nodded.

"You just need to take it easy," Nancy said, "let your body catch up. It will be a hard few days, but you need to gauge yourself and go with it. The doctors were able to repair the lung but there was extensive damage, and it will take time for it all to heal. You will have some chest pain, and it may be difficult to breathe. We will keep a close eye on you, and you'll be out of here in a few days, maybe a week. Your leg is a bigger problem. Most of the bone had been destroyed. The doctors reconstructed what they could, but you're going to have problems walking, and it won't be easy. You'll have to go through extensive physical therapy, and you'll never walk the way you did before."

"I'll be able to walk?" Ronnie asked.

"Yes, you'll be able to walk, but you may have problems running or other complications. You're young and strong, and you may be able to overcome it all." Nancy replied.

"Will I be able to keep my job?" Ronnie quavered.

"I'm sure you will," Barbara said. "Alex needs you, and I need you. Look, Ronnie, I know this is moving fast, but we need to talk right now. The timing may be wrong, but I don't want to wait anymore. I know that you like me a lot, and I like you a lot. I haven't been very fair. I know that we flirted a lot, and I know that you always wanted more of a relationship with me."

"It's okay," Ronnie said.

"Shut up, Ronnie," Barbara said. "I'm trying to tell you that all the reasons I had for not going further with you weren't very good reasons. I've spent so long trying to find the right person in my life, and you were always sitting right there next to me. I know we work together, but if I have to, I'll go somewhere else. I know your job is important to you, and you're important to the team, and I'm just a pilot who sometimes takes care of the cabin. I've seen everything you can do, and you're the voice of reason for the team. You tell the truth when others avoid it, and you do the right thing even when the right thing is the hardest thing to do. More than that, you stand up to people you don't have a chance against and somehow find a way. I don't think anyone else in the world could have faced Rachel and Jim the way you did, but you did it and, in the process, got respect from both of them."

Ronnie tried to chuckle then coughed.

"What I'm trying to say to you, Ronnie Comer, is that I want to try. We may not have a perfect relationship, but I know damn well that we could both try to have a perfect relationship. There will be days that you may not like who I am, and days that I don't like who you are, but I'll be there for you. I'll be standing next to you when no one else wants to. Am I too late? Do we have a chance? Are you willing to try with me?"

Ronnie coughed again, looked at Nancy, then moved his arm and winced a little. He beckoned Barbara closer. She knelt down and put her head close to Ronnie's mask. "What took you so long?" Ronnie asked.

Barbara smiled and raised her head just a little, her red hair falling across Ronnie's face as she kissed him on the forehead.

"I'll expect more later," Ronnie said. "We have a lot of time to make up for."

Ronnie coughed again, and Nancy said, "You need to slow down a little. This is way too fast. I know you're feeling a little better, but why don't you just rest."

"Don't let her leave," Ronnie said to Nancy.

"I'm not going anywhere," Barbara said.

Nancy left the room for a minute. Barbara squeezed Ronnie's hand and pulled it to her mouth to kiss his hand. "Thank you," she said quietly.

The door swung open, and a Kentucky State trooper walked into the room. He looked around for a few moments as Barbara leaned forward with her hand on her holster.

"Can I help you?" Barbara asked.

"Yes, ma'am," Trooper Thorne said. "I was wondering if you're okay? My name is Trooper Thorne with the Kentucky State Police."

"Yes, Sir we're just fine," Barbara noted.

"Ma'am, I'd like to take your statement on the shootings here today," Trooper Thorne said.

"I'm afraid I don't know very much," Barbara said as she realized the purpose of this visit. "What did you want to know?"

"Well, ma'am," Trooper Thorne started, "there are three bodies here, and all three were killed by a knife. Three patients are dead or dying from gunshot wounds. It appears that these men were the source of the patient deaths, but I'm trying to determine how they died. So far, I'm not getting much cooperation, and perhaps I understand that this series of events was partially responsible for saving your life. Still, we will not stand for any vigilante justice, and at minimum, I would like to question the person who killed these men. I am sure several other departments would also like to question them."

"I'm not sure I can help you," Barbara said; "We were locked in this room at the time. I didn't see anything. I can't tell you for certain who killed these men." Ronnie began coughing a little to Barbera's side. Barbara squeezed his hand and said, "Ronnie, I will be outside for a moment. I'll be just out the door and come right back in." She paused and pointed to the door, "Trooper Thorne, would you care to join me out in the hallway?"

Barbara and the trooper went out into the hallway, and Barbara pulled the door closed. "I understand you're trying to find your way to the truth. I understand you want to find the person who killed these three men, but I fully believe I would be dead right now if they had not been killed. I didn't see anything, nor did I step outside of the room when any of this was going on. Two nurses in the room with us, and I was patiently waiting with my weapon and ready to die for Ronnie. If you have a problem with any of that, please contact Alex Brown, my commanding officer. He will deal with any logistics regarding my testifying or giving any further information. I'm trying to be very cooperative, but right now, my teammate needs rest, and I have been assigned to protect him."

"I understand, ma'am, but..." Trooper Thorne started.

"There is no but," Barbara said. "If I knew for sure who killed those men, I would thank them. Do you understand what that means?"

Trooper Thorne sighed, "Yes, ma'am I do. I appreciate your time. I may reach out to your superior at a later time. We have already had quite the interactions so far."

"Then you know I'm in good hands, and I will be well taken care of," Barbara said.

Barbara turned around and was about to go into the room when she heard Trooper Thorne call out to her.

"Ma'am," Trooper Thorne said, "you know you're not supposed to have a weapon inside this hospital."

"Funny, I see you have one on right now," Barbara replied.

"I'm an officer of the law," Trooper Thorne said.

"Guess what, so am I," Barbara noted. "Have a good day, Trooper Thorne." Barbara walked into the room and closed the door behind her. When she walked to the side of the bed, she saw that Ronnie was fast asleep.

Chapter 29

"We seem to have quite the situation," Jim laughed, "as usual."

"We do," Alex said, "anytime we're given one of these strange assignments, we always end up in quite the situation. I suppose we need to find a way to talk to Michael and talk with Eleanor somewhere neutral."

Alex dialed a number while Terry drove. Alex put the phone on speaker.

"Sarah, can you get us in touch with Michael? It appears we have a lot of questions and not a lot of answers. For that matter, can you give me his phone number?"

"Of course, I would give you his phone number if it didn't change constantly. Abby gave us a burn phone several weeks ago, which is how we got in touch with them. Beyond that, it's hard to say." Sarah stated. "I will text you that number, and you can go from there."

"I appreciate that. We seem to have a situation here as well. There are unfriendlies popping out of the woodwork," Alex said. "There is also a contingent of State Troopers wanting to get involved as well as local police. It's quite the party."

"You do have a talent for attracting that type of situation," Sarah laughed. "On a more serious note, the General is very interested in how Ronnie is doing."

"Ronnie is stable right now, and Barbara is protecting him. After this latest issue, we shouldn't have any problems. If we do, I'm sure Barbara will reach out right away."

"Is Ronnie stable enough to move to another hospital?" Sarah asked.

"I'm not sure, but I certainly wouldn't want to chance it right now. This whole thing reeks of drugs that would involve DEA, but it seems like there's something else going on. Obviously, drug cartels have a significant amount of labor available, but it is almost like overkill here. Way too much for a small city like Pikeville. I'm hoping Michael has some insight into what's happening since he used to live in the area."

"Remember, it is a small town. Michael may have insight but isn't Ronnie from around there too?" Sarah asked, then paused; "hang on a second, the General wants to speak to you."

The line was blank for a few minutes. Alex considered as he was not sure how the General was going to approach this call. He decided just to wait and ride it out. Jim looked over at him and smiled, knowing what was coming next.

Alex heard the phone pick up. "Alex, you certainly know how to stir things up. I've got state troopers yelling, local police singing your praises, a mounting bill with a nowhere hospital, one of your team in a bad way again, and the hospital yelling about who will pay to clean up after all the killings. I've been contacted by DEA, and they want to know what's going on and whether they should get involved. The timer starts now. You've got forty-eight hours to get your ass in gear and solve this shit. I want to see some info flowing my way so I can shove it up the Director's ass. Keep me in the loop and start making some things happen. While you're at it, don't get my daughter killed. My expectation is that you are far better than a second-rate drug Lord. If this turns out to be something else, you get the right people there as fast as possible or eliminate the problem and send them the paperwork."

"Yes, Sir," Alex replied. "Anything else, Sir?"

"Yeah," Tarkington said, "try not to get yourself dead while doing all of that. It pisses me off that Ronnie got shot, and I don't want to hear about anyone else. My expectation is 50 to 1. I don't wanna lose anyone, but if I do, you better take 50 for every one of you."

"Yes, Sir," Alex said again, "I'll push for 100 to 1 and would like it better if we can keep that to zero."

"Me too," Tarkington snickered, "I would prefer that always."

The phone went quiet.

"A breath of fresh air as always," Jim said. "I would rather keep it to zero as well. We have lost enough."

"Yeah," Alex noted. "One is more than too many."

"I would rather my cousin not be on your list of casualties," Eleanor said. "You guys seem to talk awful tough. Ronnie said he worked with some of the best, but most of what I have seen so far is just talk."

Jim smiled for a moment. "What would you like us to do?"

"Well, how about for starters, you figure out why they wanted me dead so fast? I was up on that hill, and it seemed to be just drugs. We have lots of drugs in the hills, but why would they want to kill me for it?"

"She has a point," Sarena was looking at her phone. "We are playing pure defense, and it doesn't seem to be working. Maybe it is time to go on the offense?"

"I'd be all in for a little offense," Rachel jumped in. "Sure, we've had some fights, but the hell if I know who we're fighting. That trooper is going to take all the fight away from us, and we're still not gonna know who shot Ronnie."

"We still have the hospital to think about," Alex said. "We don't have two vehicles now, so we are a little limited."

Chapter 30

Michael was quiet as he drove the DB9 back towards the furniture store. There was a lot to consider. Michael knew that Yuri would probably be as ruthless as his father. He did not know how far his influence had grown since he was with him. The last several years could have easily allowed him to grow his father's empire, or he could have been complacent and let it slip. As it evolved, the situation appeared to point to the latter, and Michael was concerned.

"Abby, is there any way I could convince you to take a trip?" Michael asked.

"Michael, what's wrong with you? You would never have asked me to leave before today. What is different?"

"Yuri is an interesting opponent. If he has become like his father, I am concerned about what might happen to you if I miss," Michael noted dryly.

"Then you better make sure you don't miss," Abby pouted. "You have never missed before; as far as I know, why would you start missing today?"

Michael considered the question for a few moments. "Honestly, I don't think I will. I know this will sound a little bit odd but building the house and putting all this together along with our drive from Michigan to Kentucky and all of the talks that we have had has made me consider a far different path."

"A far different path?" Abby questioned, "are you thinking of leaving me, or is this about something else?"

Michael was quick to respond, "I never want to be away from you; I always want to be with you. Abby, we really haven't talked about it before, but have you ever considered marrying me?"

Abby smiled at Michael. "Of course I have," she elated; "I think about being married to you often. I know when the time is right, you will ask me. We have a fantastic life together, and we don't need a piece of paper to prove we have a fantastic life together, but I would be proud to be married to you."

"I would like to just fall off the grid and spend time with you without people showing up on our doorstep or calling us asking me to do something. It's not like anybody ever calls asking me to bake a cake."

"Can you bake?" Abby laughed. "Oh yeah, I remember you baked me a cake, and it was pretty awesome."

Michael relaxed a little. "That is exactly why I love being around you. I don't think about things very often and have them bother me, but when I do, you know exactly what to say. Will you promise me that if I need you to stay safe, you will listen?"

"I promise that I will always listen to you, but I also promise that I'm not some girly girl that can't take care of herself. I know that very few people can shoot as well as you do and that you have immense skill with a variety of weapons and combat types. I do as well. Don't put me on the sidelines when I need to be out there with you making a difference."

"I understand, and I respect that about you," Michael said. "This may get pretty brutal."

"It very well might," Abby said, "and we have dealt with brutal together before."

"I love you," Michael said.

"Wow, I love you too," Abby said.

They pulled up in front of the furniture store. "I should have put the suppressor on my pistol. Whenever we're here, I shoot someone and make Bob a little deafer."

Abby began laughing.

"You know people would think we were a little strange for laughing at this type of thing," Michael laughed.

"Most people don't have a clue about the real world. They see the world go past them and think they are safe. If only they knew about how much human trafficking, death, and worse goes on right under their noses. Maybe they'd stop fighting on the Internet about stupid political topics." Abby declared.

"You know, an outside observer would think that you had an opinion and all," Michael laughed.

Abby laughed and pointed at the parking lot. "Another car disposed of."

"You got to admit that Bob is good," Michael said.

Michael and Abby walked into the furniture store, and Bob was standing at the counter. His forehead had several neat stitches and was open to the air. Bob looked up as they walked in.

"You know, every time I see you two, I get beat up, or my eardrums threaten to burst. Did you at least get something quieter to shoot people with?" Bob asked.

"Sorry I didn't have time to pick up a suppressor," Michael laughed.

"I didn't expect you to be back this soon. What can I do you for?" Bob queried.

"I wanted to see that bomb shelter," Michael said. "I can't figure out what's so special about this location."

"Well, let me lock up so we can keep the riffraff out, and let's walk down there and take a look," Bob replied as he locked the door. Bob turned and walked behind the counter. He pulled out a large flashlight and then directed Abby and Michael to the side of the building. As they walked through the furniture, Bob said, "You know, we've got some other good furniture here, and you never know when you might need some more. If we don't have what we need, I'm happy to special order just for you."

"You have got to be one of the best salesmen I've ever met," Abby said.

"Thank you, ma'am," Bob replied. "I'm just trying to make ends meet."

Bob opened a rather old-looking door that revealed a set of ancient steps. He flipped the light switch to the side, and a series of incandescent lights flowed down a deep stairwell. Even though the incandescent lights were very bright, shadows danced on the sides and edges of the wooden frame.

Bob led the way down the stairs holding on to the railing with Abby following and Michael at the back. The stairs creaked under their weight but were sturdy and held fast until they reached a concrete floor about twenty-five feet below the furniture store. The walls were reinforced concrete and cinder block, and several doors were off to the side of the central room. In the center of the room, a pallet with a stack of boxes stood. The boxes were old, well-worn by age and marked with cryptic letter designations.

"Wanna see something cool?" Bob said as he opened a box. Inside was what could only be classified as an antique mask and Geiger counter. "These were left here back in the 50s, and the Army never came back to pick them up. Probably long forgotten, but I wasn't going to try to sell them in case it got me in trouble. If you look over in that room over there, there's about 100 more cases of these, radiation suits, and enough MREs to feed an army."

Michael looked around the room and saw no reason for it to be of any consequence. "What's behind the other doors?"

Bob laughed. "One of the doors is storage and right now is full of junk. I think there's a few old couches from the 60s, but I've never cleaned it out. Those two other doors are blocked off. They go back into the mines."

"What mines?" Michael asked.

"Well, anymore, they do strip mining and have ripped all the coal out. Up until about the 70s there was also shaft mining done here, and there are crisscrossing shaft mines all over the place. There have been a lot of grants to clean these up, and the Kentucky Department of Mines does a great job finding them and either filling them or cleaning them, but they haven't got to these yet, I don't think. They've just been here, and there was a time when they could be opened for access. They're all sealed up though, I am pretty sure, with cinder blocks. I suppose you could take the cinderblocks out and wander the mine, but I don't know why you'd want to. Some of these old mines can be pretty dangerous, which is why they're working to seal 'em all up."

"How big are the shafts on these?" Michael asked.

Bob scratched his head, "Some old ones aren't much bigger than a Volkswagen. The newer ones, the ones in the last forty years, those would be big enough to drive a truck in. It was funny when I worked nights, and there wasn't all the noise outside; you could hear the trucks driving down here going in and out with coal."

Michael looked around, "Thanks for showing me this. I really appreciate it. By the way, I don't think you'll have any more visitors, at least not for a while."

"That's a good thing," Bob said, "I don't think my ears can take any more of you saving me. They've been ringing all afternoon and yesterday."

Michael laughed.

"I'm sure it'll go away," Abby said. "I'm just glad we came when we did."

"I was just kidding ya," Bob said, "and like I said before, I really appreciate you saving me. For the life of me, I don't know why I'm such a big deal."

"You just have a nice place here," Michael chided.

"Yep," Bob replied, "I suppose I do."

They turned back towards the stairs, past a stack of boxes. Michael stopped and walked back to the wall.

"You say none of these mines are used anymore, all sealed up?" Michael asked.

"Yeah," Bob replied, "Been sealed up for years."

Michael knelt on the floor and looked toward the stairs. "No other way up from here? No windows or anything?" As Michael looked around the room, Bob answered and walked to where Michael was kneeling.

"No, Sir," Bob said curiously.

"Then why is the loose tape on that box moving?" Michael asked. Michael picked up a handful of dirt from the floor and walked to the first of the two mine doors. He slowly ground the dirt in his hand and let it fall. The dirt fell straight to the ground. Michael walked to the second and began grinding the dirt in his hand. When it reached the bottom of the door, it puffed outward.

"That's a bit peculiar," Bob said as he pulled at the door. The door had obviously been nailed shut for some time. Bob struggled, but the door did not budge. It was solid wood and painted white over time with thick coats making it look cleaner, but it was likely painted shut.

"Let me try," Michael said, pulling on the door. His muscles strained, and Bob joined in. Without warning, the door handle came off, and both men fell to the floor.

Michael began laughing, "I think we missed something there." Michael examined the hinges for other options. They were well-rusted and solid.

Bob was more determined. He walked to one of the walls and began rummaging through a large box until he pulled out two ancient crowbars. The older crowbars, made for opening crates, were worn and rusted, but still solid. "I can get a new door; this thing is coming down."

Michael stood, brushing off his pants, while Abby sat in the corner laughing at them both. "Would you like some help?"

Michael looked at her as she giggled and said, "Sure, jump on in."

Both Michael and Bob began trying to pry the door open from the edges. Abby rummaged in another box in the corner. The wood split quickly as the two crowbars pressed between the door and frame. The moldings popped loose, and Bob and Michael continued to try to get in.

"One sec, guys, let me try," Abby said from behind. The two men jumped out of the way as an eight-pound maul slammed into the lock area of the door, shattering the wood. Michael and Bob stepped back as Abby swung again and hit the door square on the lock a second time. The door buckled and broke free.

"You know the door opens out?" Michael mused.

Abby swung a third time, and the wood split inward. The door was now loose. Michael took his crowbar and pulled the door back, and this time it slid back into the room.

"You're welcome," Abby smiled as she set the maul against the wall.

Bob laughed. "You two are just the bomb, ain't ya."

"She is, not me," Michael replied.

The door opened and revealed a series of crisscrossed boards on a man-sized shaft. The walls were reinforced with thick four by fours, and the dirt floor was unused. A cool breeze was felt coming from inside.

"Must lead somewhere," Bob said. "Should be sealed off from years ago. No one has been actively mining these in a while."

"I am betting it is going somewhere else," Michael noted as he strained and pulled the boards down. He made short work of it and set the board behind him as Bob and Abby watched. It didn't take long to have a pathway through the tunnel. Michael took the large flashlight from Bob and shined it down the shaft. The light faded before it hit the end or a twist in the tunnel.

"Let me get another light," Bob noted as he walked to the stairs and disappeared.

Michael walked over to Abby and turned off the flashlight. "I love the way you mauled the door." He smiled and put his hand on her shoulder.

"I guess I know when to put the hammer down," Abby replied. Michael leaned in close and kissed Abby. It was brief, but full of passion. Abby grasped Michael as he started to pull away. "You're not done yet."

Michael looked deep into Abby's eyes. "You have no idea what you do to me."

"I think I do because you do the same to me," Abby replied.

Michael kissed Abby again. It was slow and passionate. A moment later, they heard Bob clear his throat. "I've got another flashlight."

"Then let's take a walk," Michael said.

The two big flashlights lit up the thin shaft easily. Flashlight technology had improved over time, but one of the flashlights was an old large cell spotlight while the newer one was an LED spotlight and lit up far more area. It wasn't long until they came to a T in the shaft. Michael shined the flashlight he held in both directions. One of them appeared to widen out. "Let's try this way first." The three of them worked their way down the shaft, and it did indeed widen out.

"This area looks recently finished," Michael said. "Look over there on the wall; there's a light switch."

Abby walked to the wall and turned on the switch. Brilliant LED lights lit up as far as they both could see. About twenty feet up the mineshaft, there were tables and crates.

As Michael walked up to the tables, Bob walked over to the crates. Michael looked at the maps he found on one of the tables. There was an intricate series of tunnels laid out before him. He noted the upper sheets of the map were clear and of different colors making the map almost three-dimensional. As he lifted each layer, he noted the access points where there were obviously elevators or grades that could move from level to level. On the very bottom, there was a map of downtown Pikeville, or at least this area, right in the center was the furniture store. Michael called out to Bob and Abby, who were looking through the crates.

"You might wanna come look at this."

As Abby and Bob reached the table Bob said, "Well this is pretty interesting too." He handed Michael a Kalashnikov AK-47. Abby had one as well. "There are probably ten crates of these with ten to a crate. You could outfit a small army. It looks like there is a significant amount of ammo as well."

"That makes sense," Michael noted. "If you have the perfect hideout and a protected supply chain, you will want to have weapons to ensure your safety. Take a look at this map. Note that your store is at the center, and when you lay the first clear sheet down, the shaft we just came down is the only one that intersects with any of the buildings. Now watch as I start layering the rest." Michael began lowering the pages one by one. "Do you see how this goes well out into the country? If we followed it out, I'm betting we would pop up in some type of drug field or similar. Nobody goes into Pikeville hollows unless it's their property. It's one of the reasons I like Eastern Kentucky. People are protective and loyal. Now, if they could get drugs or whatever from the country to here, they could load it on a truck, and nobody would be the wiser. If you had sold, they would have the perfect supply chain for illicit traffic."

"Good thing I didn't sell, isn't it?" Bob replied.

"What's in the lockers?" Michael asked.

"Not much," Abby said. "There are several different uniforms. Police, Fire, utilities, State Troopers, but nothing you wouldn't expect from someplace trying to blend in."

"Maybe," Michael replied, "but they may also be realistic. Bob, have any of the Police Departments changed recently?"

"Nope," Bob was thoughtful, "most of our forces been around a long time. They're good people. State Troopers come and go a lot, but I've always been told it's because Pikeville, Hazard, and the hills are training grounds that break in rookie cops. I don't pay much attention to them, and none of them visit me. The only time I see them doing anything is picking up speeders on the outside of town and showing up when there's something big going on."

"That sounds perfect too," Michael said. "A couple of Troopers could keep this area bottled up and know about any investigations before they even happen. I'd have to get to my computer and do some checking, but I'm betting there are some issues in past histories for some of these individuals."

"Should we let Alex know?" Abby asked.

"Probably," Michael said, "at a bare minimum, to clean out this area and get these guns somewhere that they won't end up pointed at me or Bob."

"Yeah, I'm about tired of that," Bob laughed. "Think they'd mind if I keep one or two?"

"I'm certainly not going to say anything," Michael laughed.

"You want one too?" Bob replied.

Abby laughed, "I think we have that area covered, but who knows. Michael always says you can't have too many weapons."

"Spoken like a true Southerner," Bob laughed.

Abby started back towards the mineshaft that led to Bob's furniture store. Michael walked to the uniforms and looked at the different groups represented. He took the time to look at each one and set them aside. There was nothing important to review right now.

Bob began walking to the mineshaft when he tripped over a piano wire. Michael glanced around and grabbed Bob. "Run!"

As they ran up the mineshaft, Michael noted several small charges on key beams they were passing. They rushed through the white door that Abby had shattered with the sledgehammer. Bob was panting fast, and Michael was helping him walk as fast as he could. Abby came back a few steps as they entered the basement room and helped Bob to the stairs to the showroom. Michael came up from behind as they ascended the steps as rapidly as Bob could walk up them. Bob gasped for a moment and stopped. Michael stopped behind him and was ready to carry him when Bob continued and reached the top step. Michael closed the door behind them just as they heard a series of shaking thrums underneath them. A puff of dust flushed under the door, but it did not buckle. It could have easily been lightning striking outside instead of a shaped explosion.

Bob fell down into a large recliner, still panting. "I guess that's my cardio for the week."

Abby laughed, and Michael opened the door to a cloud of dust that made it impossible to see the lights left on downstairs.

"That's pretty impressive," Michael said. "I only know a few people who could have shaped that explosion so well. I am betting the shafts are blocked, but it didn't cause massive cave-ins."

"I'm glad you approve," Bob said, "looks like I don't get my other rifles."

Abby handed Bob the AK47 still in her hands. "Aat least you got two."

"Two is better than zero," Bob laughed. He was red in the face, but his breathing had slowed considerably. "They seem awful serious about trespassing."

"It's my fault," Michael said. "I was careless and should have checked for tripwires. I'm not sure how we missed them when we came in. Based on the explosion, I'm guessing that a lot of the structure is still intact, and all it did was closed down the fingers to that central area. That's just a guess, though. I have no real idea what it's like down there. We should call Alex. Bob, are you going to be okay?"

"Yeah, I'll be just fine," Bob was looking pretty normal now, but still covered in sweat. "Looks like I owe you again."

"Nah," Michael chuckled. "I think we're just fine. We'll be seeing you soon."

Bob got up, followed them to the door, and locked it behind them as they left. Turning, he looked around at the mess he had to clean up again and shook his head.

Chapter 31

Ronnie opened his eyes and gasped, even with the oxygen mask on. Barbara stood and pulled her weapon, looking at the door. Ronnie started calming down almost right away and was soon asleep again. Barbara stood next to Ronnie's bed as she holstered her weapon.

A moment later, Ronnie's eyes slowly opened. He saw Barbara in the dim light of the early evening. He tried to talk but realized the oxygen mask was still on his face. Reaching up, he grabbed the mask and stopped to look at the two IVs in his hand. Ronnie took off the mask and he tried to talk. "I had a bad dream."

"I saw that," Barbara said while holding his other hand. "Was it a really bad dream?"

"I was trying to save you, and suddenly, I couldn't," Ronnie said. "It was like I was stuck in a marshmallow and couldn't do nothing to stop people from hurting you."

"You're here, and you are safe," Barbara said. "No one's going to get you or me."

"I know, but it was so real," Ronnie lamented. "There just hasn't been enough time, and all I want right now is time. Well, maybe time and a toothbrush."

"I think that's what I want too. I've spent so long searching for somebody to fill a void in my heart that I didn't need to fill. I didn't think I realized until yesterday that I don't need anyone to be happy. Not a man, not a woman, not anyone. I can be happy on my own. It's tough when you think that out and maybe I'm just now realizing it, but I want to be with you because I feel better with you. I am a better me when I am with you."

Ronnie squeezed Barbara's hand as Nancy walked in.

"You need to get that mask back on, young man," Nancy said. "I keep trying to tell you you've got to let your body heal. I bet your throat is pretty sore. I brought some ice chips when you're ready for them. Don't try to drink too much; just suck on the ice chips and swallow slowly." Nancy busied herself, checking Ronnie's blood pressure and heart rate.

She also checked several tubes that were still in his chest. "They are going to be coming in here in a little bit to get some blood and make sure everything is still okay. You make sure you have that mask on."

Ronnie put the mask back in place, and his eyes fluttered a little.

"And you, girl, you need to stop getting him all worked up. I know, I know; he's a cute young man, and you're a very attractive young woman, and things like that happen, but you need to let him rest all he can and stop letting him take off that mask."

Barbara laughed as Nancy winked at her.

"Yes, ma'am," Barbara said as she squeezed Ronnie's hand again. "I will definitely take that into consideration."

Ronnie smiled weakly as Nancy left the room. Barbara held Ronnie's hand tight. She reached up with her other hand and moved his oxygen mask for just a moment as she kissed him softly. "You need to get better," she said as she put the mask back on. "We have a lot of time to make up for."

Ronnie smiled a little and seemed to drift off to sleep. Barbara sat and thought for a moment. There was a lot to consider and a lot that she had on her shoulders. She lowered her head and kissed Ronnie on the forehead. Ronnie's eyes opened, he smiled, and she heard him rasp under the mask, "Not fair."

Barbara sat down and picked up her phone. She looked through messages and emails, and there was nothing new. She scrolled through her phone to find news of the area. There was a story about something going on in Lexington, another about how coal was slowly going away, and a few stories about the economic impact of coal mining on the Appalachians. Nothing was worth reading for her, at least.

Barbara put her phone down and stared at Ronnie. She wasn't sure she was the right person for Ronnie, but she knew he was the right man for her. Barbara heard a click in the hallway and stood up. She walked to the door and slowly opened it to see Trooper Thorne standing over Nancy. He looked her way, and she saw the pistol swing up as she slammed the door. Two more loud clicks. She heard the multiple impacts hit the door.

Her phone was next to Ronnie, and Ronnie's eyes were open. The door wouldn't lock, and there was no way she could hold off Thorne indefinitely from this position. She ran to Ronnie and pushed him to the floor. She slid the mattress and bed between them as the door began to open. Barbara fired twice at the door, and it closed again. Her phone was against the wall now. She saw it on the floor where it had fallen during her rapid rearrangement of the room. She watched the door and tried to help Ronnie as he groaned in pain. Ronnie nodded to her to keep moving as he moved painfully towards the wall.

Barbara grabbed her phone. She struggled to unlock it. The fingerprint sensor didn't seem to want to work at that moment. She placed her finger over the area several times before it finally unlocked. The door began to open again, and Barbara fired. The door stayed open this time. Barbara's ears rang from firing the shots in the small hospital room. She hit "recent" on her phone's screen and dialed Alex.

The call went straight to voicemail.

She left it running as she saw the door begin to move again.

"It is no use," Trooper Thorne said through the door. "You are a loose end. You should have never gotten involved in this. Both you and your team will be eliminated."

Barbara aimed carefully and fired one shot at the lock, which shattered as the door slammed shut again.

"We'll see how that works for you." Barbara checked her magazine and had eleven shots remaining and one extra magazine. "I don't have to kill you. I just have to keep you here long enough for someone else to kill you."

"I do have to kill you," the voice came, "and I can leave anytime I want. I have my orders. I had wanted to do this so that we could save the site, but it's obvious I can't do that now. My superiors will understand."

The door slid open only a little, and Barbara saw the fragmentation grenade bounce into the room. She looked at her phone and looked over at Ronnie. The mattress might offer some protection from the blast, but the blast wasn't what killed you. She doubted the hospital mattress would stop the pieces of shrapnel from killing them both.

"It's Thorne! Alex, It's Thorne!" Barbara screamed as she dove on top of Ronnie. Ronnie took his mask off and kissed Barbara's forehead even though there was nothing left except pain. As the grenade exploded, the pain was gone.

Chapter 32

Alex looked at his phone the moment the message came up.

"Looks like Barbara called," he said. "Wonder what's up?"

Alex pressed the buttons on his phone as he drove.

"You know that can be dangerous," Jim laughed. "You could get a ticket for using your phone while driving."

Alex smirked as the speakerphone came up. The message began to play. There was no sound for a moment, followed by a series of near explosions.

"Those are gunshots," Rachel had moved up between the seats, "turn around."

"Shhh," Jim and Alex both hissed.

"It is no use; you are a loose end you should have never gotten involved in this. Both you and your team will be eliminated." The voice was muffled, as if from a distance.

There was a pause again, a muffled movement and the click of metal against metal, then they heard Barbara say, "We'll see how that works for you. I don't have to kill you; I just have to keep you here long enough for someone else to kill you."

"She is tough," Rachel said.

"Shhh..."

There was silence for a moment again, it was deafening. Then the muffled voice again, "I do have to kill you, and I can leave anytime I want. I have my commitment. I had wanted to do this so that we could save the site, but it's obvious I can't do that now. My brother will understand."

As they listened, they heard the bounce of metal into the room and scrambling, then a moment later, the frantic scream of Barbara, "It's Thorne! Alex, It's Thorne!"

There was a loud noise, then silence.

Alex slammed his hands down on the steering wheel and spun it around, heading back to the hospital. Rachel slid to the side, pushing Elma against the door. Elma was crying. Jim's demeanor played on his face like a horrible harp. He pushed the tears back and pulled out his weapon, checking the magazine.

"Whatever happened is over," Jim said. "While we wallowed around in a car, we lost another teammate, maybe two."

"I don't care, I'm gonna be ready, and if we see Thorne, we'll sort it out later."

"We need to call Tarkington and let him know, and Michael needs to know, too," Jim stated.

Alex glanced at Jim with an eyebrow up. The roads were treacherous at the speed Alex was taking them, but they were making good time. It wouldn't be long until they were back at the hospital. As they skidded around the edges of hairpin curves, the tires barked, and the occupants of the vehicle grabbed anything they could to keep from being bounced from side to side.

"Ronnie," Eleanor said in the back seat.

Rachel turned to her and said, "Don't you worry none, we have a good team, and I'm sure Barbara is making sure Ronnie is safe.

"I wish I had never found that field," Eleanor cried.

"You need to stop crying; we will get this solved. Don't you worry," Rachel was trying to be supportive.

The car rocketed towards the hospital. There was a muffled silence inside the vehicle while Eleanor cried and wiped her tears away, choking back deeper feelings. As they found the main road, Alex dialed Michael once more, hoping this time he would answer.

Abby answered the phone, "Alex?"

"Yeah, we're on our way back to the hospital. There is a State Trooper named Thorne who seems to be at the heart of this problem. He apparently is behind most of this or at least he may have just killed Ronnie and Barbara."

Eleanor sobbed in the background a little louder.

"We'll take care of this." Alex asserted.

"It appears things are a little more complicated than we thought. I'm not sure why they are after the girl, and it may have only been for her curiosity about the poppy fields. There is a network of tunnels below the city leftover from older mines. We were just in a large area with numerous disguises and pieces of equipment. That area has partially collapsed, and we'll have to look at it later, but based on everything that's there, this was a very large operation. Whoever is behind it is not someone local. It's likely part of the Ukrainian mob. Abby and I have eliminated several of them, but we continue to run into different players. It appears they were attempting to buy out the downtown and, in the process, be able to ferry just about anything through the businesses and trucking systems in Pikeville. For some reason, a furniture store seemed to be a cornerstone, and they were willing to kill the owner to take the business. It makes sense that a State Trooper is involved simply because of the complexity and the ability to eliminate potential legal interference."

"That's real nice as we think this out," Jim was obviously agitated, "but don't think for a second that our minds aren't on Ronnie and Barbara right now. We're about five minutes out if we can get out of all these hills."

"The entire area is hills. It makes it really good for obscuring things and for keeping outsiders out. We are about five minutes away from the hospital as well; we will meet you there."

"I feel safer already," Jim was a bit sarcastic, but they all knew there was safety in numbers.

The phone hung up. There were no goodbyes or farewells, just the sudden silence of a deadline.

"Can this thing go any faster?" Jim asked.

"We're almost there," Alex said as he held on to the hand straps while they took a corner.

"It's about time," Jim saw the hospital in the distance. Behind them, Eleanor wiped tears from her eyes once more.

Chapter 33

The team pulled up to the hospital. It seemed to be quiet and inobtrusive. Perhaps a little too quiet. Although there were many cars in the parking lot, no one was milling around. People weren't wandering in and out of the hospital like you would normally see. Instead, there were two State Trooper vehicles parked out front and virtually no other movement.

Jim who spoke up first. "Well, this looks like we're about to enter a horror movie."

Rachel was strapping on a vest and watching all of the windows in the Hospital, "Y'all ever feel like a sitting duck inside a pond?"

"Gear up everyone; our people are up there, and no matter what condition they're in, it's our job to get them out."

Each of them took a pistol while Terry pulled out a rather impressive-looking shotgun instead of his usual rifle. "I figure a rifle has too much penetration inside of a hospital. We don't have any idea how many people are in there.

Sarena was the voice of reason. "You should take a second and plan this out to reduce the collateral damage. You guys are walking in after a group of troopers who could be bad, but the rest of the people inside of the room are going to think it's you. Your Army designations will not mean a lot to the standard person, and because of that, you may become a target."

Alex looked over at Sarena. "Noted. I understand your point of view completely, but in this particular case, time is of the essence. We may have to clean it up, in fact. I also don't want Eleanor to be collateral either. You and Terry hang back here at the truck. The three of us will go in pistols only and try to work this out. If something gets past us, it will be up to you to determine whether it is a friendly or not and deal with it accordingly."

Sarena nodded. She went to the back of the vehicle and pulled out a second shotgun from a rather impressive bag of weapons. Sarena's background was in weaponry. Still, she was always amazed how this team seemed to have a plethora of weapons. Working for the United States government allowed them access, and she shouldn't have been surprised, but it was unique seeing how quickly this group could gear up in a tense situation.

Jim, Alex, and Rachel walked towards the entrance. Rachel was at the rear, sweeping from side to side, watching for any distraction. Alex was in the lead, and although he walked as though he was just out for a stroll, he was obviously paying attention to everything. Jim walked two steps behind, to the right, watching the door and waiting for anything out of the ordinary.

"I don't mean to belabor the obvious, but this is pretty creepy," Jim noted as they reached the outer set of doors.

"Focus." Alex quickly opened the door and scanned the inner waiting room. "Stay tight."

Jim walked in behind Alex and caught the door. No one was at the information counter, and the waiting room was relatively empty. About four people were in chairs as though they were waiting for something to happen. A woman of about thirty-five sat looking at the ceiling like something was up there. Two men talked in the corner quietly and didn't even glance up as the three of them entered. Another man was over near the window murmuring on a cell phone.

Alex whispered into his microphone. "Strange waiting room, keep an eye on our patients."

"Stairs or elevator?" Jim was walking towards the stairwell.

"Stairs, we agree," Alex was scanning, but the earlier bustling waiting room was now very quiet. "Rachel, keep an eye on them as we pass," Alex whispered into his mic.

"Roger," Rachel glanced to the side as she followed the two men into the stairwell. "Any of you think this is really weird?"

"Still clear outside," Sarena's voice was on their comm channel. "No movement. A few cars pulling in that look like standard emergency room visits."

"Have I ever told you how much I hate stairs," Jim stated the obvious. "Stairwells are an easy trap, and I am not fond of traps."

"Would you prefer being in a tin box that can open up to a bunch of fully automatic weapons?"

"Now that you mention it, the stairs look pretty good." Jim laughed a little, but it didn't lighten the mood. Every one of them was concerned about Barbara and Ronnie.

"We need to get up there." Alex was moving up the first flight quickly; as he did, Rachel stayed to the bottom until Jim had moved up then she followed. As each one of them moved up to a floor, the other came up behind, so there were two on a landing for just a moment while one person continued to move up. This staggering allowed them to cover each other from a forward and backward perspective in the tight stairwell.

When they reached Ronnie's floor, they waited, and Rachel went up the stairwell one floor higher, watching for anyone above. She nodded, came back down, and Jim opened the door as Alex entered, watching both sides.

The lights on the floor were flashing. Although this was common in old movies because of the fluorescent lighting, the LED lights above were flashing because there was smoke. It was obvious that some wiring had been either tampered with or damaged. From a tactical perspective, the whole floor was difficult to manage. There were rooms and closed doors everywhere. They would have to check each one on the way to Ronnie's room or risk a potential ambush.

Alex wondered if everything was cleaned up from Michael's visit only a few hours previous. He knew Michael had dispatched several people, and he didn't expect it to be cleaned up so rapidly. Normally it would be a crime scene, and there would be police everywhere for hours. A lack of that activity made this scene even more suspicious. Alex looked at his two teammates and pointed behind him and across the hall. They had about eight rooms to clear before they could get to Ronnie's. It was a slow advance.

Alex pointed to the room across the hall. Rachel opened the door and walked in with her hand on her pistol. She returned a moment later with a brief nod meaning clear and closed the door behind her. Alex looked at Jim, who took the door next to him and did the same. Jim returned a few moments later and motioned that the room was clear. Alex took the next room, and a patient looked up as Alex entered. Alex smiled and put his finger to his lips. The older gentleman eased back into his pillow as Alex closed the door.

The three moved up until they got to Ronnie's room. The door was charred at the bottom but had held under the onslaught of whatever happened inside. Alex took a deep breath and opened the door. Smoke billowed out of the room, and all three ducked lower to avoid the fumes. The smell was musky and sour, like a sulfur-smoked barbeque will with dirty socks. Jim and Alex looked at each other, and Alex entered. Rachel watched outside, scanning the hallway. Alex entered a scene that would stun even Dante. The steel bed was turned sideways, and the frame twisted. The walls were covered in smoke stains and spattered with flecks of dark black. Although no flames remained, many items in the room smoldered as though over-baked in a hot oven.

Jim entered the room behind Alex. Rachel continued to watch outside but glanced inside at every sweep of the hallway. Alex walked over and saw the flattened mattress. There was little that wasn't smoking. The mattress was at an odd angle, as though blown back over the top of something, and Alex felt sick as he pushed the mattress up straight to see what lay underneath.

Ronnie was on the floor face up, Barbara over top of him. Her red hair was matted and wet. Alex knelt rapidly and put his fingers to Ronnie's neck. Alex shuddered for a moment and looked up as Jim came to the edge of the scene. Jim looked down at him, and Alex shook his head from side to side with grim purpose. A tear formed in Alex's eye. He moved his hand to Barbara and lowered his head. They were both gone.

A shot rang out behind them, and Rachel slid inside the room. She barely glanced at Jim and Alex and knew what they had found. She screamed and panted like a woman insane. Alex stood, and before either of them could move towards the door, Rachel stepped outside and fired in the direction of the shots.

"You might as well come out and get shot now because if you're alive when I get to you, you'll beg me to die." She fired again. "Come on, you coward. There is nothing in this world that is going to save you from me. You're not facing a boy in a hospital bed or the girl that cared something about him; you're facing me!"

Jim and Alex were behind her covering other angles as she walked with purpose. All three of them heard the stairwell door slam shut. Rachel broke into a run, headed towards the doors, focused on exacting the revenge that she had to have.

"Terry, we are coming down hot. We are following someone down the stairwell," Alex spoke into his mic.

"Roger," Terry whispered, "door is covered. No one is getting out."

Jim and Alex were trying desperately to cover Rachel as she ran furiously towards the door. As she got to the door, she pulled it open, and shots rang out. But Rachel pulled the door backward, only opening it while covering herself behind it. As Jim and Alex got closer, they heard someone going down the stairs in rapid staccato.

Rachel pulled the door backward and slid around it, glancing inside with her pistol before her. Like some methodical robot, as her eyes moved, the weapon trained on each spot where she looked until she was sure the stairwell below her was relatively clear. She stepped in and looked down between the rails. She was the arm of a man several floors below. She fired but missed. Rachel backed away, but shots were fired from below. She heard the ricochets above her.

Staying to the edge of the stairwell, Rachel bounded down the stairs and once again check below her. Again, she saw a shadow beneath her, but she had no clear shot and continued against the wall, working her way down as quick as she could. Behind her, Alex and Jim were trying to keep up, but she was advancing without regard to caution; only the fury inside of her gave her purpose, and that fury pressed her forward.

She came around and looked down the railings again and saw the ground floor door slam shut.

"Damn it!" Rachel screamed as she hurried her pace and came around the bottom step face-to-face with Thorne. He stood in front of the door and fired twice. Rachel fell back against the wall and pushed herself out of the view of the patient shooter.

Rachel gasped in pain and grabbed at her chest. She felt the indentations of the two bullets that hit her body armor. Although her body armor was intact, her body had absorbed a significant amount of force, and she was furious that someone got the upper hand. With a deep breath, Rachel stood back up and rapidly glanced around the corner again to the bottom of the stairwell. Thorne was no longer there.

She looked up. Jim and Alex were coming around the landing above her. She pushed forward and ran to the door.

"Rachel, wait for us!" Alex barked.

"Fuck you!" Rachel yelled back.

Jim was faster than he should have been and jumped down just above her. "Rachel, you wait; we don't wanna lose you too. Let's group up and walk out of this together."

Rachel stopped. She did not open the door and waited impatiently until Alex and Jim cleared the staircase and were soon next to her. Jim stood behind the door, and Alex and Rachel were on the opening side. Jim nodded to Alex and pulled the door open.

Machine gun fire opened fire on the other side of the door. Bullets careened inside the stairwell and sang like little chimes as they bounced around the concrete walls. Jim slammed the thick steel fire door shut with a resounding thud. "Sounds like two AK-47s on the other side."

"We seem to be a little pinned here. How many do you think are out there?" Alex asked.

"I kind of doubt all troopers were corrupt, but who knows how many others are here. I'd say we have at least three."

"It was Thorne that shot me," Rachel said; "he's mine."

"We do this by the book, or we don't survive," Alex said. "We are outgunned where we are right now, and Terry and Sarena may be in trouble as well."

"Alex, we have trouble out here as well," it was Terry. "Two vans just pulled up, and the doors are open. Looks like we have at least four men heading in towards you. Two more are firing at us. We are suppressing fire." With the last, Alex heard shots ring out on the headset before it turned off.

Alex looked at Jim and Rachel with a grimace. "Okay, that means at least seven out this door coming for us, maybe more."

Rachel moved towards the door, "Let's get this over with. If I get Thorne, it will be just fine."

"Not acceptable," Alex was more than firm. "It is time to think smart."

Alex looked at the stairs heading down to the basement level, "You two, down the stairs, get ready to fire when I open the doors."

Jim and Rachel went down a few stairs and set themselves towards the heavy door. It was quiet. The door opened to the edge of the lobby, and shooters could be anywhere when the door opened and still potentially have a clean shot. There were more shots fired somewhere on the other side of the door. Alex readied himself. The tension could be cut with a knife.

Chapter 34

Sarena and Terry were on either side of the big Escalade. Eleanor was behind a wheel of the vehicle now. The hardened steel wheel was nearly impenetrable and made a solid shield against even larger caliber gunfire.

"No idea how many more there are, but we've taken two off the playing field." Terry scanned the area behind the parking lot. "Normally, I'd try to get up into those hills and be able to take my time with the shots."

"That's not a bad idea," Sarena was scanning the hills as well. "How long of a run do you think that is?"

"Too long if there is anyone else out there," Terry noted. "It sounds like Alex is pinned down as well. Who knows how many targets are in those vans? For all we know, it could have been a bus from "killers are us.""

"Not one of you really take this seriously, do you," Sarena was agitated. "I joined this group because I thought you all were fantastic professional problem solvers for the government. Yes, you have done very well at solving some very serious problems, and yes, each of you is very talented in your own right, but most of what I see is just shy of a clown show."

"I'd say opinions would vary on that," Terry glanced over the Escalade again. "I've noted very well that you seem a little too focused on the job and not as focused on the people. It makes everyone uncomfortable to be constantly graded for their performance like some 5th-grade teacher. Do you wanna know who's smarter than a fifth grader? The answer is everyone on this team. Right now, we're in a firefight, and I have no idea how my copilot and friend are up in the hospital. As far as we know, they could be dead, so if I try to deflect with a joke here or there or Jim tries to deflect with a series of jokes, it's not because we're unprofessional or because we don't know what we're doing, it's because we do know what we're doing and we're doing it for a reason."

Sarena sat for a moment quietly. The gunfire had stopped. They both had shotguns, and Eleanor looked at her after listening to Terry.

"He's right, you know," Eleanor stated.

Sarena was obviously even more frustrated now to have a child agree with someone attacking her.

"How many shells do we have?" Sarena asked.

"I have eight left, you?" Terry was looking at the side of the shotgun that had a 12-gauge strap on it. "

"I have four and whatever is in the pipe," Sarena noted.

"We should never have agreed to just use shotguns. We need to get in the back of the truck and get out additional weapons." Terry looked over the car, and shots rang out in their direction again.

"How hard is it to get in the back from one of these side doors?" Sarena asked.

"It's pretty easy except for the fact that you're a sitting duck when you're inside the Escalade. it would be easier if we opened the back." Terry stopped and fired back, then pulled his pistol.

"Why don't you just hit the little button on your remote and open the back?" Eleanor asked.

Sarena and Terry looked at each other. Terry pulled out the keys and looked at the remote. He pressed the button for the tailgate, and it slowly began to rise.

Shots flew across the parking lot again, and Eleanor sat behind the wheel of the big Escalade, holding her ears. Sarena reached into her pocket and pulled out a small packet. She handed it to Eleanor. Inside were two earplugs made out of foam. They could be squished down and put into your ear to eliminate sound or at least deafen it so that the shotguns and pistol fire would not be so loud.

Eleanor nodded her appreciation and began working the foam earplugs into her ears.

Terry slid around the back of the vehicle as it sat, slightly angled to the van. It gave him access without making him fully visible. In the back, as he opened the case, he had access to more weapons. He threw the shotgun towards the back and pulled out two M-16s and four magazines. Sliding back to the far side of the Escalade, he handed Sarena an M16 and two magazines. Each slapped in a magazine and chambered a round as they knelt behind the truck.

"Aim low for the legs if you have a shot." Terry stood and shot over the hood of the big SUV.

The two fired fifteen shots rapidly where the men were and aimed low, hoping for a leg shot. They were awarded with screams on the other side of the van.

"Wait here and cover me. I'm not sure if we got both or just one." Terry began moving up in a low-set combat glide. It looked like he was a duck walking forward, but his weapon stayed straight and direct. His finger was on the trigger guard, not the trigger, as he came around the van to the moaning men on the ground. Both of them grasped their legs. He could tell that one man's ankle was completely shattered, the second took a shot through both calves. Terry wondered for a moment how the ricochet could have hit him that square.

In a very practiced movement, Terry swept his rifle in all directions, his gaze was always in the direction of his sites, and both eyes were open, watching everywhere around him. The two men continued moaning as he walked up and kicked their weapons away. He knelt down to the first man and pulled his side-arm. He threw that to the side as well. Terry then flipped the man onto his stomach in one movement. The man tried to resist. Terry zip-tied his arms behind his back and then zip-tied between the zip tie to make it more difficult to pull apart.

As Terry swung his weapon back to the second man, He saw a gun drawn from a shoulder holster. Everything was in slow motion as Terry tried to bring his weapon up faster. The resulting gunfire erupted from behind him. Serena shot the man several times in the chest and once in the head before he stopped moving. Terry stood.

"Thanks." Terry was already on the move checking the van. He went to the second van, and it, too, was empty. They only left two outside.

Terry began to move towards the hospital. "What about the girl?" Sarena asked.

Terry stopped and looked back towards the Escalade that was now speckled with bullet holes. "That does put a wrench in things."

"She is not a wrench," Sarena stated.

"Fall back," Terry said, "there will be hell to pay if something happens to her."

Terry and Sarena kept their weapons pointed towards the hospital as they moved back to the Escalade. As they moved around the back side, Eleanor was gone.

Chapter 35

Eleanor's ears rang as she moved around to the back of the hospital. She remembered there was a back door. She had to find a way to see Ronnie. Ronnie came here to help her, and now he may be lying dead in his hospital room all because of her.

Eleanor was careful as she opened the back door and crept inside the hospital. The rear staircase was next to her, and she worked her way upstairs. She was young and in good shape. She made short work of the few floors necessary to get to Ronnie.

As she entered the floor, there was a commotion, and in just a moment, she was confronted by both security and nurses.

"Where's Ronnie?" Eleanor tried to push past them. "I know he's up here; where is he?"

"You need to settle down," the nurse put her arms on Eleanor's shoulders.

"I do not need to settle down." Eleanor shrugged off the hold and tried to go by her, only to be stopped by the large security guard, "I need to see my cousin right now."

"I can't allow that," the nurse repeated. "Nobody can see him now; y'all need to sit down right now."

Eleanor started to tear up. "That's my cousin in there, and he is here because of me. This is all my fault. If he's hurt, it's all my fault. It's all my fault."

Eleanor pushed away from both of them, rushed back to the stairwell, and ran down the stairs. As she reached the bottom floor, the door opened for her.

Chapter 36

Thorne held Eleanor by the throat as he crouched behind her, gun to her temple.

"I know you're waiting for a time to come out. You may as well do it now, or I'll kill the girl." Thorne glanced from side to side, watching the door to the front stairwell. "I'm going to start counting in a minute, and I may shoot off her foot, just for the fun of it, if you don't get out here."

It was Alex that yelled, "How do we know you won't kill her anyway?"

"You don't," Thorne adjusted his grip. "I would say you could trust me, but you can't."

Alex stepped out of the stairwell. His hands were up, and his weapon latched to his chest.

"That's a good boy, the other ones too." Thorne waved his gun at the door. "Don't worry, I'm done with this. It seems that my outside men are no longer firing, so I will assume they're dead. You will walk me out and watch me leave with this girl, or I will kill her and as many of you as I can."

"Just kill me and him." Eleanor's eyes were covered in tears. "It's all my fault anyway. Shoot him right through me."

Thorne grabbed Eleanor by the hair and yanked her head back as he pushed the pistol into her mouth. "If you're going to keep throwing things out of it, I will put something in it. You keep quiet, and I'll take this thing out of your mouth; otherwise, that's going to be your pacifier."

Eleanor's eyes watered even more. Alex was looking for a way out but could see none. Jim and Rachel were seething. Two men ran up behind Thorne and whispered into his ear.

"It seems I was right," Thorne began moving towards the door. "It is just the three of us now, and we are going to walk out of here together. If anything happens to any of us, the girl is dead." There was some short conversation in Ukrainian, and the two men pointed their weapons at Jim,

Rachel, and Alex. "All we have to do is take a short little walk outside. Now move in front of us, hands in the air."

It wasn't a very long walk, the hospital wasn't that big. Everyone was gone as the firefight had scattered people right and left. Now their shoes made uncomfortable noises echoing in the empty chamber. Eleanor's feet shuffled as she was dragged across the floor. It was near deafening.

They reached the double sets of doors and went through the first one. The three men, with Thorne holding Eleanor tight, pistol in her mouth, came out the door behind Alex, Jim, and Rachel. They kept walking, and Alex made note of all of the carnage in the parking lot. Windows were broken, car alarms were going off, and he saw two men lying on the ground and another inside a van. A woman was sobbing on the ground with blood running from her leg. She looked up, put her hands over her face, and curled into a ball on the ground.

"Tell your people to come out," Thorne said; "if you don't, the girl and the three of you are dead." Thorne took his pistol out of Eleanor's mouth and pointed at the three of them with the barrel of the 9mm.

"What assurances do I have that my team will be safe?" Alex was looking around and saw a glint at the edge of the parking lot.

"Why none, of course," Thorne saw nothing. He was laser-focused on Alex and glancing from side to side, looking for Terry and Sarena. "Stop stalling and call them out."

Three shots rang out as one. The men on either side of Thorne fell to the ground. Thorne fell backward hard. He writhed on the ground and moved to retrieve his fallen Beretta.

Alex and Jim were on him in a second, pointing their weapons at his face. Thorne was not taken aback and instead seemed to seethe with rage. A moment later, Terry came into view carrying his rifle. He was followed by Sarena and then by Michael and Abby.

Thorne's eyes got wide. "You."

Michael looked down at Thorne. "Hello, Gaston."

"I thought you were dead or that you ran away with my cowardly cousin." Thorne was pushing up against the pain of his wound. "We thought Chekov killed our father and perhaps you as well. It was you, wasn't it? It all makes sense now; Yuri will come for me, and he will come for you."

Michael looked at the team. "I don't think so. This was all from Yuri?" Michael stood looking to the sky for a moment. "I thought you would become a good man, and instead, here we are. You have become such a silly boy. I never expected you to go down this path, but here we are."

"It took years for me to go through college here in the United States. We forged perfect papers, and I took the correct classes to get into the State Police. We have been working on this city for a long time. In these few days, it has become a nightmare because a little girl went where she shouldn't have."

"There have been drugs here for a long time; what makes yours any different?" Michael was still staring at the sky. Abby was by his side, watching Thorne closely.

"It was all new strains. It won't matter, we will find another place. I will be out of jail before I'm even processed. Even if I end up in prison here in the States, it will be of no consequence. The consequences are all on you since Yuri will know where you are. He will come for you and the girl, as well. All these people will die for what they have done."

Behind them, the Pikeville Police Department was rolling into the parking lot. It had not been far, but they were unaware of the situation right away. Everything was choreographed by Thorne so well that they were handling other issues.

Michael watched the sky, seemingly oblivious to Thorne and his story. He looked down at Abby, and she smiled at him.

"Smile while you can. She will be dead so..." Thorne never finished his sentence as Michael shot him with his FN 57 dead center between his eyes.

Alex jumped and tried to grab Michael's gun, but it was holstered so fast. Michael held him at bay with one arm.

"You can't do that. We don't know what this is all about, we have to get to the bottom of it, and you just took away our only source of information."

"I'm sure there are others floating around the city right now that you'll be able to find. I will close the rest down, and this will be done." Michael looked at Abby, "I'm going to have to take a trip for a while. I won't be gone long. It will give you time to get the things that you want for the house."

Rachel was seething. "You couldn't have even waited until I beat him up a little?"

"Take it out on the rest of them. There are several in the city, and I believe if you start looking at the businesses, you'll probably find that there are numerous fronts." Michael was sullen.

Police were now swarming everywhere and looking suspiciously at Michael, Abby, and the team.

"You should probably get out of here," Alex said to Michael, "we'll handle this. We have to bury two teammates as well."

Michael looked up and saw the tear in Alex's eye. Eleanor cried. Michael and Abby walked to the DB9, waiting in the parking lot. In a few moments, they were gone.

Chapter 37

"I have to go for a while." Michael was driving through the hills between Pikeville and Ivel. "I'm not sure how long it will take."

"What are you going to do?" Abby watched the road and didn't look over at Michael.

"I have to end this. I guess, in some ways, it's my fault. I followed the guidelines I was given, but I probably shouldn't have. Apples don't fall far from the tree."

"I suppose you want me to stay here?" Abby still looked at the road.

"I will be as quick as I can. It will give you time to put the house together the way you want it. Get whatever help you need."

"We make a good team," Abby's gaze wandered out the passenger window.

"We actually make a great team, I don't want to lose you, and this will not be a pleasant visit."

"Isn't it time to let this go? Alex and his team can handle this. I'm sure my father will make them go and exact some sort of retribution." Abby looked over at Michael, a tear in her eye. "Haven't you done enough? I thought you were retired, but it certainly seems like we get pulled into things that have nothing to do with us."

"I think I already said that. Trouble seems to follow me. I don't want it to follow you."

"You don't get that choice; no matter where you are, I should be there, and I will face life and death with you. It's not like you have to do anything alone anymore. I'm not your ex-girlfriend who didn't know anything about you. I'm not some waifish twit that can't take care of herself. I understand that you are unique in your way, but I can help, and we can do anything together." Abby wiped away the tear as she stopped for a moment.

"It may be difficult. You don't know Ukrainian. The country is currently in turmoil, and I have no idea how close I will be able to get." Michael watched the road ahead.

"At least we would be together," Abby looked back at Michael and smiled.

"I will set things up," Michael looked at the road ahead and considered his next steps.

Chapter 38

The service was simple. The Lexington Cemetery Military Garden was set up for two fallen heroes. Few people would know the extent of how much these individuals had done. Still, hundreds gathered around from the Bluegrass Army Depot and beyond.

A large group from Pikeville huddled together, and their Sunday best was prevalent in the crowd. Older suits and near-perfect hats, pulled from boxes stored with reverence and used only when such a time passed, such a time as now.

Many men were in uniform. A color guard was in formation to the side of the podium. Two coffins sat side by side, draped by the flag they loved. The graves lay below them, and the makeshift podium stood waiting for someone to stand.

A priest walked to the top of the podium and looked out upon the large crowd. People were scattered in the area, and some were beyond, near other graves, watching from a distance.

"I was told not to say much, but there is much to say. The Lord does not prepare you to take two away that were so young and full of life. I am told that Ronnie and Barbara had feelings for one another, but now they will share those feelings in heaven above. I can say with certainty that Ronnie has believed in the power of heaven since he was a small boy in Pikeville, in our church."

In the crowd, Alex stood and walked to the podium. The priest cleared his eyes as Alex took to the microphone. "I know you're all here looking for closure. We all are. The senseless death of our two friends is not acceptable. No death is acceptable this early, and I cannot find it inside of me to forgive or forget. I am told it is said that vengeance belongs to the Lord, but there is no closure in that. There is no way to let go." Alex looked over at the priest. "You are right, Sir, that both of these young people should never have died. They have cheated death a dozen times, but to die the way they died is not fair, nor is it right."

There was a sudden clamor from the group from Pikeville. Alex looked over at them and nodded as many whispered but kept their eyes on him. Alex noted Ronnie's uncle and Eleanor in the crowd. Behind them, Ronnie's cousin from the Pikeville Police Department stood with several other men in uniform. All were sullen and obviously affected by all that was going on around them.

Alex bowed his head, "I said we wanted to keep the service short because Ronnie would want to be remembered for who he was. Many of you knew him, but you didn't know the honorable, intelligent person that he was unless you were with our team. Ronnie kept honor above all else except one thing. Ronnie held Barbara in an even higher regard. He idolized her from afar and believed in the good of mankind because of her. They may not have been married or even boyfriend and girlfriend, but the love they shared is a love we should all reach for. It's a love that I wish I could have known." Alex looked into the crowd. "Most of you know I can say nothing about what happened or what will happen, but what I can say is that justice will be served. Even though I can find no solace in what has happened, it will be made as right as it can be."

Rachel had not moved as she stood in the front in full uniform, but this time at those words, she whispered, "You're damn right."

Alex looked out at the crowd again. "Share a moment of silence with me for our two lost comrades." He bowed his head again, and everyone bowed their heads with him.

The service continued with Jay playing *Amazing Grace* on the bagpipes. People felt deeply, and Jay was covered in tears as he played. No one else stood, but as Jay played, many began singing until the chorus could be heard easily for miles around.

There was a short prayer and a 21-gun salute. As people walked by, the two flags were folded. One was given to Ronnie's uncle, and the flag for Barbara was given to Jim. Jim held it tightly and showed little emotion.

The crowd slowly began to dissipate while many walked to the graves, cried, and then left. The small team huddled together for a moment.

"When are we going to take care of the rest of this?" Rachel asked. "I know Thorne is dead, but whoever started this has gotta go."

"Not our problem," Alex looked down at the ground and then scanned what was left of his small team. "Tarkington decided not to put any of us at risk. Besides, the person with the most knowledge was sent to deal with all of this."

"This is our problem!" Jim said.

"I agree with him for once," Sarena chimed in.

"Guys, I agree too, but we have our orders. This will be resolved within the week."

"Tarkington is going to make Michael even richer?" Rachel was red-faced with anger.

"No, Tarkington offered Michael a lot of money, and Michael refused. He said this was personal and he would do it for free. I think Michael's exact words were, 'no one fucks with my friends,' but that could have been a Tarkington translation."

The team sat looking at the ground as people slowly filtered away. Twilight began to come, and they worked their way to the Suburbans as workers finished covering the two graves. As they drove away and left the Lexington Cemetery, the magnificent steel gates closed behind them, and with that, their two friends were gone.

Chapter 39

Getting into Ukraine was very easy. Americans were very welcome, and there was a certain camaraderie between the countries. Although that camaraderie was also filled with distrust didn't really matter. Michael and Abby traveled under forged passports into a country filled with terror.

War was consistent, and a gun control advocate in the United States would have a stroke and die with the number of fully automatic weapons roaming the streets of the city. Michael had the taxi driver drop them off at the edge of the business district, and he and Abby began to walk, each carrying a small backpack. They packed light, and much of what they needed was hopefully still at Michael's warehouse.

"Don't expect much. I haven't been here in quite a while." Michael scanned the streets as they walked, but the roads were empty, and not a person could be seen.

"I never expect much, but you never cease to surprise me." Abby smiled and looked up at Michael. He looked down for just a moment and continued watching the area.

Several blocks in, they came to a large brownstone warehouse. Michael took out a key and worked it into multiple locks on the door. Though old and rusty, the locks opened easily. He opened the door, and the two of them walked in. Closing the door behind them, Michael made his way to the elevator and was surprised at the lack of decay. There was dust everywhere, and a person would be hard-pressed to note anything as even slightly clean. Still, the foundations and structure were solid, and nothing had degraded. Michael did note, as the elevator rose, that several rat traps were full. Those would have to be emptied and reset if he was ever to use this place again. He had set over 100 traps, and by now, he supposed they were all triggered.

The elevator went up slowly until it reached the top floor. Michael opened the elevator doors, and they creaked as they revealed his home for a few weeks years ago.

Abby looked around. "Nice, but it could use a woman's touch."

"I seriously doubt there's a Home Goods in the area," Michael laughed.

Abby looked at the car to the side. "Does it run?"

"I absolutely have no idea. I planned to work on it but was forced to leave rather rapidly. This was to be my project while I waited for the heat to die down, but instead, I had to leave suddenly."

"Things didn't quite go as planned?" Abby kept surveying the area and dropped her bag on the bed, creating a plume of dust in the air. "At least you still have electricity."

"I had the bill paid indefinitely just in case, and no one has ever tried to trace it. I don't think anyone knew I owned this except the one person who found me."

"What happened to them?" Abby sat on the edge of the bed.

Michael nodded to the freezer, "I let them move in, they don't pay rent, but they don't take up much space."

"Well, at least we know where they are. I'm kind of glad the power is on."

"Me too." Michael pulled out an old tank vacuum cleaner and plugged it in to a socket on a beam. "I think the smell would have been horrible if the power had gone out. The freezer will probably work forever; it's a 1960s model, back when they made everything impervious."

Abby and Michael laughed and spent some time cleaning up the living space. When they were done, Michael looked down at Abby and pulled her close.

"I have to tell you that I didn't want to bring you here; this may not be safe. Actually, I can assure you it won't be safe, but it is good for you to be here. At least you get to see my nice warehouse." Michael smiled.

Michael lowered his head and lifted Abby slightly; as he did, they kissed softly, and he held her tight. When he let her down, he said simply, "143."

Abby laughed, "I remember when you were in Texas and told me that you loved me. It was the only time I have ever been worried."

Michael walked to a dresser, pulled out a drawer, and put it on the bed. The bottom was false, and he folded it out. Inside the drawer was a P90 and two FN Five-Sevens. He pulled out a second drawer and put it next to the first. In the false bottom of that drawer was a series of magazines for both weapons. He began assembling and checking all three. Abby picked up one of the pistols and broke it down expertly. Michael handed her cloths from the drawer and a small bottle of oil. In a matter of minutes, all three weapons were cleaned and lightly oiled, ready for what was next.

Michael put the drawers back and opened a third drawer. From it, he pulled out a tack vest and several holsters. He looked at Abby, "I will go to the house and scout it out. You wait here. I will just take one 57 in case anything heads this way."

"You know nothing will head this way, so take both pistols, and I will keep the rifle. If they haven't found this place yet, they're not going to in the next few hours."

Michael nodded. "Depending upon the situation, I will either resolve it or come back here for you to assist. I know you want to come with me, but please let me do this alone first."

"I understand. I expect you back here with some dinner," Abby laughed again, this time with a little nervousness in her voice.

"Don't worry, I'm not sure anyone will even remember me," Michael smiled. His blue eyes seemed to sparkle in the halogen warehouse lights."

"I'll keep myself busy." Abby looked around.

"I'm sure you will." Michael finished putting on his vest and mounting the pistols. He put a jacket over top of it all, and it looked like he was just a little bit bigger.

"I'll be back soon. If you get hungry, there are some old cans of stuff in the kitchen area. Just don't feed the rats."

"Be careful," Abby looked at him as he turned to go.

Michael turned back and then kissed her softly again. Then Michael walked to the elevator, went to the bottom floor, and locked the doors behind him. Michael cinched his coat and headed out into the Ukrainian afternoon.

Chapter 40

Yuri's house could only be considered a palace. As Michael watched from two blocks away, he tried to blend in and not look like a tourist or an American. The problem was there was nothing close, and many of the homes were silent. Michael mused to himself that he probably looked a little out of place, but he rapidly came up with a plan and wandered to the giant gates of the estate.

Michael counted four guards so far. Two of them were at the front gate, and he saw too at the door. Michael guessed there were at least another dozen, but he had no idea. He wandered to the gate, and the two guards approached him immediately.

Michael looked up at the two men. He spoke in Ukrainian; "Is Yuri available?"

The two men looked at Michael suspiciously. "Get out of here; Yuri sees no one."

"Yuri will see me," Michael noted. "Tell him Michael is here."

The two men from the house had walked down to the gate as well. Michael saw no one else. Two men were inside the gate, and two men were outside. All four men were uneasy now because Michael did not immediately leave. "Yuri sees no one; he is grieving for his brother at the cemetery again."

"Thank you," Michael said in English as he drew the silenced FN 57. As each man attempted to draw, Michael put a single shot into their foreheads. He holstered his weapon behind his back, and it was hidden again.

Michael knew the cemetery where Anton was buried was only six blocks away. The Petrikov family had a very large section of the cemetery. It is where everything would happen. Michael walked with his hands in his pockets and headed to the cemetery. He considered if he should wait for Abby or to do this alone and realized he was already committed because of his actions a few moments ago. Once the bodies were found Yuri would have many more guards and be on guard.

It didn't take long to get to the entrance of the cemetery, where two more men were waiting. As Michael walked up, they moved to block him. "The cemetery is closed right now; come back later."

"Sorry, I feel the need to grieve right now." Michael pushed forward, and the men put their arms out to stop him. Michael pulled the Hibben from his pocket and sliced the neck of the first man. As he grabbed his throat, in one fluid motion, Michael turned and put the blade into the temple of the second man. Both fell to the ground. Michael sat them up against the gate and walked in. He saw no one but knew there would be more.

As Michael crossed the first hill, he saw three men standing at a grave. The cemetery was huge, and Michael could not see another person. He walked slowly towards them, and the two men pulled their weapons and shot without questioning. Trees were abundant in the cemetery, and Michael ducked behind one as shots rang out as large clicks in the air. There was a pause. Michael rapidly looked around the tree and then swung around to the other side. In a swift motion, he fired two shots, and both men fell. The third man stared. He made no move as Michael walked forward.

"Michael," Yuri said as Michael was ten feet away. "Of all the people responsible, I did not expect you. There are 100 foolish drug Lords that all want to topple me. Chekov was right, wasn't he? When both of you disappeared, I was unsure. I thought perhaps Chekov was covering for himself and escaped, but I never knew what happened to you."

"I suppose I do owe you the truth." Michael watched the area waiting for anything to show. "Your father was a terrible man, and I was paid to kill him. I became friends with you accidentally because you were a good person, but now not so much."

Yuri looked down at the ground. "No, not so much anymore. After Father died, I had to take care of my brother. I finally sent him off to the United States. But to keep the family together, I also kept the family business together. I would like to say that it was a bad thing for me to do, but it was the only thing I could do. A good person does what they can but a responsible person does what they must. When you killed my father, hundreds of people were unemployed unless I did something. I took over, and things got better. I tried to be less brutal, but I am sure you know that doesn't work. I'm sorry that you will have to die now."

Michael looked around and still saw nothing. "I'm not expecting to die today. Care to enlighten me?"

Yuri pulled a small button from his pocket. "The guards will be here momentarily. They will come over the hill as you did, and whether I am alive or dead will not matter. You will be dead in moments."

Michael got behind Yuri and held him facing the hill. It was the only easy way into the cemetery, and at any moment, there would be men rolling over the hill. The two men waited.

"Have you checked the batteries in that thing lately?"

"I don't understand. I don't understand at all."

A figure began walking over the hill. The pace was slow and deliberate. The figure was dressed all in black and blonde hair flowed to the side. The P90 was in her hands, her finger on the trigger guard. She walked forward. It was Abby.

"Aren't you glad I followed you?"

Michael smiled. "I guess you took care of my problem." Michael let Yuri go and pushed him down towards the ground.

"There were only eight of them; it was a small problem," Abby said. "Why do men always think women are defenseless until they pull out a fully automatic rifle and plow them down?"

"I never thought of it like that?" Michael smiled at her.

Yuri reached into his pocket, but Michael lifted his FN 57, and with a loud click, Yuri was dead.

"I'm hungry." Abby looked down at Yuri and shot two more shots into him.

Michael and Abby worked their way back to the gate and disappeared into the city. In the distance, the sirens screamed and would soon cover the area, but Michael and Abby would take their time and enjoy the warehouse for a few days.

Epilogue

The 1969 fastback Mustang drove into downtown Pikeville. The thrum of the engine echoed around the furniture store as Michael and Abby parked. They walked in to find Bob sitting at the counter.

Bob looked up at the two of them and smiled. "Y'all know I got a burst eardrum because of you?"

"Well, if you had better clients, your eardrum would have never burst."

"You got that right." Bob laughed and came around the counter. "Did y'all come for some more furniture? I'm sure I can make you a good deal."

"I think we may want to get a few more things here. We're meeting some friends here in a minute, and I was thinking about a new couch."

"You already bought a couch; I expect it's already set up at your house." Bob glanced around as the door opened, and Alex, Jim, and Rachel entered.

"We did already buy a couch," Michael nodded, "maybe we'll just look around."

Alex was the first to speak. "I'm told you took care of things."

"Everything is done, I'm sure there will be some mop-up, but it's not our problem. Yuri is gone along with a number of his men."

"The General said that you did this for free," Jim nodded, "I wouldn't expect that from you."

"That's because you still see things from a smaller point of view. I expect more out of you Jim; after all, you should know with your Eastern philosophies, but sometimes there is a much larger picture to be seen. Ronnie was a friend, I did not know Barbara well, but I knew Ronnie cared about her. I could not let this stand. The people of this area now know what's going on, so it won't come back. I wish you had been with me, but I needed to do this alone because, in a small way, it was my fault."

"And that's it?" Rachel was slightly indignant. Her fists were crumpled up. "You get to deal with it while we sit on our hands? You're lucky you've never fought me because I would pound your little ass."

Michael's eyes sparkled. "I think we can do something about that."

It was Bob who ran into the middle of them. "Please, no more; my ears can't take it. If you want to start a gunfight, go down the street or just go somewhere else. I don't mind y'all killing each other, but I still have ringing in my ears from this guy."

The five looked at each other and then at Bob, and all of them started laughing.

"If you want to come back to the house, I have a sparring mat."

Rachel nodded.

"The good part is we have BBQ," Abby said, "and potato chips, and maybe some popcorn. I'm all for sitting on the side and watching. Maybe we can take some bets."

Alex put out his hand to Michael. "Thanks for taking care of this, even though I would have liked to have done it."

"Thanks for letting me," Michael walked out the door, and after they were in front, they heard the door lock as Bob turned the sign over to 'Closed.'

About the Author

Andrew Allen Smith was born in Anderson, Indiana. Until the age of fifteen, he moved at least once per year and finally settled in Lexington, Kentucky. Andrew spent a significant amount of his teenage years reading and writing short stories, attempts at novels, and poetry. He published his first book, "A Slice of Passion," in 2005. It was a book of poetry compiled from dozens of years of work.

In 2015, Andrew published "The Theft and Other Short Stories" as a collection of some of his favorite portions of his writings after he was challenged to self-publish a book. Challenged and excited about his success, he published his first novel, "Vengeful Son," in 2016 and began building a franchise with that book. "The Masterson Files" (the series containing "Vengeful Son") now includes five books and has fifteen in outline form. The story follows an ex-assassin that is reluctantly engaged in helping others while trying to retire.

In 2020, after a tragic event, Andrew co-wrote "What NOT to Say to People Who Are Grieving." This book showcased emotions and an approach to helping others be more mindful of their words during grief.

2021 gave us "A Slice of Fear" followed by "Another Slice of Fear" with short stories focusing on fears of all types. "Another Slice of Fear" won Andrew a Literary Titan Award and has been reviewed positively for several stories in the genre.

As Quality Leader and System Architect, Andrew's work gave him credit for a series of instructional manuals for site relationship management systems, various quality documents, and development lifecycles. In Andrew's spare time, he has a passion for many hobbies and his family, which he considers paramount. For more information about Andrew, please visit **andrewallensmith.com**.

Books by Andrew Allen Smith

Fiction

A Slice of Passion
A Slice of Fear
Another Slice of Fear
Yet Another Slice of Fear
The Theft and Other Short Stories

The Masterson Files Series

Vengeful Son
Sinful Father
Deadly Daughter
Fateful Friend
Silent Sister

The Eternal Forever Series

Adam

Non-Fiction

What NOT to say to People Who are Grieving

Books Containing Andrew Allen Smith's prose

Monster Hunter Intern and Other Tales
The Gift and Other Stories
Simple Things: Moments of Isolated Gratitude
The Portrait of Herbert Losh and Other Stories
The Drifter and Other Unusual Tales

Coming Soon

Burial Ground
Stealth Drive
The Masterson Files Book 6 - Curious Cousin
The Eternal Forever Book 2 – Morgan
Another Slice of Passion